W9-APG-127

"I'm starting to remember things... things I'm not supposed to."

He squeezed her hand tight, and she could feel his torment. "You've got to help me, Molly. If you can't, no one can. I trust you."

"With your life?" she whispered.

His smile was visible through the pain. "I remember a date—the 7th. That's when I'm supposed to kill."

The 7th? It was less than a week away! "But who? Alec, you've got to remember."

As he looked at her, his blue eyes turned icy. "It's someone I know...someone I'm close to." He swore in frustration. "I can't remember...but I'm beginning to think there's no way I can stop myself...."

ABOUT THE AUTHOR

California native M.L. Gamble thought her old neighborhood in Pasadena provided an ideal setting for her fourth Intrigue. A believer in the philosophy "write what you know," this Bayville, New York, resident is hard at work on her fifth Intrigue. An avid fan of mystery and romantic suspense, she conducts creative-writing workshops and is busy raising her two children, Olivia and Allen.

Books by M.L. Gamble

HARLEQUIN INTRIGUE
110—STRANGER THAN FICTION
146—DIAMOND OF DECEIT
153—WHEN MURDER CALLS
172—IF LOOKS COULD KILL
226—DEAD MAGNOLIAS

Don't miss any of our special offers. Write to us at the following address for information on our newest releases.

Harlequin Reader Service
U.S.: 3010 Walden Ave., P.O. Box 1325, Buffalo, NY 14269
Canadian: P.O. Box 609, Fort Erie, Ont. L2A 5X3

Trust With Your Life

M.L. Gamble

Harlequin Books

TORONTO • NEW YORK • LONDON
AMSTERDAM • PARIS • SYDNEY • HAMBURG
STOCKHOLM • ATHENS • TOKYO • MILAN
MADRID • WARSAW • BUDAPEST • AUCKLAND

If you purchased this book without a cover you should be aware
that this book is stolen property. It was reported as "unsold and
destroyed" to the publisher, and neither the author nor the
publisher has received any payment for this "stripped book."

With love for two beauties, Kathleen Rose Seaman and
Sara Kathleen Seaman.
Also for Beulah Mae McKinney Curran Beckland,
the dearest Valentine.

ISBN 0-373-22321-8

TRUST WITH YOUR LIFE

Copyright © 1995 by Marsha Nuccio

All rights reserved. Except for use in any review, the reproduction or
utilization of this work in whole or in part in any form by any electronic,
mechanical or other means, now known or hereafter invented, including
xerography, photocopying and recording, or in any information storage
or retrieval system, is forbidden without the written permission of the
publisher, Harlequin Enterprises Limited, 225 Duncan Mill Road,
Don Mills, Ontario, Canada M3B 3K9.

All characters in this book have no existence outside the imagination of
the author and have no relation whatsoever to anyone bearing the same
name or names. They are not even distantly inspired by any individual
known or unknown to the author, and all incidents are pure invention.

This edition published by arrangement with Harlequin Enterprises B.V.

® and TM are trademarks of the publisher. Trademarks indicated with
® are registered in the United States Patent and Trademark Office, the
Canadian Trade Marks Office and in other countries.

Printed in U.S.A.

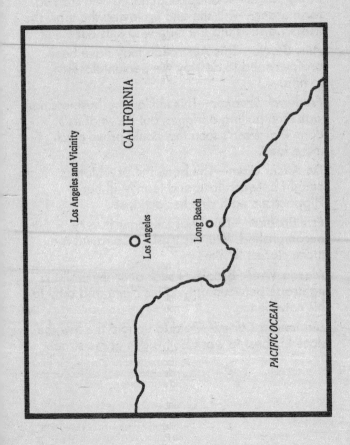

CAST OF CHARACTERS

Molly Jakes—Kidnapped, chased and framed for murder—will she end up loving the man she trusts...or trusting the man who kills her?

Alec Steele—This Australian may have been brainwashed to destroy the person closest to him.

Frederick Brooker—This millionaire businessman was seen pulling a trigger, but it's what he's done that wasn't seen that could prove much more fatal.

Dr. Alicia Chen—The beautiful psychiatrist caught between love and fear. Will her Hippocratic oath rule her actions?

Eric Brooker—This deaf teenager is very accomplished. Will his trust be betrayed by those closest to him?

Mason Weil—Brooker's slick attorney walks a tightrope between duty to his client and duty to his conscience.

Lieutenant Cortez—Paid to uphold the law, he does his best to work both sides of the street.

Prologue

Molly Jakes grabbed her cellular phone out of the front seat compartment and slammed the car door. She glanced at her watch, grimaced at the 11:53 reading and stuck the phone in her purse. Slinging the strap over her left shoulder, she shivered and buttoned her coat.

Fog drooped down like gray flannel from the starless sky, refracting light from the surrounding buildings into a bright blur. Molly shielded her eyes against the glare. She could just make out the shape of the Summer Point Towers office complex a few yards away to which she had been summoned.

Checking to be sure she had locked her car door, Molly headed toward the bulky form ahead, holding her arms close to her body. It was February and forty-two degrees—cold, very cold for California.

It was also one of the last places Molly would have wanted to be if she had been given a choice. Handling service complaints against her telephone installation crew was part of her job. But being called out on Valentine's Day from the warm bed she had collapsed into three hours before seemed above and beyond, she thought grumpily. As she got near enough to the building to see the glass doors of the entrance, she attempted to shake off her rotten mood.

But her brain wasn't through grousing. It was bad enough to be thirty-four and to go to bed alone on the traditional lovers' holiday because there was no likely lover within a hundred yards of her life. But to finally get to sleep only to be awakened by a shrill phone ring followed by a leering, male voice that taunted, "Hey, Jakes, I hope I'm not interrupting your big night..." Those sweet words were spoken by Jerry Williams, one of the more obnoxiously chauvinistic dispatchers, a man she had less respect for than a cockroach.

The heavy glass door swishing closed behind her, Molly finally managed to lay to rest her slightly self-pitying thoughts and take a deep breath. Hey, even cockroaches were entitled to their fun, she reminded herself. Another day, another buck. Think of the town house you want to buy. That's why you took this promotion, remember? So you could earn enough money to buy some overpriced California real estate all by yourself. And this is how you do it. So be quiet and be happy you've got such a good job when a couple of million people are out of work.

Standing in front of the lobby directory, Molly searched out the office number for the alarm company she was seeking. She found Inscrutable Security listed in Suite 330.

She pressed the elevator button with a finger stiff from the cold and rode up alone, composing an all-purpose apology for the owner of Inscrutable, one Frederick Brooker, which she hoped would serve the situation.

Williams hadn't been clear about the problem but said that the foreman was having dial-tone problems with another telecommunications line carrier, that the crew was going to blow the installation deadline and that they "requested, as per union guarantee, you know," Jerry had crowed, "a manager type ASAP to run interference" with an unhappy client.

The steel doors slid open and Molly disembarked, peering to the left, then the right. Small painted numbers on the marble-faced wall across from the elevator directed her to the left.

Just her luck. The hall lights to her left were off. She took a few tentative steps into the gloom and stopped. A door eight feet away was marked 320, which meant 330 was several yards farther along into the unseeable.

"It was a dark and stormy night," Molly muttered into the silence. She squared her shoulders and headed down the carpeted hallway. The air inside the building smelled of salt water as strongly as it had outside. The Pacific was only a few blocks away, and the building's decor was typical of the growing beach town of Summer Point, sixty miles from L.A. Seascapes, painted rattan pictures and a collage of hemp and polished shells hanging on the walls she passed reinforced the style.

She stopped in the darkness and peered at the information on a doorway.

Suite 328
California Psychiatric Clinic, Inc.
Dr. T. Kahn/Dr. A. Chen/Dr. S. Thompkins

Molly grinned. "Not a bad time to get my head examined," she said aloud, immediately feeling foolish to be talking to the woodwork. She also scolded herself for feeling so ill at ease. She was an experienced professional. This was a safe part of the county. Chill out, Molly, she ordered her thoughts.

Hurrying to the next door, Molly practically had to put her nose to the wood to read.

Suite 330
Inscrutable Security

A thin line of light escaping under the door spilled over her toes. She allowed a sigh of relief. Resting her hand on the doorknob, she turned it, eager to get inside even if it was to confront an angry client.

But the door was locked. Molly turned harder, but the knob didn't budge. She raised her fist to knock, then heard the sound of a small chime and snapped her head to the right in the direction of the elevator. Someone was coming up. She was quickly reminded of the fact that she had not seen the security guard in the lobby her dispatcher had told her to check in with.

Was it the guard?

The hiss of the elevator's air brakes told her she would soon find out. Despite her earlier admonitions to herself, Molly's heart began to race. She remembered she had pepper spray in her purse, as well as her phone, which had nice, big buttons. She banged her knuckles against the door in a more frantic rhythm than she had intended and glanced toward the elevator. A husky, dark-skinned man wearing a black jacket and black pants, carrying a bright orange gym bag, stepped into the shadows and began walking briskly in her direction.

She only saw his face for a second, but it shocked her, mostly because she recognized him even though they had never met. The man with the bag was Paul Buntz. He had been a local sportscaster in Los Angeles when she was growing up, though she hadn't heard anything about him for years.

Reacting to her fears, Molly reached into her purse. At that moment, the door she was leaning against opened and she gave a little yelp. Off balance, she nearly tumbled inside. A tall, very tanned blond man stared at her, his blue eyes narrowing when he caught the movement of her hand into her purse.

"What's this about then, miss?" he demanded, his deep voice full of the lilt and music of a native Australian.

"I'm—I'm sorry, Mr. Brooker, is it?" She removed her hand and extended it, then threw a glance down the gloomy hallway. Paul Buntz was nowhere in sight.

"No, I'm not Brooker. You got business with him?"

Molly noted that the man seemed to dig his boot-clad heels into the thick carpeting, while managing to lean back and tower over her all at once. He crossed his arms and looked more angry than wary now.

"I'm sorry. Yes, I do have business with Mr. Brooker. My name is Molly Jakes. I'm a field supervisor with Pacific Communications. I've got a crew of men on the premises, and they called me out to assist with a problem."

Her hands fell to her sides and she tried a smile out on the stranger. "I'm sorry if I startled you, but there was a man in the hallway and I got a little spooked."

The blond man quickly brushed by her and stuck his head out for a look, then he took her by the arm and moved her into the office. He closed the door.

He locked it.

Molly took a few steps toward an empty receptionist's desk, watching the Australian lean against the wall and quite openly appraise her from head to toe.

His very blue eyes finally came to rest on Molly's face. "No one there now, love. Shouldn't be sending a chit like yourself out alone in the dead of night, if you ask me. What's your boss thinking?"

Molly straightened her back as the muscles in her face tightened. It was the nineties, but some men still lagged a century behind in their regard for women, she reminded herself. But why did a modern-day Neanderthal have to look like this guy?

"Well, this is only a guess, but I'd say he's thinking he had a job to get done so he sent the person responsible for doing it. Are my men from Pacific Communications here in this suite, do you know?"

His smile grew wider at Molly's challenging tone. "Just me. But I saw a van and a crowd of chaps with hard hats and the like around back at the receiving dock when I came up a few minutes ago. Probably your crew. Can I walk you down?"

"No, thank you," Molly replied, not liking the fact that her voice held more sarcasm than was really necessary. She realized the stranger was getting the brunt of what she'd wanted to say to her dispatcher. Molly prided herself on doing a great job in a field overwhelmingly populated by men—the majority of whom felt pretty much like this guy did about women—without letting their jibes rankle her. She tried hard to smile sincerely and reached into her bag for a business card.

With a snap, she left it on the desk. "If you see Mr. Brooker, would you mind telling him I'm down with the installation crew?"

The stranger raised his brows, which were bleached white by the sun. He grinned. "I'll do it if I see him. Have a good one, love."

Molly nodded, then hurried past him out of the office and down the dark hallway. She pushed the button for the elevator and glanced back into the darkness. She made out a tall shape and was a little annoyed to realize that the Australian stranger was watching her.

He's being kind. Chivalrous, one side of her brain said.

He's getting a last look at your fanny, the other said, with a bit more conviction.

Molly stepped into the elevator and stabbed at the button marked *B* as well as the Door Close command. Staring straight ahead, she thought about the Aussie. It wasn't until the other passenger made a noise that Molly realized she was not alone.

Paul Buntz looked more frightened than she felt, Molly realized after the initial jolt of adrenaline surged through her. His eyes were wide and his mouth tense. She had the distinct feeling he had been expecting someone else.

His left hand was in his jacket pocket. Molly had a fleeting thought that he was carrying a gun. The orange gym bag she had noticed earlier was on the floor at his feet, as if he had dropped it.

"Hello," she offered, her pulse racing as the elevator chugged slowly to the basement. "I'm sorry if I startled you. I've done that twice tonight."

"No problem," Buntz replied, then leaned down to retrieve the bag. He jerked it quickly upward and two computer disks tumbled out. "Damn," he muttered, hurriedly grabbing up the small black squares as if he didn't want Molly to see them.

She turned her eyes away, in the hopes that that would calm him down, but not before noting that the labels on the disks said Inscrutable Security. As the elevator doors opened to reveal the concrete basement, Molly stepped forward. Without looking back at the ex-sportscaster, she hurried into the well-lit garage area. No footsteps echoed behind her, so she assumed Buntz was riding back up to the lobby.

Molly heard men's voices echoing off the thick walls, smelled gasoline and the sea and spotted a group working across the huge, open space of the office building's basement. Rafe Amundson, foreman of the crew, was watching three other installers wrestle with a five-hundred-foot spool of cable.

"Hello, gentlemen," Molly called out. "How's it going?"

Three heads turned. Rafe's didn't. When she got to him she saw he was scowling while the installers grinned and kept working.

"Those g.d. frame rats at Gutless Electric, Inc. refuse to call out anyone to help us get dial tone, that's how it's going, Boss," Rafe said as he kept his eyes on his men. "Which means out of the sixty-six special circuits we're supposed to cut in here tonight, thirty-eight are dead. What the hell Gutless is doing still jerry-rigging its old-fashioned switching equipment is beyond me."

"Gutless Electric" was the way Rafe and several others referred to the other local dial-tone carrier well-known for its less-than-timely resolution of problems. "I'll go out to the van to call and get the district level out of bed," Molly replied. "But before I do that, where's the client?"

"Mr. Brooker disappeared with his block-long limo about an hour ago." Rafe met her eyes and slid the wad of gum he was chewing to the other side of his mouth. "That's one weird puppy, you ask me. Ranting and raving, strutting around, the whole time his kid sitting in the car looking like he wanted to drop off the face of the earth. He told me to tell you he had to go to meet some people who were moving his boat down to San Diego but that you weren't to leave until the problem was fixed."

Rafe chuckled and cracked the knuckles on his huge hands, which for thirty-five years had so ably serviced telephone customers throughout Orange County. "Guess he didn't realize you had to get your makeup on and comb your hair before you could get out here with us peons."

She smiled and looked pointedly at Rafe's crumpled T-shirt, which was untucked from his grimy jeans. "You know how appearances count toward making good first impressions, Rafe."

"Hell with that, says my union rep. The brass wants me to dress up in a monkey suit, they can give me a clothing allowance, Ms. Jakes." Rafe spat out the gum into his hand, wadded it up and shoved it into the pocket of his jeans, then lit a cigarette and stuck it in his mouth.

Molly bit back the two dozen criticisms she was ready to voice, well aware that the three installers were listening to every word. She gave Rafe an "I'll deal with you later" look and asked, "Where did you park the van?"

Rafe made a motion with his hand, dug out a set of car keys and handed them to her, then turned his attention back to the diagnostic equipment on the cart in front of him. Molly walked out onto the loading dock, descended the steep stairway and crossed into the nearly empty lot. The Pacific Communications van was parked in the middle. She unlocked the back doors and climbed in.

Settling down for some intercompany unpleasantness, she located the home phone number of the district manager for repair in Rafe's call-out book. A groggy woman answered on the fourth ring and then a sleep-filled male voice picked up, a this-better-be-good edge to each word.

After five minutes of tense conversation, Molly gained his agreement to dispatch a second-level supervisor—Molly's equal at Garrett Electric Telephone, which was Gutless Inc.'s legal name—to help the frame people fix the circuit problems.

Molly hung up the phone, turned off the van lights and sat quietly in the dark. Her neck and back ached, and the headache she had fought off announced its reappearance with a vengeance. She hugged her coat close and looked around the van for a thermos. Molly knew a cup of coffee at this hour would give her a stomachache, but she needed a hit of caffeine to shake off the fatigue.

Grabbing a badly dented, old-fashioned aluminum thermos she knew to be Rafe's from the front seat, Molly poured coffee into a foam cup and tried to relax while she waited for reinforcements.

Her mind wandered to the blue-eyed Australian stranger on the third floor. She met a lot of men on the job. Customers, fellow employees, lawyers from the megafirm that shared the Pacific Communications building in downtown Mission Viejo. But this guy seemed different from most. While few got her blood running during an initial meeting, this man had.

Despite his beak of a nose and the craggy lines around his eyes, he was handsome in what might be described as a dangerous way. A way that made her forget what she was doing. A way that got her thinking about things she would like to be doing—with him.

He was powerfully built and what her grandmother called cocksure of himself. Molly blushed and smiled at the X-rated thoughts racing through her mind.

But there was no denying the attraction she'd felt toward him. Could it have been fate willing them to meet on a night like this? If she went upstairs later, would he still be there?

The Aussie was fresh and a bit arrogant, but very, very sexy. Definitely dangerous for a serious-minded professional woman with a plan for the next couple of years that called for hard work and all the overtime she could stand.

"Heck of a guy to meet on Valentine's Day," Molly murmured, then laughed aloud at her silly fantasizing. The sound of an approaching car cut short her thoughts, and she peeked out the window, wondering if Frederick Brooker was ready to reappear. Sure enough, as she watched, a long, cream-colored Lincoln limo rolled past. It stopped near the dark side of the loading dock.

Molly put her hand on the door handle, but stopped as a shape emerged from the darkness. From twenty yards away, she could not make out the face of the person in black, but the bright orange bag the man carried told her it was Paul Buntz.

The back door of the limo opened, Buntz got in and the car sped off.

So much for her confrontation with Mr. Brooker, Molly thought. With a sigh, she stepped out of the van and headed back to the crew for what she feared would be a long night.

AT SIX-THIRTY in the morning, Molly pulled out of the parking lot of Summer Point Towers. Sixty circuits into Inscrutable Security from various commercial- and residential-alarm customers were at last up and running.

Frederick Brooker had not returned, though she had endured a terse phone call from him at 2:00 a.m., during which he'd promised to "report you and your crew to the Public Utilities Commission, the Better Business Bureau and the mayor's office if those circuits aren't up as promised!" After all, Brooker had continued, hadn't he paid a huge advance installation bill because the credit office of Pacific Communications had requested it?

Molly had done her best to soothe him, imagining that a man like Brooker had taken it personally when his business's creditworthiness had been questioned by her company's business office. But despite that edge of ego, she had been able to calm Brooker down remarkably fast.

The supervisor from Garrett Electric had shown up and been effective with his technicians; all in all, it had not been a bad night's work. As she pulled off the Orange Freeway and headed up the already busy streets toward home, Molly figured she could shower, sleep for a couple of hours and be back in the office by noon.

She turned off the soft-rock station and flipped to an all-news station. The first story was a frightening one about more turmoil in the Middle East, a car bomb and dead children. The second story was about the murder of ex-sportscaster and football player, Paul Buntz.

Molly stared at her radio as if she could see the story unfold, while the broadcaster filled in the details. Shot five times in a deserted parking lot near the Summer Point Marina, Buntz was found floating in the Pacific by an unidentified man at approximately 2:00 a.m.

A suspect was being sought by the police, the radio voice added. He was a wealthy Orange County businessman identified as Frederick Brooker, owner of Inscrutable Security in Summer Point. An eyewitness reported seeing Brooker speeding off in a beige Lincoln limo, in the direction of Mission Verde.

Chapter One

Like most women, Molly Jakes was good in emergencies.

The sight of blood, particularly other people's, did not freak her out. Which is why, without hesitation, she was ready to help as soon as she spotted three wrecked cars and four people scattered across the sloping concrete freeway off ramp, a mile from her home.

As she braked, she noted it was 3:00 a.m. exactly by the car's clock. Above her in the damp, late-summer air, ribbons of fog wound around the thousand-watt fluorescent bulbs atop the light poles lining the double-laned expanse, giving animate and inanimate objects alike the spooky blue tint peculiar to the middle of night.

The accident had occurred just a minute or two ago, she estimated, reaching for the cellular phone in the car console. Her fingers brushed the cold leather where the mobile unit was usually nestled and she swore under her breath. The phone was being repaired, and all she had in her purse was the antiquated pager that gave her no ability to call out.

She glanced in the rearview mirror, hoping to see the reflection of oncoming headlights, but caught only a blank swatch of asphalt. Clearing the incline, she braked and rolled past a red-and-silver Bronco, its wheels still spinning. From her location she saw a handful of twinkling lights from the sleeping houses lining the hills of Mission Viejo. The town-house development where she lived was just beyond. For a moment, she considered driving on and calling for help from home, then returning. But the smell of burned rubber and the sight of people tossed like rag dolls thrown by a malicious giant changed her mind. Years of first-aid training had taught her that in many cases five minutes' delay could cost a life.

Molly judged that the wreck had started in the left lane, for the Bronco had left a long trail of skid marks that cut across both lanes at an angle. The car it had run into—a small blue compact—was smashed into the two-foot-thick abutment on the right, facing east in the westbound lanes. It was hooked into the Bronco's door panel by its rear bumper.

There were four people on the pavement. Two were facedown near the back of the Bronco, which was spitting out a threatening plume of white smoke from under its hood. One lay on his back in a strangely restful pose, the fourth a few yards over against the abutment.

He was the only one she knew for sure was dead. Even at a distance of twenty feet, Molly's brain registered his missing limb and the bright smears on the ground.

She slowed and scouted a safe place to stop past the carnage, a shot of fear immobilizing her for a second before giving her brain a tremendous rush. As a phone company manager with eight employees reporting to her, Molly had completed over a hundred hours of emergency training. She even knew basic sign language commands. Traffic accidents, electrocution, cuts, poison, burns and broken bones, she had studied how to handle them in films and handbooks. Monthly newsletters, called *Flashes,* parked themselves weekly in her In box, and over hurried lunches she had made it a point to read them all. There were countless examples of how death resulted because the most basic safety rules weren't followed.

Thanks to her training, all the procedures for keeping herself safe kicked in together in her head. She continued past the accident for twenty yards, leaving room for the cops and ambulances, and parked cleanly off the road. She was directly in front of a call box, right under a light. While waiting for the operator to answer, she removed her dark windbreaker to reveal a more easily seen white T-shirt. Molly noted more skid marks and a flattened safety fence lying on its back just ahead of her and glanced down the steep hillside.

Imagining another night's vehicular violence gave her a chill, but she remained cool and gave the necessary information to the operator, whose sole responsibility was to communicate with motorists in trouble. A minute later, she hung up and grabbed two blankets she always kept in the trunk, looked both ways and dashed into the traffic lanes at the edge of the mayhem.

At that moment, a man in a black pickup truck rolled toward her. He stopped in the left lane and jumped out, yelling, "Did you call it in?"

"Yes. They're coming," she answered. "Do you have any flares?"

"Good idea." The guy ran back to his truck while Molly hurried to the man lying on his back. He was young and preppy-looking, dressed in a white polo shirt, khakis and one deck shoe. The emblem on his shirt wasn't an alligator, though. It was a face, a smiling Oriental face. She threw one of the blankets over him, smacking her knuckles on something hard as she tucked the cloth around his knee.

Her fingers wrapped around the object and she scooted it out from under him, recognizing its shape before she saw it, even though she had never held one before.

It was a gun. Small, heavier than she would have guessed, it was warm to the touch.

For a second, Molly couldn't think what to do with it; panic squeezed out all thought. Finally she took a big gulp of air and stuck the thing into the pocket of her denim skirt. In the fullness of the fabric, the pocket swallowed the gun.

Molly pressed her hand against the man's neck. No pulse. She pulled his eyelids up and found his pupils were dilated and motionless.

He was dead.

Molly drew back, suddenly cold, noticing how incredibly noisy it was near the truck since its engine was still running. Her train of thought was probably born out of reflexive self-protection, she realized, remembering people say that in times of great tragedy it's possible to put one's emotions on hold and take them out later when there's more time for a nervous breakdown. Which is what Molly felt she might have someday when she recalled how lonely it felt to sit beside two dead men.

These were the first corpses she had ever seen, and her eyes filled with tears. They were so still. And heavy, as if gravity was sucking their bodies down into their graves already.

A few months ago she had been circumstantially involved in a murder case, but it had not saddened her like this. In that matter, Molly had been witness to no mayhem, had not been privy to dead eyes and wounds and blood. Because of that, she had remained calm. She had given the police various coherent statements, had coolly appeared before a grand jury, was set to testify next week at the trial. Molly had not even spent one sleepless night because of images of corpses.

Something told her that this time things were going to be different.

Now that she was face-to-face with violence, all she could think about was the car's engine, the pebbles digging into her knee, the weight in her pocket, the sound of her heartbeat echoing in her ears and her own mortality. If she had been driving on this stretch of road only a few seconds earlier...

Molly stared at the dead man beside her, finally forcing herself into action. Carefully she leaned over the figure and started CPR.

Five puffs in, then push, push, push.

"Let me help you." A man in a blue mechanic's jumpsuit touched her shoulder and she nodded, not allowing herself to wonder what was going on around her, never missing a breath. She blew expelled air into the stranger's body, while the other good samaritan pushed down on his chest.

The stranger remained dead.

"There's one alive by the Bronco. I don't think the car's a risk to blow up. Do you want to try him?" the man asked, gently squeezing her arm as he coaxed her to her feet.

Molly stood up and nodded, feeling her lip tremble and her eyes sting. She moved away as if walking through sand. A rock, zinged out from under the tire of a vehicle on the freeway above, smacked into her forehead above the eye. It hurt like mad, but for some reason Molly welcomed the pain.

She heard a squeal of tires behind her and shouts, then two young women, dressed in bicycle pants and U.C.L.A. T-shirts, ran past her. They began working on one of the other accident victims, an older man with white hair. When he lifted his hand, all three women grinned.

Encouraged, Molly fell to her knees next to the remaining man. He had on a heavy windbreaker zipped up tight. His pulse was so weak she could hardly feel it, and his dark skin had paled, particularly around his mouth. Glancing back at the off-ramp entrance, she saw both lanes were blocked by cars and several people were running around.

The pickup driver and a teenager with dreadlocks were working together and lighting a string of flares around the blocked lanes.

Molly tilted the man's head back, then blew sharply through his dry lips. Her hands fumbled with his windbreaker, stopping at the hard lump over his heart.

Damn if he wasn't wearing a gun! A bigger one than she had picked up before, to judge from the outline of it. The weapon was strapped against his chest.

"What in the hell was going on out here?" she asked in fear and anger. No one answered her.

Visions of high-speed chases and deranged drug dealers flooded her brain. She blanched, but pushed on. A second worry, that this scene somehow had something to do with the murder trial she was going to testify at, Molly dismissed. Get a grip, she scolded. Lives were depending on her.

The scream and whine of emergency vehicles began to fill the air.

The girls had saved the white-haired man, Molly thought. Maybe she could save this one, too.

"Please stay in your cars and proceed." This static-tinged command blared out of a patrol car's loud-speaker as two black and whites rolled up and parked a yard from Molly. She left the gun where it was and slipped her hand beneath the holster to do chest compressions. Suddenly the man's body jerked, and he inhaled and began to gag.

Molly turned him on his side so he wouldn't choke, which was when she saw the hole. It was about the size of a pencil, neat and clean, right in the center of his left shoulder blade. Blood soaked his entire back.

"We'll take over, miss."

The paramedic's hand on Molly's shoulder made her gasp. She stood. "His pulse is low, about thirty-three. I've been doing CPR for three minutes. And I think he's got a bullet in the back," she added.

Hearing this information, the paramedic didn't even blink, but turned and ordered, "Get me an IV and plasma. Possible gunshot."

A uniformed cop beckoned Molly and the two co-eds. They followed, and Molly saw there was now an entire fleet of police and rescue trucks. The authoritarian honk and blinking lights of a fire engine clogged her senses along with the sounds of radios, dispatchers, air brakes and the whacka, whacka, whacka of a hovering news helicopter. It buffeted the group below with hot gusts of air.

"Hell of a job, ladies," offered a smiling highway patrolman, his beige uniform impossibly clean. "We could have used you after the last earthquake."

The group stood silent, watching as the ambulances loaded up their badly battered or lifeless cargo. One of the policemen, a man about sixty with a precision salt-and-pepper haircut and a fat polyester tie, took Molly aside to ask a few questions.

"Molly Jakes. I work for Pacific Communications," she answered.

"Phone number?"

She gave him her work number, craning her neck to look at the firemen, all yellow jackets and boots. They were spraying foam on the Bronco, and she thought of herself sitting next to it five minutes before.

"What were you doing out at 3:00 a.m., Miss Jakes?"

"I was going home. I live just up the road, in Mission Verde."

He stared at her. "Didn't you have something to do with the Brooker murder case?"

Weakly she nodded, cursing the fact that she was now so well-known by the authorities in her own town. She had preferred her law-abiding, anonymous life. Being known by sight by a cop gave her an odd feeling. She explained that she was a witness, though only a material one. For a moment, she was afraid he was going to make her go to the station. But he let it drop.

Molly gave him her address, telling herself that the edge in his voice wasn't really thankless. Molly had a tendency to apologize for other people; it was her way of retaining her optimism about the human race.

This guy is obviously tired, she told herself. He seemed to be near retirement age, and Molly imagined he was sick of being called out on these middle-of-the-night disasters.

"Where were you coming from?"

"Summer Point Towers. Eighteen ten Summer Road. I got a call that there was an emergency at that location where my phone crew was doing an installation."

"How long were you there?"

"Not long. It turned out the call was a mistake by the dispatcher."

"That happen often?"

"No, thank God." It had never happened before, not to Molly anyway. But she wasn't going to get into that with the cops. She was going to raise hell with dispatch, but it certainly wasn't a big deal.

The cop raised his eyebrows, then glanced in the direction of her parked car. "You went alone?"

"Yes." She swallowed the words "I'm a big girl, Officer," and with this little defiance felt her equilibrium take a turn for the better.

"Okay, Miss Jakes. We'll be calling you tomorrow, I mean later today, to get you to come in and give a complete statement of what you saw here tonight."

"Fine." She wanted to ask what he thought had caused the accident, but the cop took a couple of steps toward one of the coeds, probably to ask her the same basic questions. Molly clasped her hands over her forearms and looked down to see why they felt so dry and tight. She had brown splotches on her T-shirt and skirt, and all over her arms. For a moment, she was nauseous, but forced herself to breathe deeply and headed for her car.

A red-haired patrolman nodded as she passed, his eyes flickering over her. More than anything, Molly wanted to go home and take a hundred-and-fifty-degree shower, then soak in a bubble bath.

"You can go ahead and get back on the freeway, ma'am," the officer told her. "They're setting up barricades so they can get the fuel hosed off, but you can make it if you go now."

Molly smiled and kept walking, wishing someone could drive her home, wishing she had someone waiting for her there. Now that the emergency was over, that initial rush of strength was dissipating and her bones felt like rubber.

Sliding into the car, Molly sat for a moment and stared in disbelief at the ignition. Her key ring, holding house keys, office keys, the whole shebang, was hanging there. She never left her keys in the car! If it had been stolen, the insurance company wouldn't have paid off, good samaritan acts notwithstanding. So much for patting herself on the back earlier for following safety rules, she thought.

The car started immediately. Molly buckled her seat belt and hit the door-lock button. Accelerating, she turned right at Verdugo Boulevard and headed for home. She wanted off the freeway. Out of this scene of mayhem that was much too real to ever forget as one could an upsetting movie or even a tragic news show.

As MOLLY DROVE AWAY from the accident scene, the man in the blue mechanic's jumpsuit gave his name and telephone number to Lieutenant Cortez. He was also thanked and sent home.

The man returned to his car, but before driving off, he reached for his cellular phone and punched in a number.

"Hello," a male voice snapped in his ear.

"Nothing went down as planned," the slight man reported, wiping a bead of sweat from his thin mustache. Despite the cool night air, his being that close to a cop had made him nervous. "I was waiting for your guys, but all hell broke loose. They were ambushed or something. Both of your vehicles were in a wreck. When the girl arrived, she dived right in to help. By the time I got out of the car, there were three other cars stopped and I never got a clear shot."

"Why didn't you take them all out?" the man on the other end demanded. "I would have covered you for the extra work."

"It never would have worked. There were too many people."

"Well, where the hell is Steele? Is he dead?"

"I don't know. Probably. Two guys are. The two live ones I saw were an old dude and a black guy. He ain't either of those, I guess."

"Well, at least he's dead. That changes things, but..." The man's voice trailed off. "Well, tomorrow I'll send someone for the girl. You go back home. I'll be in touch."

The man in the blue coveralls hung up without answering and drove off. He saw the girl's car up ahead, wondered if he could get a clean shot through the window, but discarded the thought. Too chancy with all the cops around.

He'd get her later. Or someone else would.

A BLOCK AWAY FROM the accident scene, Molly leaned back into the seat. It was then she noticed the dash light on. The tiny red diagonal line in the box indicating the silhouette of a car was blinking brightly, Detroit's high-tech way of telling her that one of the car doors was ajar.

"For criminey's sake," she muttered, feeling the driver's door with her left hand. She thought she had closed it tight and realized she was more wiped out than she feared.

"Put your hand back on the wheel."

The man's voice boomed out from the back seat in a ragged, angry command. It was deep, with an accent Molly's terror-frozen brain did not immediately place.

Reflexively, her leg stiffened and the car lurched.

Her chest ached from the increased speed of her heart, and the muscles in her neck screamed out as if they were encircled by a noose. For a second, Molly felt as if she had suddenly died and floated above herself.

"I've got a gun aimed at your back. Put your hand back on the wheel."

Molly trembled as the unseen passenger roughly pushed at her hand, and she cried out in a little whimper. The door that was ajar was on the passenger side of the car, she realized in horror!

While she was out helping keep a fellow human being alive, this guy had crept into her back seat with who knew what brand of crime on his mind.

She was too afraid to look around but risked a quick check into the mirror. It told her nothing. He must be hunkered down in the corner of the seat, or on the floor. How could I not have seen him when I got in? she asked herself. Molly damned the fact that she owned a two-door car. You could never see into the back seats.

With her hands now growing sticky with sweat against the leather steering wheel, a million possible actions to take flew through her mind. She could honk, slam on the brakes, run into a car. Anything to get someone's attention. The traffic light a few hundred yards ahead changed to red, and Molly slowed down and stopped.

"What are you doing in my car?" she demanded.

The stranger made no response, though she heard him gasp as if in pain, then swear softly under his breath. Molly caught the image of a muscular forearm, and a glint of metal around his wrist. Then she saw his gun.

"Drive."

She jerked her eyes straight ahead. The light had turned green. "Where to?" she asked, keeping her foot on the brake.

"Drive home. That's where you were going, wasn't it?"

He was Australian. The Crocodile Dundee inflection was there, though all the wit and "g'day, mate" humor were ominously absent.

"I'm not taking you to my home." Molly knew she sounded insane, but even terrified, she had no intention of driving some maniacal murderer to her front door.

For a moment, it was quiet. Another car passed on her left, the driver peering in his mirror to get another glimpse before pulling his vehicle in front of her. The light ahead changed to yellow, then red again.

Molly realized she was holding her breath. Then she heard the gun click. Suddenly the man in her back seat jerked her head back by the hair. "Drive to your house or I will. I know the address, Molly, and I know Mission Verde. You have three seconds to decide what happens next."

Tears stung Molly's eyes from the pain of his grip, as well as from sheer physical terror. The fact that he knew her name scared her much worse than when she thought she was a randomly chosen victim. Some bell of recognition was ringing in her brain, though through the fog of fear she couldn't tie it to a specific piece of information.

With no other alternative, Molly eased her foot off the brake and hit the gas, sending the car rushing through the red light.

Chapter Two

A half mile from her home, Molly's heart rate slowed down a bit, and anger joined forces with hysteria as a leveling force. Most people she knew would agree that she wasn't a tough person, but she also did not allow anyone to push her around.

If a waitress was snooty, Molly asked to see the manager. If she paid eighty dollars for a silk blouse and the seam popped open the first time she wore it, Molly took it back. So, now that it appeared she had been kidnapped, she decided to be what her nephew, Tyler, would call a "hard case."

Her passenger had made no further comment the past few seconds, but she could hear his breathing. She thought he must be injured and wondered if he'd been a passenger in one of the wrecked cars. Molly kept picturing the gunshot wound in the one man's back.

Was the guy in her car the shooter?

Clenching her teeth to stay calm, she let the car coast as she rounded Isabella Avenue, weighing if she should call the guy's bluff and go straight instead of turning on Plaza Viejo, where her town house was. She stopped at the light two blocks from her house, slanting her gaze to the mirror again.

"You can turn right on red in California, doll. I suggest you do it."

"I need to get gas."

"If you run out, you'll wish you hadn't."

Someone else knew all about being a "hard case," she decided.

One minute later, Molly turned left into the steepest driveway in town, cursing the fact that she hadn't seen one cop or one burly trucker.

The car groaned as it usually did at the incline, and Molly shifted into low. Her home was one of sixty, ten rambling groups of blocks cut into terraces in the hilly countryside of Mission Verde, fifty-six miles south of Los Angeles. It sat at the edge of some of the last undeveloped land in the area, where skunks, raccoons and rabbits poked around on the patio where Molly sunned herself.

Killing the headlights, Molly heard the coyotes bragging out loud about their night's catch of slow house pets, and a shiver of empathy for their furry prey ran down her back. She reached for the door at the same moment her passenger again grabbed her hair.

"Take it nice and slow, Molly girl. I wouldn't want to wake up your neighbors."

"Stop pulling my hair," she replied, surprised when he let her go. Slowly she stepped out of the car. Her skirt caught on the edge of the door and she tugged at it quickly, unable to place the weight in her pocket. Then she remembered.

Holy night, Molly thought as her scalp prickled with fear. I'm armed.

She turned toward her captor and got her first look at him as he stepped out of the car. He was big. Well over six feet, he had shoulders like some lumberjack and longish blond hair. He wore jeans and cowboy boots, a red T-shirt with an Aussie flag over his heart and a tiny gold earring in his right ear.

"Oh my God," Molly gasped. "It's you."

"Hello, Miss Jakes. Long time no see." Despite the words, he didn't smile.

Impossible as it seemed, standing in front of Molly, gun in hand, was the man she'd met briefly in the office of Inscrutable Security, the night Frederick Brooker was alleged to have shot Paul Buntz. Molly felt her stomach flip as a rushing, ringing noise rattled through her brain. My God, she thought, as her face flushed with embarrassment and anger, I fantasized about this guy! Talk about poor judgment!

She stared at the big man. He was sporting handcuffs this time. Or handcuff, if the singular is correct, Molly silently corrected. His right wrist was encased in one metal circle. The empty one hung down like a punk rocker's bracelet.

The gun was big, too, with a long, black barrel.

She met his eyes. "Who the hell are you and what's this all about?"

"Let's go in. Then we'll talk."

"Oh, sure. I'll make coffee," she snapped.

The man's deep blue eyes narrowed. "I'd rather have tea. Or don't you Yanks ever drink the stuff?"

"I've got tea. I save it for *invited* guests."

"Yeah, well consider me invited or we'll finish this right here." He moved the gun slightly, his face deadly calm.

The weight of the pistol in her skirt felt enormous, and Molly wondered if he could see the outline of it against her leg. The last thing in the world she wanted to do was close herself in her house with this maniac, but she couldn't think clearly enough to decide what else she could pull off.

Molly nodded toward the path winding around the parking garages. "We need to go that way. Should I go first?"

The man seemed to detect something in her eyes that racheted his anxiety up a notch, because he reached out and grabbed her arm. "Who's in there?"

She could smell the fear on his skin and began to panic. He had kidnapped her, for heaven's sake! What was he so afraid of? "My marine husband and six Dobermans. So why don't you take off now?"

Molly regretted her smart answer but not the look on the man's face. He looked shocked. But the shock quickly turned to arrogance. "Nice try. Get going. I'll take my chances."

"I don't think so," she replied. "Not until you tell me what's going on." An obvious answer to her question suddenly occurred to her, and she felt weak. "Does this have anything to do with Brooker?"

His grip on her arm tightened and he waved the gun in her face. "Shh. I don't want you waking anyone, understand?"

When he drew closer to her, Molly realized with a shock that she had memorized his features from their last meeting. Up close she saw deep fatigue lines in his face. But it was the same firm chin, the same aggressively curved nose, the same pale eyebrows, silky above eyes a clear sea blue. He had a tiny, uneven cleft in his chin, which she did not remember. He was as tanned as when she saw him months ago, as if he worked outdoors, and his teeth glimmered white in the light from the security lamp next to her front door.

"I understand. But don't you see how ridiculous this is for me? I can't let you in my house. I'm afraid," she added, the very real sentiment coming out without her thinking it.

"Yeah, well, I'm sorry about that. But I'm not standing out here in the open with you. Now get going!"

He pushed her, and she took a few steps toward her door. "Look, I live alone. But I don't have any money in the house. Why not take my purse and the keys and my car and go. I don't have anything else of value inside." She heard the plea in her voice and felt tears welling. She thought the man looked regretful for a moment, but his expression changed quickly.

"Go. Now, Molly, I don't want to shoot you."

"How nice you remember my name," she couldn't help retorting.

"Don't flatter yourself. I didn't, but we've got mutual friends who reminded me."

For the first time, Molly considered screaming, despite the folly of it amid these thick-walled, high-windowed units that were touted for their soundproof qualities. But she knew it would get her killed, as well as possibly some of her neighbors. The man released her and she walked toward the door, prompting the lizards who lived in the bushes to do their usual rustling through the ivy. The noise made the man next to her tense, but it was a comfort to Molly.

Molly's neighbor above, Jerry, was never home during the week. She considered going up to the wrong door in the hopes of alerting someone but discarded that notion as the man's gun pressed into her back. Though she wasn't crazy about most of her neighbors, she didn't dislike anyone enough to risk getting them killed.

Molly turned the key in the dead bolt, then in the lock, and suddenly she and the man were inside. He rested for a moment while his eyes grew accustomed to the dark. Neither of them made a move to turn on the light, but enough of it poured in from the twelve-foot wall of windows on the opposite side of the living room for him to see the layout.

Molly stared at her comfy chairs, the shawls to drape over legs in cool evenings, the pillows her friends had made, and felt none of the joy she usually did. Her big splurge items since she'd bought the town house were pictures. She loved art, and the walls held a few lovely paintings. The man didn't seem too interested in any of it, though.

"So where's the tea?"

"Why don't you tell me what's going on and what you want with me?"

"I need something to drink, that's why," he replied. He gestured with the gun. "Why don't you pour?"

Molly moved to the left, and he followed through the archway into her kitchen. Large by the area's standards, it held cupboards floor to ceiling, a center work island with a stove, and a pass-through to the dining room on the opposite side of the wall.

She was more scared than she ever imagined a person could be. She had no idea what was going to happen next, and the suspense was making her dizzy with fear.

"What kind of tea?" she whispered in a ragged voice.

"Kind?" he asked.

"I have Lipton, decaf orange spice and Earl Grey." Her hand rested on the canister and her eyes met his. She saw then how dry his lips were; the bottom one was cracked and bleeding at the corner. He was still pointing the gun at her, but for the first time she felt her terror recede a degree.

He didn't seem the type to shoot a woman at close range, or at any range, really. He looked exhausted, frightened and, unless Molly was completely wrong, in pain.

"Lipton will be fine, doll. Two sugars and milk."

Molly snapped on the flame under the teakettle. "I don't have milk." She did have, but she didn't feel hospitable.

Disappointment flashed across his face, and she thought how stupid this scene was. Here she was with a stranger, acting like some domestic couple, discussing what was needed at the grocer's. Just then he groaned and rested his hands on the tiled counter of the cooking island.

Molly stood two feet away from him and for the first time noticed how badly bruised he was. He seemed to have some kind of bandages on his neck, below his collar.

She moved around the counter toward her front door but stopped when his head snapped up. The stare he gave her now was one of a man clearly in pain, and his knuckles were white around the grip of the gun. "Stand still, damn you. I don't want to hurt you."

Carefully she put her hands into her skirt pockets, hoping the bolt of fear that rammed through her arm muscles didn't show when her fingers made contact with the gun secreted there. "I'm not going anywhere. What's wrong with you? Have you been shot?"

"Don't concern yourself with me, doll. I'm fine."

She nodded at the keys lying on the counter. "Why don't you just take my car and go? Lock me in a closet or something."

"I can't go anywhere yet. I need you to help me get this thing off." He held up his arm with the handcuffs dangling.

"That's why you kidnapped me?"

The man's eyes went blank and suddenly he raised the gun and pointed it directly at her throat. "No. That's not why. I know you, from before. Why don't you talk for a minute? Tell me how you know Fred Brooker. Did he send you to get me tonight?"

"What are you talking about?" she replied, taking a step backward. "I told you the night we met that I work for the phone company. I was in his office on business. I never even met the man. So why would he send me to get you?" Molly stopped talking and leaned against the counter. "And how would he know you were going to be in a wreck tonight?"

The man didn't seem to be listening to her. He was gazing off over her shoulder. It gave her the creeps, and a fresh wave of anxiety that he might be on drugs crashed over her. "Look, you can't stay here. I've got to go to work this morning. I've got a big job to supervise in San Clemente. If I don't show up, my crew will be here looking for me. So will my boss."

The man caressed the trigger with the pad of his thumb. "Supervise?"

"Like I just told you, I'm with the phone company. I'm a manager. We're putting in a new system at the administrative offices of Green Grocery Stores today, and I'm in charge." Molly blinked, trying desperately to remember if he'd locked the door behind her. She decided he hadn't. "So have your tea and I'll take a shot at the handcuff, but then I want you to leave."

He flinched when she said the word "shot." He lowered the gun a few inches.

"I know you must be scared, Molly," he replied in what in other circumstances would be an apologetic tone. The stranger's glance rested for a moment on Molly's face. "I'm sorry I'm frightening you. It seems, however, that it can't be helped."

The teakettle began to wail.

When the man turned his eyes toward the noise, Molly pulled the gun from her pocket as if she had practiced the move for years. "Throw that gun down and move over against the wall."

The man's face registered no surprise, which scared Molly worse than if he'd cursed at her. "Well, now, that changes things, doesn't it, doll?" He placed the gun on the counter, then reached both hands behind his head, grimacing slightly when his fingers touched his neck.

Molly's hands were sweating and her arm ached from the weight of the gun, or from the tenseness of her grasp. The kettle's screams were full volume now, and the hot steam escaping from its mouth began to fill the cool room like fog.

Her plan was to direct him to her bedroom, which could be locked from either side of the door. After she locked him in, she could call the police. Which meant she had to get him to walk about thirty feet out of the kitchen, across the foyer and down the hall. "I want you to walk out of the kitchen and turn left."

His eyes flickered toward the dark hallway. "To your bedroom, Molly? I'd go there at your invite even without the gun."

"Very funny. Just walk." Her voice was too loud and she glared at the still-wailing kettle.

He made no move.

Nausea churned her stomach, and her skin began to turn clammy from all the steam. Could I just shoot him? Molly asked herself. She was too nervous to look down at the gun to see if it had anything like a safety on it. A knot of pain was throbbing in her shoulder blade.

"Start walking, you creep, or I'll hurt you." The insulting word zapped out of her mouth, surprising Molly and the man both. He made a noise deep in his throat, and a dangerous glint came into his eyes.

All at once he lunged, hurling the red-hot teakettle off the stove directly at Molly, a shout of pure animal anger erupting from his throat. She banged her body against the cabinet to duck the kettle, then turned and ran for the front door. He tackled her and grabbed the gun before she got three feet.

They rolled on the floor while Molly clawed and screamed, kicked and cussed at him, remembering most of her self-defense moves but executing none of them with any effectiveness.

Even injured, his six-foot-three, two-hundred-and-twenty-pound frame found no match in a woman almost a foot shorter and a hundred pounds lighter. They smashed into the foyer table and onto the floor, where Molly felt his body all over her. His hands were so quick she couldn't get a blow in. She kept yelling, though, and he moved a knee over her arm and covered her mouth with his hand.

"Shut up, damn you. Shut up!"

Molly looked him right in the eye, then used every ounce of strength to bite his hand. He didn't yell, but he did slap her head back against the floor, sending her sliding into a fuzzy pit of pain and unconsciousness.

Chapter Three

Alec Steele stood in Molly Jakes's kitchen berating himself for allowing a bad situation to get so much further out of hand. He never should have abducted her; he should have walked off the freeway and found another car.

But seeing her had given him such a start. He couldn't believe it was the same attractive woman he had last seen on the night he had stood on Fred Brooker's boat and watched as the businessman shot and killed another human being.

Alec had thought of her several times in the months between that night and this, especially when he was alone on his boat, the *Strewth,* in the blue-green waters off Australia's coast. He had even planned to look her up when he was in the area, having kept the business card she had snapped down so primly on Fred Brooker's desk.

Could it be a coincidence that she was here? In a city of millions, what the hell had she been doing leaning beside the corpse of a man who had tried to kill him?

With a shiver, Alec threw down four aspirin tablets and took a long swallow of water. The single handcuff pinged against the glass and he frowned. It was time to check and make sure Molly Jakes was recovering from that bonk on the head he had given her.

As well as to find out if she was as innocent as those warm brown eyes made her seem.

MOLLY CAME TO SLOWLY, wanting to believe what she was remembering had not really happened. But, judging from the throbbing in her head, it had.

She was lying on her bed, the afghan, knitted by her best friend's mother, tossed over her bare legs. She was still wearing her stained T-shirt and skirt, but the Aussie had washed her hands and arms.

The thought of some man washing her down while she was out cold sent a wave of anger and embarrassment spilling down her body, an emotion quickly replaced by the terror of the situation. Molly struggled to sit up, which was a bad move, for immediately her stomach contracted and her head felt as if it had been used as a strike ball in a bowling alley.

She wiggled up against the headboard, sank back onto the thick pillows and stared at the door. It was closed, and she guessed, locked, as well. She was now a victim of her own nesting instincts, which had her install old-fashioned locks with keys sporting lovely silk tassels. Trouble was, they could lock a person in as easily as out.

This imprisonment in her own home made her angry enough to attempt to sit up again. She remembered in time to avoid the pain and made herself lie quietly and smolder. Her gaze roamed the room for help or protection. The Aussie had unplugged and removed the phone. Her windows did not open, except for the louvered ones eight feet up the glass.

The town house faced a hill and was alone in the last unit save for her upstairs neighbor, who drove a long-distance rig and was never home on Thursday. Of course, today was Thursday.

Molly swore when she was really frustrated. She knew it was immature, but the vulgar phrases passing her lips relieved some of her anxiety. Only for a moment, however. Fear returned like a growling bear at the sound of the doorknob turning. The tiny hairs on her arms rose above the goose bumps, and she drew her legs up defensively.

She was scanning the room again, trying to focus on something she could use for a weapon, when in walked the person about whom all the curses had been uttered. The stranger looked as bad as Molly felt. For the first time, she noticed that his clothing was also soiled, probably from the deep scrape down the side of his right arm.

It was after six. Sunlight streamed through the white linen drapes. The intruder squinted at Molly and walked toward the bed, halting about two feet away.

She wanted to spit at him but settled for yelling, "You son of a bitch. Do all the men from down under beat women, or just scum like you?"

"Well, glad to see your sweet personality wasn't altered by our little ruckus." He took a step closer and Molly flinched, which stopped him in his tracks.

"Ruckus?" she sputtered. "Let's use the right word here, *mate*. In the States, we call it kidnapping, assault and battery, attempted murder."

"Now hold on. I never meant to hurt you. I was just trying to get my hand away from your damn teeth."

He held up his hand, showing how he had bandaged himself with some adhesive tape and gauze. He'd made a real mess of it; the tape was all lumpy where it had stuck to itself before he'd got it stuck to him.

"I bit you in self-defense."

He made a grunting sound. "I'm sorry you got hurt, Molly. I really never meant to do that." He ventured a step closer and stared intently into her face, not to see into her thoughts, she realized, only her eyes.

"Your pupils are the same size. I'd say you don't have a concussion."

"Are you a doctor?" Molly demanded.

"No," he countered. "Are you?"

"No. For the tenth or so time, I work for the phone company. Remember my boys with hard hats?"

"Hard heads, as well, if they're having to work for you, Molly Jakes." The intruder flushed under his tan as his voice roughened. "If you don't mind me saying, you're out of your mind, acting like some damn female John Wayne. Don't you American women have any sense at all? Don't you know enough not to attack a man twice as big as you? If I were a criminal, I could have killed you when you pulled that gunslinger stunt of yours."

Molly glared. "Who the devil do you think you are, lecturing me like my dad used to? And what is all this John Wayne stuff? Don't you get any current movies in Australia?"

"I think you're being hysterical, Molly."

"And what are you talking about, saying *if* you were a bad guy? If you're not a bad guy, what do you call what you've done to me the past few hours? If you're not a bad guy, call the police and get them out here, and we can all listen to your explanation together."

He rose abruptly, walked over to the bedroom window and peered through the curtains. Molly felt her fear flare up again as she realized just how big he was. The man rubbed at his ribs, which obviously pained him, then turned as he ran his long fingers through his hair. "My name is Alec Steele. I'm surprised you don't know that."

"Why would *I* know your name?"

"For the same reason I know yours. For the same reason I can't call the police. And I can't let you call them."

The single handcuff still dangled from his wrist, making the incongruously comforting sound of a dog's license clanking against a choke collar. His name seemed familiar, but she couldn't place where she'd heard it before. "Why not?"

"Because I can't trust the bastards, that's why not."

"Why not?"

Molly's redundant question hung between them while he got a very odd look on his face. "They may be trying to kill me."

For several seconds, Molly examined this statement, wondering if she was correct in detecting honesty in this very macho man's voice. She was a woman who genuinely liked men but wouldn't claim to know a whole lot about them.

One thing she did know, after working with them for twelve years, was that they didn't like people to know they were scared. Which meant this guy must have been frightened big-time to admit such a thing to a female.

"Does this have something to do with your being at Frederick Brooker's office the night he was supposed to have murdered someone?" Molly remembered that she'd told the police about their meeting. During her interviews with them, the cops had acted as if the man was of no interest to them at all. One of them probably mentioned his name to her, she decided.

"You're a material witness at the trial, aren't you?" she demanded.

"Yes."

"What was all that stuff last night? The wreck and all. Does it have something to do with the trial?"

Alec Steele stared at her for several seconds. "I don't know. Why do you ask?"

"Because I don't understand how we both came to be at the same place at the same time when you live in Australia and I live here."

"I don't understand that, either, Molly. I was hoping maybe you could explain it."

"Me?"

"What were you doing out at three a.m.?"

"My job. What were you doing?"

Alec felt confused, then angry. He had half a mind to tell her the truth. That he had been abducted. Drugged. That he had been sitting with two thugs in a car on the freeway when their car was rammed from behind and all hell broke loose.

But he couldn't tell her any of that. If she was involved with the people who had abducted him, he could be playing into their hands. He stared hard at the fresh-faced beauty in front of him. She couldn't be involved with the guys who had grabbed him. But she must have been targeted, or why else would she have been there?

The questions in his mind made him angry because he knew he couldn't answer them now. Angrily he shook his finger at Molly. "Tell me what you're going to testify about."

Molly opened her mouth, then closed it. She had no intention of doing anything like that, she decided.

While she was no longer afraid Alec Steele was going to kill her, he did have a gun in his waistband, and he seemed to have no intention of leaving. And while she thought he was gorgeous, she had no intention of spending any more time than she had to in discussing whatever it was that was bugging him.

She had to get to the authorities. She had to get help.

And to do that, she had to get rid of him. "First I need to go to the bathroom," Molly announced as a plan began to take shape in her mind.

Alec blinked as he thought it over, then finally nodded his head in agreement. "Sure." He walked to the door and opened it, let her walk past but followed close behind.

She stopped at the bathroom door. "Where are you going?"

"With you."

"Thanks. I think I can manage."

His glance swept over her bathroom and came to rest on the high windows above the sink. He looked back at her intently as if he was measuring something, then backed out of the room and closed the door with a resounding snap. Molly knew he was standing in the hallway, which really ticked her off. She turned on the water in the sink and left it running while she took care of things.

Her head didn't hurt all that bad now that she was up, and it felt good to brush her teeth. She also went after her hair, glad for once that the thick brown mane was straight. Since she had found someone to cut it decently, it hung well, framing her round face and looking shiny and healthy, though her skin showed the results of a sleepless night of shock and fright.

She scrubbed her face and rubbed in a dollop of moisturizer, then stripped off her soiled clothes. Even without clean underwear, Molly felt human again as she wiggled into the one-piece terry jumper she wore around the house in the summer.

Just as she zipped it over her chest, Alec rapped his knuckles against the door. "You okay in there, love?"

"Love, doll, chit. Don't you ever stop with the cutesy labels? You would never be able to hold a job with an equal opportunity employer in this country."

"Have me working for a woman?" he challenged through the wooden door. "No thanks. Come out if you're done. We need to get a few things settled."

Yeah, sure, she answered silently. "I'll be out in a minute. Why don't you make us some tea?"

This false, friendly chattiness was a calculated gamble on her part. While the guy was obviously a danger to her, she couldn't believe he wanted to kill her, which allowed her some options. She was eager to get to a phone, though she knew she would have no chance of that with him in the same room.

Since Alec Steele had made no protest in response to her cheeky suggestion, she reached down and flicked the lock closed. Still no reaction. That meant he'd headed for the kitchen. She turned on the shower, then scrambled up onto the counter and cranked the window completely open. It was plenty big enough, she decided quickly.

Molly had not yet installed new screens, so she didn't have to worry about pushing them out and having them crash into the thick ivy. She hoisted herself up, wondering if the ivy was thick enough to save her own body.

The outside of her town house offered a sheer drop twelve feet to the pavement. Her neighbor Jerry's front porch was directly above the window and Molly hoped she could sit on the window ledge and pull herself up enough to get a leg over his railing. Her nerves were buzzing when she stuck her head out the window and looked around.

None of the other neighbors was out yet. She considered screaming but decided they would have a much better chance of hearing her out in the open than from inside. Just then, the bone-jarring noise of jackhammers exploded in the late-summer air.

Great, Molly thought. Just peachy. They're finally patching the potholes from last winter's mud slide. With all the racket, she was definitely on her own.

Her fanny stung from the sharp lip of the window, and Jerry's rail was farther away than she thought. She didn't have much room to maneuver so she swung one leg over the windowsill and tried to reach sideways for the rain gutter.

Her fingers slipped just as the pounding on the door started. She couldn't hear what Alec Steele was saying over the drone of the shower and the work crew, so she yelled back, "I'll be out in a second. Make some eggs."

Something about her voice must have alerted him. Maybe he could tell she was way up off the ground, she realized, because he tried the door. Molly heard him rattle it, then hit it a couple of times with his fist when he realized it was locked.

The sound of his fury made her rush. Using all her strength, Molly pulled herself completely out of the window, balancing her toes on the ledge. Because the windowpane opened in, she had nothing but the frame to hold on to as she tried to stand, though she found she could reach the railing now, with about six inches to spare.

Gritting her teeth, she forced her right hand to release the window and made a grab for the metal slat of Jerry's rail with both hands. With much effort, she started pulling her body up the side of the building.

The stucco against her skin hurt like the dickens, pricking the soles of Molly's feet. She was breathing through her mouth, concentrating on pulling her rear end up even with her shoulders when she slipped. Her knees skidded and banged against the rail and she slid down, though she somehow managed to hold on despite now sweating hands.

She knew she didn't have much more time. Her shoulder blades and every muscle in her back screamed for relief, but after five or six seconds, she managed to grab the rail with her left foot and hoist herself up.

It was exhilarating, but only for a moment. The front door opened below her and she flattened her body against the wall. Alec Steele was most likely searching the ivy, figuring Molly had dropped down and been killed, considering his unspoken but guessably low opinion of women's physical abilities.

But the man was no fool. She knew it wouldn't be long before he checked upstairs. Molly had a feeling he wouldn't be nearly as calm as he'd been a minute ago. She grabbed the knob on Jerry's door and turned it, but of course the door was locked. She had a key to his place, but it was hanging downstairs on the key keeper in her kitchen. She dropped to her knees to feel under the slimy green welcome mat. Amazing how people leave their keys in such obvious places, she thought as her heart pounded faster. A yell of victory nearly escaped as her fingers found the cold piece of metal. Still on her knees, she leaned over and slipped the key in, shivering as the door creaked open to admit her into the safe haven of her neighbor's empty home.

Molly shut the door behind her, surprised at how badly her hands were shaking. The skin on her face felt taut and unreal, and she had a funny hollow sound in her ears, like the one she got on some carnival rides. She knew enough about shock, however, to realize that it probably accounted for all these bizarre symptoms.

The dead bolt seemed nice and sturdy, and for good measure she fumbled with and finally engaged the chain. She turned and ran into the kitchen and picked up the wall phone. It seemed to take forever to punch in 9-1-1, but finally a man answered.

"I need help, please," Molly said.

"Give me your name, phone number and location, please."

Her tongue felt like leather. She swallowed, then ran it over her dry lips. But before she could speak, an urgent pounding began at the front door a few feet away.

"Molly! Open the door. Please, I need to tell you something about last night you need to know. Please, I don't want you to get hurt."

"Right," she yelled in a sarcastic voice. Alec Steele's voice was clear even through the plaster and wallboard that made up most of the residential buildings in California. *He is insane,* she thought. *Why doesn't he just run away?*

"Miss? Are you okay, miss? Please give me your name and location," the emergency operator's voice insisted in her ear, but suddenly all Molly could hear was the echo of Alec's words of a few minutes earlier, saying he couldn't trust the police.

"Molly! Please, I don't have much time." Alec's voice was louder.

Molly didn't feel afraid, only confused somehow. He was pleading with her as if they were friends.

Which they weren't.

The man had kidnapped her at gunpoint, for crying out loud! Still, how did they happen to be at the same place last night? Had Alec Steele planned it?

Had someone else? Fred Brooker?

None of it made sense to her. Molly's internal argument had slowed her reflexes, but she had come to a decision.

Err on the side of the sensible, she told herself. Swallowing hard, Molly spoke into the phone more loudly than she had intended.

"My name is Molly Jakes. I live at 2001 Plaza Viejo. But I'm in the town house at 2003. Send help immediately. I think there's a very dangerous man with a gun by the name of Alec Steele outside. He kidnapped me. Please hurry."

Chapter Four

Thirteen minutes isn't a long time if you're waiting for a taxi, and it's a short amount of time if you're waiting for a doctor. But if you're waiting for the cops, Molly decided, it feels like a day and a half.

Alec pleaded another minute or so while Molly stayed on the emergency line, and his voice grew a little more desperate, then trailed off. She assumed he had departed. Normally very civic-minded, she decided there was no way she was going to make an attempt to try to stop him.

As she sat with her head pressed to her knees and her back against Jerry's front door, it passed through her mind that she should probably call all the neighbors and warn them. But she didn't know any of their numbers and wouldn't have known what to say in any case.

The police were efficient and polite when they showed up, two young Mission Verde cops, ringing Jerry's door and calling out nicely, "Miss Jakes. It's the police."

They dutifully checked her town house, walking in and out of every room after they had thrown open her front door, but Alec Steele was nowhere in sight. The three were joined a few minutes later by two additional officers, one a woman.

Ten minutes after that, four Orange County P.D. members arrived, one of whom was the plainclothesman Molly had talked to at last night's freeway accident scene. He obviously hadn't had any sleep, either, and his manner had deteriorated to a point where even the excuses she made to herself on his behalf didn't allow her to like him.

"You're telling us you drove this guy from the accident scene out to your house?"

"He held a gun on me, Officer. And as I've told all eight of you, I didn't know he was there until I was too far away from any cop to yell for help."

At that, Lieutenant Cortez, as Molly had heard one of the others call him, turned and yelled for the rest of them to start searching the area for Alec. Molly described her car, and the female cop went to look and see if it was still in her car space. Molly didn't see her keys anywhere but couldn't remember what had happened to them last night, so really had no idea if Alec Steele had them or not.

Cortez and Molly stayed put, she on her pink-and-green flowered couch, he pacing in front of the fireplace. "So when did you know this Alec Steele from before?"

Cortez had called Lt. Lester DeWitt of the Summer Point precinct and run the whole story by him, and DeWitt was frantic over this new development. He had asked to speak to Molly.

She repeated her story about the night Paul Buntz was murdered.

"So how does this Alec Steele fit into the Brooker case, Lieutenant?" Molly had demanded.

The cop had given her no answers, only promised to come by with an assistant district attorney that evening to explain "what you need to know about this."

Molly handed the phone back to Cortez. He listened for a minute, then slammed down the receiver, about as happy as Molly over the Summer Point detective's stonewalling.

Cortez resumed his questioning. "And you didn't see Steele get into your car?"

"No."

"Did any of the other men involved in the accident mention his name to you?" Cortez stopped and stared at Molly, his hands on his hips. His coat jacket was pushed back, and she could see his holster.

"The only guy I worked on who was alive didn't do anything but gag after I gave him mouth-to-mouth." Molly folded her arms across her chest, wishing she had not been barefoot. There was something about talking to this angry cop without wearing shoes that made her feel guilty.

Cortez started pacing again. "Okay, let's take this from the top, Miss Jakes. Tell me everything Alec Steele said to you."

She started with Alec's "put your hands back on the wheel" and kept talking, all the while wondering where he'd gone to. He wouldn't get far with that handcuff hanging from his wrist, even if he did take her car. Once the police put out an alert on the plates, they would catch him.

That conclusion made her feel uneasy as she got to the part in her reconstruction where she was making tea for a man holding a gun on her. Just as she was figuring out some way to explain how she had forgotten to tell Cortez last night about the gun she had accidently carried off from the wreck, thereby having it to pull on Alec Steele, the female cop came running into the living room.

"He's taken her car. It's not in her carport."

"Great. He'll be out of the county by the time we get this on the air." Cortez glared at Molly, then turned back to the patrolwoman. "Call the car in and put out an APB on Alec Steele. Get his description from the others." He turned to Molly. "You did give them a description?"

"Yes." She was anxious to ask Cortez why Alec thought the cops were out to kill him but decided to keep her questions for the district attorney this evening.

Molly listened as he gave a few more gruff orders to the other officers as they returned. "And bring Miss Jakes into the station. We'll get her complete statement there."

"Wait a minute. I have to go to work today."

Cortez faced her again, his pockmarked skin oily and pale with fatigue. "We need your statement, Miss Jakes. A very dangerous individual is on the loose, and you may have important information. It's your duty."

"I don't think I need or deserve a lecture on civic duty, Officer," she replied.

He seemed to soften a bit and used a more civil tone. "This is for your own good. If he has your keys, he could get back in the house. He's very dangerous."

"How dangerous? What did he do?" Molly thought of the guy with the bullet in his back. A cop, maybe this one in front of her, might kill Alec if he resisted their efforts to apprehend him. "Did he shoot that man in the wreck last night?"

Cortez ignored her question and ordered the uniformed officers out on assignments, then turned and crossed his arms over his broad chest. "No one was shot last night."

He had very dark eyes, making his pupils nearly invisible. Molly began to tremble suddenly and clenched her fists at her side. "Don't b.s. me, Lieutenant. I saw the wound. The guy lying by the Bronco who was wearing a gun. He had a hole in his left shoulder—"

"You're mistaken, Miss Jakes. No one was shot. But one of the men who was killed in the accident was a police officer. He was a good man. He had been out looking for Alec Steele the last time the station heard from him. He must have been bringing him in when the wreck occurred. Steele was lucky to get out alive and find your accommodating car to hide in."

"Looking for him? Why? Has it got something to do with the Brooker case, too?"

"I can't comment on that."

"Can you comment on the fact that it's too much of a coincidence that, in a county of seven million people, two witnesses in a murder trial were involved in the same fatal car wreck?"

Cortez blinked. "No, I can't. You got any explanation for that coincidence?"

"None."

"Then we'll leave it there. For now."

Molly sighed, stood and walked over to Cortez, unable to shake the feeling that the cop was lying. "I'll come in, but it'll have to be later this afternoon, after I check on my men."

Quickly she explained about the crew of installers, ending by pointing to the mantel clock above the fireplace. "It's already almost eight. I have to be there by nine, so if you'll excuse me, I need to get dressed and call someone to come pick me up."

Cortez took a card from his pocket and handed it to her. "That's my address and phone number. I'll be back in around two. Be at the precinct by then, or I'll come and get you."

"Don't you ever go home?" This small attempt at a more human interaction was ignored.

"I'll see you at two, Miss Jakes. And let me take this opportunity to advise you that if you fail to appear, I have the authority to issue a warrant for your arrest, despite your friends at the Summer Point Precinct."

What a jerk, Molly thought. A real hardball player. "You won't need to do that, Lieutenant. I'm willing to cooperate, even though you're treating me like a criminal."

For a second, Cortez's face softened, the wrinkles in his forehead slackening into his thick head of hair. But then he turned away and headed for the door.

Molly watched as he walked away. He never turned around or said goodbye, just slammed the door shut behind him.

Molly put Cortez's business card on the coffee table and reached for the phone. She called Rafe Amundson, her installation foreman, at the shop. He agreed to send someone out, then proceeded to give her an earful about the new female cable puller, who didn't pull fast enough to suit Rafe.

Rafe was sixty-three, one of the last icons of the pre-breakup days of Ma Bell, when "men were men and women stayed home," as he was fond of saying.

Rafe loved stirring up trouble, especially over equal rights and E.E.O. regulations, and hearing that he was in a balky mood threatened Molly's last remaining hold on mature behavior. He enjoyed baiting her. She decided to give him a big thrill this morning and really get into it with him.

"Tell you what, Rafe. Why don't you come here and get me yourself? We'll discuss Sandra Jackson's abilities on the way out to the client's."

Molly hung up and headed for the shower. As she cranked the window closed, her mind replayed Cortez's denial that anyone had been shot. Though she was no medic, she was sure of what she had seen, and the round hole in the victim's shirt didn't look like anything he could have picked up from being bounced out of a car.

There were so many questions.

And there was Alec Steele.

Molly shook her head hard, wishing she could shake the thought of him away. He'd terrified her. And yet compelled her. Something told her he wasn't truly a kidnapper and killer.

But what the heck was he then? Sexy as hell, some demented part of her brain answered. Disgusted with herself, Molly soaped up and washed her hair, running the water as hot as she could stand. She cut herself twice while shaving her legs and swore loudly over her lack of concentration. Ten minutes later, she was wrapped in her baggy robe heading for the bedroom.

With any luck of the bad variety, Rafe would be here before she was ready, and he'd have "women are never ready on time" ammunition to use against her during her planned consciousness-raising session.

She threw the towel and bathrobe onto the carpet in a heap, and wiggled her damp legs into panty hose. With a snap she put on her bra, then opened the closet and stared at clothes while brushing tangles out of her hair. Business suits, silk blouses and tailored dresses filled most of the space. But this morning she wanted something different. She sorted through an assortment of "mistake" buys: tweed culotte pants that made her legs look fat, a blue angora sweater dress that shed worse than a cat, a leather miniskirt that bunched up at the waist.

Finally she grabbed a beige silk dirndl and its matching cropped jacket. With a white sleeveless blouse, the outfit enhanced her skin, moderately freckled with typical brunette undertones of peach and brown. She hung the clothes on the doorknob and dropped to her knees to hunt in the bottom of the closet for beige pumps.

The bells from the front door chimed merrily. "Damn." Molly was beginning to suffer from the lack of sleep. She suddenly felt furious, for the mistaken call for help that had halved her sleeping time, for the gruesome accident, for the damn Aussie stranger who didn't seem at all suited to his adopted role as a criminal.

The door chimes called a second time. Rafe must have traveled ninety miles an hour, Molly thought. She pulled her robe on and headed for the door.

But instead of finding her craggy-faced foreman, her neighbor across the way, Steve Troy, was leaning against the front railing, wearing his favorite arch smile. "Good golly, Miss Molly. Want to explain why your car is in my space?"

"What?"

Steve rolled his eyes and puffed his cigarette lustily, never removing it from his mouth while he talked. "I bet you had a sleep-over who parked in your space, and that's why you used mine, right?"

Molly blinked, trying to absorb what Steve was babbling about. He must be hung over and completely wrong about whose car was in his space. "You think my Chrysler is in your carport?"

This question really cracked him up. "Snap out of it, Moll. Just say no next time if you can't handle your drugs any better than this. Yes, it's your car, and it's wearing my car cover. That's rather personal, don't you think?"

"I'll move it, Steve. Let me get dressed." Molly shut the door in his leering face, wishing for an instant that Southern California wasn't populated with so many nut cases.

Cursing the cops' lack of thoroughness, she pulled off the robe and searched the dresser and her purse for her car keys. She still had no idea where they were and couldn't remember if her extra set were in her desk at work or with her upstairs neighbor. The question of why Alec Steele had moved her car and covered it, and where he was now, made her pulse race.

He must have wanted to throw them off. Have him look for one car while he beat it out of town in a different one. The questions were bubbling in Molly's brain as she bent down to look under the bed for her shoes. The cops had really blown it by jumping to the conclusion that Steele had left in her car just because it wasn't in its assigned space!

Molly flipped up the edge of the bedspread and felt beneath the bed. Nothing. She moved to the other side and slid her hand farther in.

At that second, she got the kind of chill that warns you that you've got about two seconds to live if you don't act fast. She had touched something unexpected under her bed.

Something that felt like a person.

She rolled her weight onto the balls of her feet, but before she could move, she was captured.

Just like in the scariest, most wrenching horror movie she had ever seen, fingers wrapped around her ankles with a deadly serious grip.

Molly fell and screamed and nearly dislocated her arm. The hand on her right ankle moved to grasp her around the calf as the man crept out from under the bed. Molly screamed again and beat at his fingers, clawing at the exposed hairy wrist that nearly broke her own with a grab.

The man slammed his body on top of hers, knocking the breath and the strength to get away right out of her.

IN THE SUMMER POINT JAIL, in interview room number one, Frederick Brooker was conferring with his attorney, Mason Weil.

Frederick Brooker was a short, powerfully built man of fifty-two. He had a full, thick head of black hair, with a predominant widow's peak. His small hazel eyes were framed with thick short lashes, giving his face a slightly feminine appearance. But his voice was very masculine. Deep and gravelly, it commanded attention with very little effort.

"I told you not to worry about the trial, Mason."

"You're not answering my questions, Mr. Brooker. If you are engaging in activities that are going to cast my efforts on your behalf into speculation, I want to know about them now."

Mason Weil touched the perfect knot of his gray-and-mauve silk tie.

"So this is about you, then, Mason."

"I don't follow you, Mr. Brooker."

Frederick Brooker leaned forward, resting his hands on the scarred and battered table in front of him. "I thought you came here to brief me about the progress you've made discrediting the D.A.'s evidence, Mason. But instead, you're sitting here, at three hundred and fifty dollars an hour, whining to me about what I think are your imaginary worries over your reputation. Is that what's bothering you, Mason? Just because a cop and a thug were wiped out last night on the freeway doesn't mean I had anything to do with it."

Weil, to his credit, did not blink an eye, though his uncallused and freshly manicured hands were damp. "I'm glad to hear that, Mr. Brooker. I'm sure you understand my concerns. The police are hollering that you hired someone to kidnap their star witness, you see."

"Do they have any proof of that, Mason?"

The lawyer shifted in his chair and finally shook his head. "No, they don't. That I know of. Yet."

Frederick Brooker smiled, and his eyes hardened. "Well, why don't we talk about the defense then? Since you're on the clock and all. If you don't mind. I want you to make sure the district attorney doesn't try to call my son. I won't have that!" Brooker's voice rose and his eyes blazed.

"We've filed the necessary doctors' reports to keep that from happening, Mr. Brooker."

With that, Mason Weil picked up his briefcase and placed it on the table. It had been searched. He was annoyed that the guard had smudged the gold plate engraved with his initials, MMW, but was satisfied that he had cleared his conscience of any conflicts of ethics questions that might arise. He smiled and handed Frederick Brooker a catalog of radio-controlled model airplanes his client had requested, then said, "Well then, let's begin. The district attorney plans to make his case on the point that you lied in your initial statement to the police. You told them, when they recovered the murder weapon from your limo, that you killed Paul Buntz when he approached your car and threatened to kidnap your son."

"Yes."

"You pulled the trigger when you saw him reach into an orange gym bag. You thought he was armed."

"Yes. I'm still surprised he wasn't."

Weil looked up, but then continued without comment. "The prosecutor will counter this claim with an eyewitness report that puts you and Paul Buntz in your car at midnight. A second witness, Mr. Steele, states he heard you call Paul Buntz's name, and when he approached your car, you shot him and drove off when Mr. Buntz fell dead into the water."

"I'm quite tired of going over this material, Mr. Weil. I know the facts."

"I appreciate that, Mr. Brooker. But when these witnesses take the stand, you must be prepared."

"*If* the witnesses take the stand," Frederick Brooker corrected. "If I was a betting man, I don't think I'd bet the house on that happening anytime soon, Mason."

For a long moment, Mason Weil stared at his client. His conscience was kicking him in the ethical ribs again. But if he didn't ask Brooker directly what he knew about the disappearance of Alec Steele, then he was off the hook.

So be it. Weil droned on about other administrative court matters. While the attorney talked, Frederick Brooker thumbed through the pages of the catalog, barely listening, barely able to wait until he would be out of jail and back with his son.

His son, Erik, was a good boy, always did what he was told. Too bad more of his employees weren't more like him, he thought. Too bad Erik's mother wasn't more like him.

This thought caused Brooker's brow to crease, but he kept on reading, kept on half listening to his attorney, kept on dreaming of the time, very soon now, when his plan would come to fruition and this nightmare of isolation would finally end.

Chapter Five

Molly pulled the sandstone lamp from the night table onto Alec Steele's head, but he managed to stay conscious despite the resounding crack to his skull.

He responded by pinning Molly to the bedroom floor and clamping his bandaged hand across her nose and mouth, his touch much rougher than it had been hours ago in her foyer.

She stopped struggling at the sight of the threat in his eyes, for it was one she didn't feel like challenging.

"Are you ready to listen to me now, Molly Jakes?"

She nodded, opening her mouth to gulp air, tasting the moist, soapy flavor of his hand. He loosened his grip only slightly.

"All right, then. I'm going to let you up. You're going to get dressed. Then you're going to drive me somewhere and let me off. You'll be done with me for good then."

Molly blinked and nodded again. Alec rewarded this movement by removing his hand.

"Why didn't you just take my car and drive yourself this morning?" she demanded. "Why add kidnapping to your list of crimes?"

"I thought you might have something to do with the men who—" Alec stopped himself short.

"What men?" she probed.

"Never mind. Look, I don't have time to explain anything to you, Miss Jakes. And anyway, you're better off not knowing. Now get up and get dressed—" his eyes glanced at her chest, then hastily away "—and we can get going."

"Get going how far? To the end of the street?"

"Farther, if we leave soon."

For some reason, Molly felt compelled to reason with the agitated intruder, in the hopes, she had to admit to herself, that he would tell her what men he'd been referring to. She had started to get a very bad feeling that their meeting on the freeway hadn't been so random. Which could only mean that since Frederick Brooker's crime was the only thing they had in common, those dead men last night and Alec's wound must have something to do with that.

She lowered her voice, trying to sound reasonable. "But the cops are looking for *my* car. Even if I'm driving it, we're going to get pulled over by the first CHIP who's awake."

"I know that. Which is why we're taking Rafe's car."

These words didn't make sense to Molly for a second, then they made horrifying sense. Rafe was due any minute; obviously Alec had heard her whole conversation. "You were going to stay put until Rafe showed up, but when I decided to check if my car was at my neighbor's—"

"You're a smart girl. I planned to take one of your neighbors' cars tonight, but when I heard you on the phone, I decided Rafe's was a better plan. I knew you'd send your man away. That's why I had to stop you. I need his car.''

Molly's chest was beginning to ache from his spread-eagle hold on her, and her robe had slipped open during their struggle. She wasn't excruciatingly modest, but she damn sure wasn't going to give him a bigger eyeful of her breasts, she promised herself. ''Will you let me up now, please?''

Alec released her and she sat up.

They stared briefly at each other. ''Are you okay?'' he asked.

''You're awfully polite for a man wanted for murder.''

Alec paled at these words. ''I didn't murder anyone.''

''Then who were those men? Did you shoot one of them last night?'' she challenged.

Alec looked as though he might answer but clamped his lips together tightly and stood. ''Get dressed.''

''Did you kill someone?''

''None of your bloody damn business.''

That sounded like a confession to Molly, and a new surge of fright fanned out through her veins. Alec Steele disappeared through her bedroom doorway.

Since there was no way out but to follow him, she did. Besides, her curiosity was as aroused as her anger. ''It *is* my business. You're jeopardizing my life. If you want any more help from me, I deserve to know what Lieutenant Cortez meant when he said you were dangerous. I think he thinks you murdered those men last night. Did you?''

They were standing in Molly's kitchen. She watched as Alec picked up the dented teakettle from the floor, rinsed and filled it. Slowly he turned on the flame under the front burner of the stove and set the kettle down.

He ignored Molly and walked around the island and looked in the refrigerator, then set some milk down with a thunk in front of Molly. "I thought you didn't have milk."

"I was wrong."

"So you were. And so is Cortez. I didn't murder anyone."

"I see. The police are lying?"

He leaned toward her. "Cops don't ever lie in the States, doll?"

"If you hate the United States so much, just what are you doing living here?" She folded her arms, suddenly as weary as she could ever remember being in her life.

"I don't live here. And for your information, I love you uptight, overachieving, never-know-when-to-be-happy Yanks. I'm only here to do my honest duty and testify in a trial to help the good old U.S. of A. Although it appears now that my testimony isn't going to be worth a pile of dingo dirt."

"I know you were at Brooker's office the night of the murder. Is that all you have to testify about? Or is there something else you saw that you've managed to avoid telling me?"

Alec glanced away at her surprisingly correct guess and rubbed his ribs. He thought for a moment, then turned his gaze to meet Molly's brown eyes. "I was a witness to Paul Buntz's murder."

Molly felt as if someone had landed a punch in her midsection. The cops and the district attorney had led Molly to believe that there were *no* eyewitnesses to the crime. Suddenly, she remembered a recent tabloid-television report that had hinted about a surprise witness who could hang Frederick Brooker with what he knew. She had dismissed it as unfounded.

Was Alec Steele that witness?

The case was a lurid one. Frederick Brooker, it had been revealed, had been blackmailed by ex-television sportscaster, Paul Buntz. It was rumored that Buntz had connections to organized crime, but as far as Molly knew, which was only what she read in the papers, no one had discovered the reason for the blackmail.

Some speculation arose over a rash of burglaries of Brooker's customers. Immediately after the crime, the media had been full of theories, but the coverage of the trial had been overshadowed by other grisly murders across the country, and Molly had not been able to find anything new about the case in the papers for several weeks.

"I've never read your name in any of the news stories," she said.

"Yeah. Well, I'm the surprise witness, you might say."

"You actually saw him shoot the guy?"

Alec's eyes narrowed and he leaned against Molly's kitchen counter. He still had one of the guns in his belt. Though he'd stopped pointing it at her, she still felt his prisoner.

"Yes. Poor bastard."

"How did you come to be at the murder scene?"

"It's a long story. I knew Brooker. Was going to deliver his sailboat to San Diego. I won't bore you with the details. But when I saw what happened, I got to the coppers as soon as I could. There was a bit of a stink, but they finally decided I was telling the truth and kept me under wraps back home in Melbourne while Brooker's lawyers tried to buy their way out of murder one. I was sent a ticket and told to report here for the trial next week. But that's looking real chancy right now."

"Why?"

"You really don't need to know any of this, Molly. The less I tell you, the less trouble you'll have sleeping tonight."

Alec was about a foot away from Molly, and she felt more than heard a tremor of regret in his voice.

"I'll judge that for myself, Alec. I'm a witness myself, you know. And the cops haven't told me anything except that my information about seeing Paul Buntz get into Brooker's car at midnight is crucial to their case. How much more is there to know?"

He seemed to weigh something, then shrugged his massive shoulders. "I meant it when I said I couldn't trust the cops, Molly. Brooker's money has turned one of them, I think. It may be dangerous for you to know this."

Her mouth went dry, but Molly wanted, needed to know. "Keep talking, Alec. I think I deserve to hear what's going on."

"When I landed at LAX, four guys with badges met me, but they weren't the real helpful sort, if they were cops at all. Unfortunately for me, I didn't catch on till they'd cuffed me and driven me out to some shack to begin their dirty work."

The kettle began to boil, and Alec poured the water into two mugs. Molly's brain felt filled with fog.

"What dirty work?" she whispered.

"Those boys tied me up and whacked me about a bit for the past few days." He pointed to his ribs. "I got in a few licks, but four against one ain't the best odds."

"Talk about John Wayne."

Alec grinned, but then his voice became more serious. "Anyway, they doped me up, too. Then the real fun began." His whole body went still, as if he were reliving the moments. "If I'm not mistaken, they brainwashed me. Or tried to anyway."

"Brainwashed?" Molly blinked and thought of POWs, Chinese water drips and medieval stretching racks. "They tortured you?"

"That's enough, Molly."

She couldn't let him stop now. "But why did they do that? Why not just kill you? Did they try to get you to forget what you know about the murder?"

"I'm not sure what they were up to. There was a skinny little bloke with a hooded mask who was directing everything." He bowed his head as if suddenly very tired. "I can't remember much of it."

She thought that was probably a good thing. "Alec, what were they trying to brainwash you to do? Change your testimony? Were they Brooker's men? Did they mention him?" To Molly's ears, her own questions sounded like silly television cop-show scripts, but she had to ask these things.

"That would make sense, wouldn't it? Especially since I'm the only witness. But no, that's not what I'm remembering from it. What I can recall is that I'm supposed to do something for someone. Be a hired gun for someone when they give the order."

"Hired gun?" she repeated. "You mean you're..." Her voice trailed off. She couldn't put the absurdity of what she was thinking into words.

"They want me to kill someone, love."

Molly took a gulp of tea and seared the inside of her mouth. She set the mug down. "But that's so absurd.

Who is it? Surely the person's identity would explain what's going on."

Alec stirred three sugars into his mug and rested on his arms as if his entire weight might collapse onto the counter. "I don't know who it is. Every time I concentrate, that bit floats away. The blokes were taking me to do it last night, I think. We parked on the side of the freeway. I heard one of them say 'his target should be here about three.' But something went wrong. I heard another car pull up, and some shots. The car started moving, then we got into the crack-up on the freeway. I was drowsy during the ride, but I could swear I heard a woman's voice screaming just before we crashed. At any rate, I was cuffed to the car door and managed to get loose when the Jeep we were in rolled. I ran off the highway and hid in the bushes, then saw you park your car. I have to tell you, when I recognized you from Brooker's office, I didn't know what to think."

"You mean you thought I was involved with them?"

"Yes."

"Do you still think that?"

"Should I?"

The kitchen was very quiet. Molly moved her mug half an inch forward, sloshing some of the contents onto her hand. She felt ill. "I'm not, Alec. I was there by coincidence."

She knew, however, that this wasn't quite true. The Brooker case had to be behind the phony call-out. Someone must have planned for her to be on that stretch of highway in the dead of night so that they could . . . they could what?

Have Alec Steele kill her?

That would be a ridiculous plan. They had no guarantee she would be there at the right time, that she would stop even if she was there. It would have been a totally ridiculous plan, wouldn't it?

Her conviction turned on itself. Actually, it would have been brilliant. Brooker could have then said Alec Steele was lying about what he saw. Molly felt her legs trembling, and she moved a step back from Alec, wishing she could run away.

Because Alec Steele was programmed to kill.

He'd been waiting near the freeway. Waiting near her home.

Waiting to kill someone.

Was it her? If it was, maybe he would do it now.

Molly met Alec's eyes and saw the anguish and fear she felt mirrored there.

"Don't be afraid of me, Molly. I'm not going to hurt you."

Her chest tightened with nerves, but something rang so true in his voice, she found herself believing him. "My God, what are you going to do? We should call the district attorney. He'll know—"

"How do I know it's not the D.A. who's behind all this?" Alec interrupted. "No. I need to hole up awhile. I know a place I'll be safe. But I may need some medical help. To get deprogrammed, or whatever the hell you call it. Maybe a psychiatrist is what I really need...."

Everything Alec had recounted sounded outlandish and unrealistically dramatic, even though his delivery was calm and deliberate.

Which made everything too believable. This fact made Molly feel like throwing up. Murder was something she had been exposed to daily, at least through the media. She thought, particularly after her experience with the Brooker thing, that she was hardened to fear.

She thought if she was cautious, didn't walk down dark alleys or pick up hitchhikers, she would be okay. Gangs, freeway snipers, drug raids, psycho slashers, all of those front-page *Times* headlines she devoured calmly each morning with her cereal happened to other people.

She always assumed—hoped, really—that the people who did those kinds of things would have a certain look about them. Some glint in their eyes, or tone to their voice, that would identify them as vicious.

Alec Steele had no outward characteristics of a violent person. He appeared sane and had a charismatic personality when he wasn't bashing a person around. He seemed very decent.

But who knew what evil lurked inside his heart? That thought tempered her empathetic rush of emotion. Was this guy honestly going to let her go if she helped him get the handcuff off and drove him someplace safe?

His voice brought Molly out of the clouds and back to reality. "You better get dressed, Molly." He again had a gun in his hand, though he wasn't pointing it at her. He seemed to sense that she wasn't as resistant to helping him as before.

Not that he trusted her very far, however. She turned and went back to the bedroom, eyeing the phone in the front alcove, knowing he was watching her every move. Molly hastily pulled on clothes, then applied minimal makeup and brushed out her tangles just as the front bell chimed again.

Rafe. Molly walked out of the bedroom and nearly ran into Alec. He put his finger to his lips. He was still holding the gun, and the second was tucked into his waistband.

She glared at him. Alec pulled her into the hallway. His voice was a ragged whisper. "Ask him in. Then tell him you need his help to move something in here."

"I'm not going to let you hurt one of my men."

"You never let up, do you?" He looked as if he wanted to bite her. "I'm not going to hurt your chum. I'm going to tie him up, and we're going to take his car."

"Maybe we don't have to do that. I'll tell him to take my car, and I'll use his truck. That way—"

"That way you'll be an accessory to murder. Don't give me more help than I'm asking for, Molly. Just move."

She frowned but headed for the door. Alec followed her closely, slipping into the foyer closet at the last second. She wondered again how much his looks belied his true nature. The front door opened to the left and in, and she flung it wide, deciding only at the very last half second not to scream for Rafe to run.

But Rafe wasn't there. Instead, a young man about twenty-five stood in the doorway. Nice-looking with neatly groomed brown hair gelled into spikes, he was wearing a denim shirt and jeans, both hands crammed into a windbreaker-type cotton jacket. He smiled at Molly.

"What do you want?" she nearly yelled.

"Miss Jakes?"

"Yes. Who are you?"

"Tell Alec Steele he has a caller." He pulled a gun out of his pocket, his lip curling up viciously. "Move back. And don't scream or I'll blow you away."

It was just like in the movies. Molly's jaw dropped open. For about two seconds, she simply stared, but then the punk put his hand flat against her chest and pushed. It flashed through Molly's mind to haul off and hit him, but before she could do anything, a movement outside caught her eye.

The gunman caught her motion and glanced sideways. They both saw Rafe at the same instant, just as the jackhammers out on the street quieted.

"Well now, Miz Jakes. Did you call for a real man to come to your rescue?"

Molly realized the big old fool was halfway down the walk, and he had not even noticed the gun in the punk's hand. "Rafe!" she screamed, but he never heard her. The gun exploded with a spurt of fire and smoke the same instant the jackhammers started again.

Molly kept screaming, unheard by anyone, and watched helplessly as the best cable puller in the Southern region hit the ground a dead man.

With a blind fury, Molly turned on the gunman, her arms and fists flailing against him, but he hit her on the side of the face with his gun, and she slumped onto the floor. He started to kick her, but Alec grabbed him by the shoulder and smashed him against the foyer wall.

Her vision blurred, she watched him hammer the killer into the floor.

"Who sent you?" he demanded.

"Stuff it—"

Alec savagely twisted the younger man's arm behind him. "Listen, slime, you're dead meat. Now who are you working for? Brooker? One of the cops?"

Instead of answering, he kicked Alec and managed to knock him sideways. Alec's gun spun out of his hand and the guy grabbed for it. Molly also crawled toward it, blinking until her vision cleared.

Maybe I can sink my teeth into his ankle or something, she thought. But then she saw Alec pull out the second gun and heard it fire. Alec rolled away, then rose and came to her.

Molly was crying and whimpering and generally falling apart. Alec was shaking, and his breath rattled in his throat. He pulled her close to him and tried to comfort her, though he was as shaken as she. Rafe was dead, as was the new intruder bleeding at her feet.

Suddenly it seemed to Molly that every single thing in her life was screwed up forever. She began wailing, but Alec jerked her to her feet. He pointed to the door that led to the back patio. She looked where he was staring and, through the glass, saw two men coming down the slope, guns drawn.

"We've got to go. Now!" Alec pulled Molly outside and they ran away from the corpses lying across her welcome mat at her sun-splashed, open front door.

ALEC DROVE LIKE a little old lady, never pushing past fifty-three miles an hour.

Molly stared out at the brown layer of smog that was eating into the clean morning air, craving the cigarettes she had given up the past year. As they drove by the massive hunk of granite beside the road at Eagle Rock Monument, Molly realized that the hole gouged out of the middle of the thing really did look like an eagle's profile.

Funny what you notice when you're trying not to be hysterical, she thought. For the past few minutes, she had sat in a stupor. Alec had stopped long enough to confirm that Rafe was dead. They had then taken his keys and stolen his truck.

Molly thought about how for all his thirty-five years on the job, Rafe had never left his keys in the ignition. For all the good that safety rule had done him today.

They approached the Summer Point Marina turn-off, and Molly had no idea at all where they were heading. The direction was north from San Clemente, but since half the world is north from there, a guess would be a waste of energy.

"I don't think any of my neighbors heard the shots. You didn't see anyone looking out their window or coming to their door?"

"No," Alec replied softly. "But I'm sure the police will find your friend's body soon."

Molly was watching the side of Alec's face because the motion of the passing scenery was making her dizzy. He glanced at her, and she felt like slugging him. He had caused her friend's death. She hated him for it.

Alec knew she was in pain and could feel the waves of rage and guilt over Rafe's death rolling out of her. It wasn't my fault, he wanted to say. But he didn't, more than a little afraid it really was.

Molly turned away and gingerly felt the side of her face. It was sore and a lump was rising. She turned and faced forward, then swung the visor down. The cut was small, but ragged. She already had a bruise.

"Where are we going?" she asked, feeling numb. She told herself she had to stay sharp. The police were going to ask a thousand questions sooner or later, and it was going to be tough to answer anything that started with "Why did you . . . ?"

"I know of an empty boat at Summer Point. We'll go there and I can lie low, ditch the truck and try to contact a doctor, or someone else who can help."

"Do you know any doctors?"

"Yeah. One. She's a police psychiatrist. Maybe she'll suggest something."

"I thought you didn't trust the cops," Molly retorted.

"I don't. But Alicia's not really a cop. She does contract work for them. I got to talk to her when the D.A. checked me out to see if I was a competent witness. But I've known her for quite a few years. I can trust her."

"That's a pretty rich taste in people to trust. Can you pay a psychiatrist to help? Or get money from your family?"

Her hostile remark brought a small chuckle from Alec. "No. I've a bit of cash, but I don't expect I'll have any problem with her bill. As for my family, I never knew my mum. Dad's a cowboy. Drives cattle down at the Alice Springs station. My dad's how I know Alicia, actually. He was married to Alicia's mum for about ten minutes a few years ago. Alicia and I never really knew each other then, but we got to know each other when I crewed for a team in San Diego during an America's Cup race five years ago. Like I said, she's a good egg. Not really family, but as close as I get to it."

Molly regretted being so petty with him, but she felt as if she was going to explode with grief. She was suddenly convinced that she shouldn't have gone along with his plan. "Let me out, Alec. Take the truck. I won't tell anyone. But I need to get out. Now."

Alec gripped the steering wheel more tightly. "No. I can't stop now, Molly. You saw those two men on your patio. It's too dangerous, for both of us. They could be following us, for all I know."

Molly peered out of the truck's back window. Five lanes of traffic glimmered in the morning sun. Shiny, metallic, like a molten snake, the vehicles cruised behind Rafe's truck as far as the eye could see. "You can go to hell," she said quietly, staring down at the floor where she thought he'd concealed the guns. "I want out! I'll take my chances with the cops. They'll find out what's going on, and who's behind it, even if it's one of their own. This isn't Nazi Germany, for God's sake. And I am not your prisoner, you know."

"No, you're not, Molly. But I can't stop now. We've got to find somewhere safe, and I think we better stay together."

"Why?"

He turned his cool blue stare at her. "A man just tried to kill you, Molly. He knew where you lived. Probably knows where you work. Can't you see that you're part of this somehow?"

She realized at that moment that Alec had been constantly checking the rearview mirror. "Great. So now you've got the counterfeit cops and the thugs after you. Why don't you just push me out of the car, Alec? I'd probably have a better chance of living through that than if I stay with you."

"I didn't plan this any more than you did, love. And there's nothing I can do to change any of it now. I'm sorry I got you involved last night. But my being sorry doesn't change the facts. And the facts are that we've both got to put some distance between ourselves and the friends of that little twit who tried to kill us."

Molly clenched her teeth but said nothing. She knew what he said was right. "So who do you think that guy was working for? Brooker?"

"I don't know."

"Can't you guess? Or do you have a variety of people gunning for you?"

Alec didn't answer for several seconds, then he sighed. "I know you're upset, Molly. I don't blame you. But I can't let you out, and I can't explain everything because I really don't know what the hell is going on myself. Try to relax. Be patient. I won't let anything happen to you.''

She made a snorting noise and folded her arms across her chest. ''Boy, I feel better already.''

''You should.''

His retort took the wind out of Molly's indignant sails as she sat in silence mulling over the implications of fleeing with him. Lieutenants Cortez and DeWitt would both be annoyed with her, of that she was sure. Pacific Communications would make her file nine hundred pages of reports. And her neighbors would probably never approve her for permanent ownership of the town house she was leasing under a lease-to-own contract.

But worst of all was that Rafe was dead. Tears began to fall, hot and fast, down her cheeks.

Chapter Six

Molly cried for a few seconds, then Alec surprised her by reaching over and giving her arm a squeeze. She pulled away from his touch, and he had the decency to look ashamed.

"Look, you're a right spunky chit, and too stubborn for common sense. But things will work out. Just give me a little time to think this out, decide who we can trust." He drove a few silent miles then asked, "So you never married?"

"No."

"Why not?"

Molly sighed. Her brain hurt too much to try to explain how her career had been her number-one concern for a long time and that men had come and gone without leaving much of a mark. "I haven't had time," she finally blurted out, more than a little uneasy that the answer was truer than she cared to admit. "You don't have a wife, or ex-wife, or kids?" she asked quickly.

"No. Never married. After watching Dad rat around and marry three times and never have it work out, I decided the Steeles aren't really the nuptial type." He grinned at Molly, forgetting for a moment their dicey situation. "Looks like we have a bit in common. On the lam from the law, and not able to make it in a marriage.''

He was teasing. Under any other circumstances, Molly would have risen to the occasion and given as good as she got. Instead, she looked out at the traffic, wishing she was asleep, alone in her bed. "We're sure in this thing together, aren't we?" she replied softly.

"That's right, Molly. You have to trust me."

"With my life, eh, mate?"

He looked at her, but didn't answer.

With my life, her mind echoed silently, not liking the sound of it at all.

The miles passed with no more conversation. Several road crews had closed lanes during the rush hour, naturally, and it was bumper-to-bumper traffic when they turned off at the Summer Point exit. It was Thursday and not yet the end of the tourist season. Alec found a place to park by some condos about three-quarters of a mile from the marina.

They left the truck and started walking. The air was cool and salty, and the tang of it coated Molly's dry lips and filled her nostrils with a briny promise of relaxation. Despite the mess she was in, her shoulders slackened. The beach had always had that effect on Molly.

But not on Alec.

He was stiff, somewhat favoring his right knee, and he knew his demeanor was tense and distracted. As they approached a fast-food drive-through, the smell of coffee and french fries made him realize how hungry he was.

Molly had the same reaction. "Can we stop and get something to eat?" she heard herself ask him as if she were a child. "I'm famished."

"It's not a good idea to be seen. I'm sure my mug will be splashed all over the news any minute now. Yours, too, once they find the bodies."

Rafe. Somehow Molly had managed to put his death out of her mind these past few minutes, but she felt the shock of memory and immediately lost her appetite. The man was dead. Because she had asked him to come and pick her up.

"Molly? You okay, love? You're going a bit pale." Alec didn't touch her, but his voice was kind.

"I'm fine. Where's the boat?"

"North slip 111. I don't have a key to the dock ramps, so we may have to jump a fence. You game for that?"

His voice was half tease and half challenge.

He was trying to make her relax, she realized. As if either of them really could, a thought brought home by the fact he was still armed and still checking behind them every few seconds.

"Yes. I should have worn pants, though."

Alec glanced at Molly's legs and shook his head. "Nah. That'd be a real crime to cover up those gorgeous legs." Before she could say anything to put him in his place, he wrapped one arm around her shoulders and gave her a hug. "Now don't start moaning at me. I'm a man who doesn't think much before I talk. It's just the way I am, Molly. One good thing about it is that I don't lie. I never leave myself enough time to think of one."

"I'll remember that," she mumbled, enjoying, despite her anger and misgivings, the feel of his warm strength.

They didn't have to jump the fence, which was all to the good. It was six feet of chain link, with those twisty little topknots designed to rip skin. An older man dressed in natty white cashmere slacks and a blue jacket unlocked the gate at that moment, holding the door for Molly and Alec because they acted as if they belonged there.

The man stopped at a shining new Cal 34 yacht, where a bikini-clad girl about nineteen was polishing a brass winch with a toothbrush. Alec allowed a wolfish smile of appreciation as he nodded. She swooned, and Molly shook her head. California. Despite earthquakes, fires and riots, the general population was always ready to respond to someone with hot looks.

They walked the length of the dock. All the boats were bobbing in the low tide, decks shimmering above sleek, polished hulls. Above them, the boats' halyards, whose job it is to hoist the billowing sheets of sails into the wind, snapped tautly against jutting masts.

They slapped in rhythm with the triangular yacht-club pennants, called "burgees." Fluttering at the top of the masts, they announced the wealthy owners' social connections for all to see.

As they walked farther down the dock the size of the boats increased. "They're all so incredible, Alec. But it looks like you'd need a crew of ten just to get them out to sea."

"Not if a bloke knows what it's about, love." He came to the end, which faced the calm, protected water. Alec walked up a short set of stairs. "Here we are. Get ready to board the *Geisha Empress*."

The boat was gorgeous. Forty feet of teak-bedecked artistry lolled in the water, the vessel's beamy cockpit big enough to seat eight with room for a servant to pass the hors d'oeuvres. Though Molly belonged to the working-class, money all by itself didn't impress her much. She worked in Beverly Hills, Glendale and Pasadena, and saw too much of it thrown around to have it hold instant glamour. But when it was wed to good taste, she felt her envy beeper go off. Beep, beep, beep, it said now. And she couldn't even swim.

The lines of the ketch-rigged beauty were simple and pure, proclaiming speed and comfort.

"Whose boat is this?" Molly asked in admiration.

"Fred Brooker's."

Molly reeled back a step. "What? Are you nuts?"

"Yes, I may be. But he's in prison and I still have the keys. If they work, I'd say we've picked the perfect place where no one would think to look for us. In the lion's den, so to speak." Alec jumped aboard spryly, then reached for her hands. "Take off your shoes, Molly. It's a rule with wooden boats."

"I don't think this is a good idea. Are there any life jackets?"

"I'll get you one," he replied. "Now come aboard and I'll fix you something to eat."

Reluctantly, Molly slipped off her shoes, holding tight to Alec's hand as she followed him to the galley hatch. "She's beautiful."

"That she is. The *Empress* is a classic Cheoy Lee. Built about sixty years ago. You can't get them like this anymore." He spun the combination lock easily, then pushed back the hatch cover and stepped inside.

Molly peeked in after him, marveling at the compact efficiency below. A kitchen and dinette, complete with stereo and television mounted into the wall next to a microwave oven, beckoned invitingly. Alec drew back curtains and opened windows, then turned and smiled the first genuine smile Molly had seen since their surreal second acquaintance began.

"Come on down, Molly. I'll make you some grub, then we'll call Alicia."

She threw her purse and shoes, along with the satchel into which she had stuffed a company directory, onto a chintz-covered sofa and walked backward down the stairs. Beside her was a shelf full of pictures, and her gaze was drawn to one with Frederick Brooker and a teenage boy. Their arms were around each other's shoulders, while people in the background were pouring champagne onto their hair.

Molly picked up the leather-framed photo. "I didn't know Brooker had any children."

Alec looked over his shoulder. He was opening up a canned ham. "Yeah. A son. I met him once in Brooker's office. He's a good kid. Deaf, however. Goes to a special school in the East, I think."

Before Molly could ask anything more about Brooker, a piercing noise clamored from the direction of her purse. The pager. God, she had forgotten all about having it. With the cellular in for repair, she had been relying on the pager to keep up with her crew. She should have grabbed Rafe's phone, she realized.

Someone was probably beeping her from work, she figured. Wondering where the hell she and Rafe were, if they hadn't heard the news. Before Molly could grab her bag, Alec moaned. There was no other way to describe the sound, unless it would be to call it a wail. The intensity of the pain in his voice paralyzed Molly for a second, then she ran to him.

She stood helplessly as Alec clutched his neck and fell to his knees, whacking his arm on the counter as the handcuff caught on a drawer knob. He began to have what looked like convulsions, his eyes closed tight. "No...no-o-o-o!"

For a second, she was too stunned to move. Finally Molly went to him, searching for an explanation for his fit. Just then, the pager went off again, and he yelled a second time, collapsing onto the floor as he broke into a sweat.

Though Molly didn't understand how, it seemed his pain had something to do with the pager, so she grabbed it and turned the ringer off. She leaned down and felt for Alec's pulse. It was racing. He was white and clammy, and she feared he might have suffered a heart attack. She placed a pillow under his head, then pulled a throw blanket over his legs.

After about five minutes, his body lost its rigidity, and his eyes opened. They were bleary and unfocused. All the good humor and playfulness of a few minutes before had left his face. He swallowed, then grabbed her arm tightly. "Molly. You didn't run out while the getting was good."

It was true. It had occurred to her to flee, but she was so full of worry over his condition, the thought had flown out of her mind. "No, I didn't." She flipped some blond hair off his forehead. "What happened just now, Alec? Do you know?"

He closed his eyes for a second, then a long shudder shook his body. When he looked at Molly, his gaze was not there on the boat, but someplace else. A place full of terror and pain. "The guy with the hood. He had some electrical gadget hooked to me. And he used some sounds." His voice sounded hollow and echoed in the air. "I thought I had dreamed that part."

The rotten, no-good, ruthless creep, Molly muttered to herself. They had tortured the man. Despite her prior anger at Alec, the emotion she felt now was rage that one human being could *willingly* inflict so much pain on another.

"Hang on, Alec. We've got to get you to a doctor. You must have been hypnotized or brainwashed or something to respond to that sound. A doctor will be able to figure it out."

"I bet I am, love. Just like Pavlov's pooch. But not completely. I'm starting to remember things. Things I'm not supposed to."

"Things? About—" She didn't want to say "about who you're supposed to kill?" but she knew that was it.

He blinked and let go of Molly's hand, gingerly using his long fingers to poke at the bandage on his neck. "Something's really nicking into me, Molly. Under the tape. Can you see what it is?"

She pulled his shirt open and, as carefully as she could, pulled up the adhesive. It took all her stiff-upper-lip training not to cry out at what she saw. On his neck were welts, like those on the back of a sailor who'd had a hundred lashes from a wet whip. But that wasn't the worst. He had two black needlelike objects embedded right into his flesh, covered with clear surgical tape.

Alec knew from her expression she had found something awful. "What is it?"

"They've got needles in you, Alec. Tiny ones, like an acupuncturist would use. Maybe that's part of the treatment." Molly met his eyes. "We've got to get these things out."

"Take them out."

"Me? I won't. I can't. I could hurt you more."

"You have to, Molly. If some other electric thing goes off, I'm liable to go berserk."

"I can't, Alec." She stood and measured the doorway with her eyes, trying to imagine how she could possibly manage to drag him up on deck. "We've got to go to the hospital. I'll drive. So what if the police show up? Those guys last night were surely the only bad cops. We're miles away from them. This is too dangerous to fool with."

He squeezed her hand tightly. "I'm not leaving here, Molly. Besides, if you can't get these things out, no one can. Give it a try, kid. I trust you."

"With your life?" she whispered.

He smiled despite his pain. "If you don't help me, who knows what might happen." He swallowed with effort. "I still don't remember who I'm to kill, love. But I remember when. Tuesday. Tuesday, September 7."

"That's less than a week away."

"It's the day I was summoned to be available to testify."

It was also the day she was scheduled to appear. "Who are you supposed to hurt, Alec? Try to remember who it is. That's the key to this whole, insane thing."

He closed his eyes and sighed, and the vulnerable sound made her shudder. "I can't remember, love. I think it's someone I know. But I just can't remember who."

"Do you think you'll do it?" Molly couldn't help but ask.

"I don't know," Alec replied in a whisper. It was the thing he feared most, he realized. That he might kill someone, that he was capable of it. "I almost killed a man in a bar fight in New Zealand ten years ago. There had been a storm and my crew was cooped up for sixteen days. They had done too much drinking to pass the time. My head winchman was hit in the face with a bottle. Nearly lost an eye. The man who hit him came after me when I broke it up.''

Molly's eyes were huge as they sat huddled together in the gently rocking yacht. ''But that was different, Alec. I read once that hypnotic suggestion can't make a person do anything they aren't already capable of doing. Doesn't that story show you that you're not that kind of man?''

''I don't know,'' he repeated.

Molly had to admit she didn't know, either.

Chapter Seven

Leaving Alec to rest on the floor, Molly searched around for the tool kit he said was stowed outside. The wind was picking up and the sky was a vivid, cloudless and perfect blue. Shimmering reflections glared off the water, making her scrunch her eyes to slits, and she became aware of a slight headache pounding at the back of her skull.

She found the tools and went back down to work on the handcuff. Alec watched and didn't talk; he just lay still with his other hand on his forehead. The screwdrivers wouldn't trip the lock mechanism, but her third try with an ice pick and hammer did the trick.

"Goodonyer, Molly!" Alec grinned weakly, rubbing the thick indentation on his wrist.

"You're welcome, if that was a thank-you."

"It was, love." He reached up and touched her chin.

She liked the feel of his hand on her, she realized then. Even when they had been adversaries, she had sensed an underlying gentleness, the full force of which she was experiencing now. As he touched her, his expression became tender, as if her face were a delicate piece of china.

"You'd better call Alicia," she said, suddenly eager to get back to business.

Alec blinked and dropped his hand. "You're right." He turned and hit a button on the couch arm beside him. Out popped a cordless phone. Pulling up the antenna, Alec nodded at the food on the counter. "Do you feel like running up to the marina store for tucker? That ham doesn't look too edible."

At this mention of food, Molly's stomach growled out loud and they shared a laugh. "Tucker, huh. Sure, I'll go for tucker anytime." Molly stood up. "Are there any women's clothes on board, d'you think? Jeans, maybe?"

"Should be. I heard tell Brooker fancied himself quite the ladies' man. Check in the rear stateroom. Lockers are under the kip."

"Kip?"

"The bunks."

"Great. I'm going to borrow some."

He nodded, then spoke into the phone. "G'day, love. Is Dr. Chen around?"

Molly paused, wondering why that name sounded familiar. It was a common enough Chinese name, she realized. Deciding it wasn't important, she went down the narrow passageway past one stateroom, though that word didn't really describe the closetlike sleeping area it was comprised of. The rear compartment had bunk beds, and she got on her knees and pulled open one of the two drawers under it.

It was crammed full of clothes, mostly shorts and T-shirts, caps and white sweaters of all sizes. She found some bleached jeans that looked as if they'd fit her and hurried into them and an emerald green shirt. Everything smelled faintly musty but was clean and very expensive.

There were some shoes in the other drawer, but Molly drew the line at other people's foot germs thanks to an overzealous seventh-grade gym teacher. She decided to slip her pumps back on for the trip to the store and added tennis shoes to her mental shopping list.

She was getting a little claustrophobic inside the boat and wanted to get back out into the sunshine so she could plan what to do. It was clear now that Alec had to see a doctor, or at least a psychologist of some kind. Molly was counting on his friend, Alicia, to help convince him that they had to go to the cops. Even if they were both arrested, once the facts were known about what happened at her house today, they would be set free.

Right? Molly mulled over that conclusion, not as sure as she had been that it was correct. Especially if what Alec said was true about Brooker's people getting to one of the cops…or even worse, *being* one of the cops.

At any rate, she decided the best thing to do now was lie low and see what showed up in the media, if anything did. It was sad, but all too true, that news about two men found murdered wouldn't necessarily end up on the front pages.

"Very fetching, Miss Molly."

She whirled around and met Alec's stare. He looked a lot better, and he was standing. The toll the attack had taken showed in his paleness despite his tan and in the slight twitching under his right eye.

"Thanks. Did you reach Dr. Chen?"

"She's on her way. I gave her the address of the motel I stayed at in February. It's a few blocks from here. If she makes it there okay, meaning without anyone following her, she'll call us and I'll give her the directions to the boat.''

"Then what?"

A strange look passed over Alec's face. "What do you mean?"

"I mean, when are you calling the cops? At some point you have to explain that you're being framed by several creeps who are chasing us around with guns." Molly felt clammy and weak all of a sudden, and hot. "I really have to get some air, Alec. Can we finish this outside?"

He didn't move, and his softened expression disappeared. It was replaced with an intense look, of the type she had experienced the previous night. "I told you I can't trust the coppers. You're not going to turn me in, are you?"

Molly had no intention of doing that, but suddenly she questioned if she had too easily chosen not to. She looked away and noted for the first time the tiny design on the pocket of the borrowed shirt. It consisted of a simple circle with three Chinese symbols inside. "No. I hadn't planned on doing that."

Molly felt his breath on her hair and looked up to meet his blue-eyed stare. "Like I said a while ago, I'm on your side, Alec."

His smile returned. "I have a lot to thank you for, Molly. Sorry I sounded so gruff. Come on up and get some air. You're looking as green as your shirt."

She followed him out, aggravated that she kept having to rebutton the top button of the borrowed jeans. She would go to buy food, but might not be able to eat it and keep these pants on. Outside, Molly slipped on her pumps and a blue-visored sun hat while Alec turned on the boat's generator.

They both stopped and watched as two coast-guard helicopters flew low over the marina but relaxed as they headed out to sea.

"I think it would be wise, as soon as Alicia leaves, to head out to Catalina Island. Brooker has a lodge there. It'll give us a day or two to see what hits the paper."

"And to get you deprogrammed. Hopefully, Alicia can give you a shot or some pills. Or something," Molly added lamely, at a loss over how one went about counteracting brainwashing.

"Yeah. If that's possible."

His voice was expressionless, but Molly felt a certain charged tension between them. She didn't allow herself to dwell on the fact that she had just agreed to be alone with Alec for the next couple of days. "Okay. Any special dietary requests?"

"Tea. Loose breakfast leaves, if they have any. And dark beer. That yellow water you Yanks drink is impossible."

Alec helped her onto the dock, then reached into his jeans and handed over twenty dollars. "I don't have any more on me, love. The rest of it is in traveler's checks in my coat, which I didn't think to take when the car turned over. I asked Alicia for a small loan, and she'll have the cash when she gets here."

"That's okay." Molly smiled. "You can pay me back when this thing's over."

"I'll have a big tab by then, girl."

His face now wore an intense, intimate look, like the one he'd given her earlier, and Molly couldn't help reaching out to squeeze his arm. That embarrassed them both, and she quickly turned and headed up the dock.

When she got to the gate, Molly was surprised to look back and find he was still watching her. She waved and

Alec responded, his arm sweeping in a caressing motion it seemed she could feel across the breezy air between them. A shiver ran down her spine.

He cupped both hands around his mouth and shouted, "I'll unlock the gate when you get back. Just ring the bell."

"Okay," she yelled, then started off. The shops were only a five-minute walk. She passed quickly by the pay phone and reached for the door of the tiny Galley Grub food market but stopped and stared back at the phone. Her mind was whirring through the facts of what she had been through the past eight hours. She once again tried to analyze the rightness of her decision to throw in with Alec Steele.

Molly walked to the phone and impulsively dropped a quarter in. She punched in her office number and waited while the smell of diesel oil wafted around her on the wind, making her stomach tighten and complain from hunger. Above her, gulls screamed from their perches near the outside eating areas, advance scouts for their hordes of feathered friends waiting on the masts of boats surrounding the buildings.

"Answer the phone, dammit," Molly muttered.

Her clerk at the office, Sara Gillem, picked up. "Mission. This is Sara."

"Sara, just listen and don't talk. This is Molly."

"My God," Sara gasped, despite her orders. "Are you okay?" the woman whispered.

"Yes. Now listen, a terrible, terrible thing has happened to Rafe." Molly, despite herself, began to cry. "He was shot, Sara. I don't know what the news or the police are going to be saying about this, but I want you to call Rafe's daughter and tell her for me that I'm so sorry. He died a gentleman, coming to my aid."

Sara was softly crying on the other end. "We just heard a little about it. The police are here now," she whispered. "What should I do?"

"Don't tell them I called unless they ask you directly, Sara. Go to the ladies' room and calm down. I'll call you later. I think I'm going to need your help running down some information. You going to be okay?"

"Yes." The clerk, her assistant for five years, sounded in control of her voice once again. "Thank you for calling. I've got to run now. I'll talk with you later."

The line went dead. Slowly, Molly hung up, taking a moment to wipe away her tears before she left the phone.

Lieutenant Cortez must have beaten a path to the Mission Verde installation office trying to find her, Molly realized. For a moment, she again considered calling him and exiting this whole scene, but the memory of Alec Steele's farewell wave stomped out common sense.

Molly walked into the market and looked around. The shelves groaned with exotic munchies priced three times higher than normal. She grabbed an assortment of canned items, as well as a variety of perishables and an armful of breakfast fixings. She even grabbed an $8.00 bottle of wine that was marked at a special buy at $14.99. For Alec she added four bottles of German beer.

A young girl in a pink T-shirt rang up the items, eyeing Molly as she counted out $63.68 in cash.

"The *Empress* is setting sail today?"

"Excuse me?" Molly said, caught off guard.

"The *Geisha Empress*. You're crewing on her, aren't you?" she asked, pointing to the insignia on the borrowed shirt.

"Yes." Molly started thinking fast. "We're taking her down to Redondo Beach tomorrow for repairs." If the police, or anyone else, showed up looking for them, the least she could do was give out a few false leads.

"So you're having a little party tonight, right?"

"Right. Thanks for your help." Molly picked up the bag and left the store. She felt a blister forming on her heel, which reminded her about the tennis shoes. Molly detoured across the plaza, heading toward the shops opposite the market.

At Trader Ric's, which she decided should be renamed Pirate Ric's, she paid $38.00 for pink sneakers and $12.50 more for two toothbrushes, a tube of toothpaste, deodorant, one pair of underpants and three pairs of cotton socks. She was all set to be away from home for a few days, though she was completely out of cash.

Molly was hurrying up the boardwalk toward the boats when she spotted a man scanning the crowd. He was leaning against a white Mercedes, his dark-skinned arms folded across his light-colored shirt. Though he was dressed for it and sported tinted sunglasses, his body stance told her he wasn't on a carefree outing to the beach.

As Molly approached, he lowered his arms and rubbed a spot on his thigh, and she felt herself nearly panic. The outline of a gun was clear through the thin chino of his baggy shorts. She glanced up again to meet his eyes, but he'd turned his head in the opposite direction. It was then she noticed the design on his shirt. A tiny, smiling Oriental face was painted on the pocket just above the heart.

It was identical to the shirt worn by one of the dead men on the freeway last night.

Was it the same logo she had noticed at Inscrutable Security all those months ago? Molly couldn't remember. Her legs stiff with fear, she hurried on. A few yards past the man, she risked a check in the direction he had been looking. Just as she did, a tall, younger man in a white cap and shades, wearing a red L.A. Rams T-shirt, came out of the market she had visited a short time before.

The second man motioned for the first to come inside. A hot stab of premonition shot through Molly. She had never believed in intuition or visions, but at that second she knew these guys were looking for Alec.

Without running, Molly made it back to the gate, groceries and all, in three minutes. Mr. Cashmere Pants was leaving with his teenage girlfriend, and she ticked them both off when she hurried by without a word as he held the gate for her.

Her lungs hurt from the quick, jerky breaths she was taking, and her arms ached from the twenty pounds of junk she was lugging. But she kept up the pace down the long walkway toward the *Geisha Empress*. As it loomed closer, Molly searched for Alec's figure, but he wasn't anywhere in sight.

She got to the stairs and dumped the bags into the cockpit, taking a moment to look toward the gate. At that moment, the white Mercedes pulled up.

"Dammit. Alec? Alec, where are you?"

Molly stuck her head through the door and looked around the galley, then stumbled down into the boat. Alec wasn't on board!

She pulled back the curtains and looked out to the dock walkway just as the black man and his companion sauntered through the gate.

The gun, Molly thought. I have to get the gun Alec had yesterday.

Frantically she searched, but couldn't find it. Finally she pulled a knife out of the drawer and took a deep breath, then peered out the window again. The two men were nowhere in sight.

She had to go out, she decided. There was no other way to keep track of this probable new wave of assassins and try to warn Alec without showing herself.

Draping her jacket over her hand, Molly ventured out onto the deck. Beneath her, the boat creaked. Ducking down even with the cabin, she spotted the men. They were on the *Geisha Empress*'s bow. The black man was hanging over the bowsprit, holding on to the railing with his right hand. His left hand was stuck in the pocket where she had seen evidence of the gun.

Slowly Molly crept up another rung on the ladder leading to the top of the *Geisha Empress*. The guy with the hat was talking in a low tone and pointing to the water. She looked around hurriedly but saw no one else on their boats. Down the channel, she spotted a coastguard cutter moored, and she wondered if she could somehow get their attention.

At that second, the guy in the hat turned and looked right at her.

"Hey! What are you doing?" he yelled.

The second man turned and withdrew the revolver from his pocket, curbing her notion to run. With a bolder attitude than she felt entitled to, she shouted, "I'm a friend of Fred Brooker. What the hell are you two doing trespassing? Leave now or I'll call the coast guard."

They walked toward her, the man in front motioning with his gun for her to stand still. He had taken off his sunglasses and Molly could see he was older than she'd originally thought, very handsome and sympathetic-looking despite the gun. "Stand still, miss. No one is going to hurt you."

"That's damn straight, mister." Molly dropped the jacket covering the knife and raised the weapon slightly. "Get off this boat. Now."

Both men looked surprised and a bit shaken at her show of force. The guy in the hat held up both hands. "Take it easy, lady. I'm not—"

"You heard me. Get off this boat now." Molly raised the knife higher and allowed what she hoped was a demented look to take hold of her features. The waves splashed the keel of the *Empress* and Molly felt her roll slightly with the current. She was getting very nervous, sure that at any second the two men would rush her.

"What in the bloody hell.... Molly?"

She turned at the sound of Alec's voice. He was standing in the cockpit, dressed in a wet suit.

"Get the gun, Alec!" she yelled, then whirled back to the men. The one in the Rams shirt grabbed her and knocked the knife into the water. The other stepped closer, a very serious look on his face.

"Alec Steele? You need to come with us."

"I don't think so, mate," Alec replied, pointing a gun at the man's face. "Now drop it and let the girl go."

The older man dropped the gun and nodded at his partner to release Molly. She ran to Alec and picked up the discarded gun. "Now what?" she asked.

"Keep them covered while they come down," he said. "All right, chaps, inside now."

The men looked grim, but respected Alec's fire-power and hastily descended the narrow steps. Molly kept the gun trained on them while Alec tied their hands and legs with sailing line and covered their mouths with adhesive tape. He had asked them several times who they were, but they refused to answer.

He searched them, found wallets with no identification but plenty of cash, dragged them to opposite sides of the galley, then motioned for Molly to go back up on deck. Alec followed, then sat on the steps where he could keep an eye on his "guests."

"We're going to take the boat out and moor her," Alec whispered. "Then we'll take the dinghy back in and use their car." He handed Molly the keys. "Make up a couple of bags of supplies. We'll get another boat. Be safer than using the *Empress,* now that we've been spotted."

Quickly Molly told him about the girl in the store recognizing the shirt. Alec swore and shook his head. "I should have thought of that. Well, too late now. Hopefully, she's a typical beach bunny and won't recall your face. Get the supplies together then, love. We'd better wait a bit before we bring them up on deck again, just in case any friends of theirs turn up. In the meantime, if you don't mind, I'd love a cup of tea."

While Molly worked, Alec stripped off his wet suit and kept an eye and a gun trained on the two men. They stared back but remained complacent. This bothered him more than anything, for he had the distinct impression they were waiting for reinforcements.

Molly handed him two canvas bags, her purse and a bundle with warm clothes in it, all the while taking in Alec's appearance. He looked much stronger and more alert. He wore the bandage over his neck wound, but save for a skintight yellow swimsuit, he was bare. His body was incredible. Well-developed calves, muscled thighs and a flat stomach glistened under a matting of softly curling blond hair in the California sunshine.

Molly found herself distracted from her fears for the moment as she stared at his nipples, which were small and hard from the bite of ocean breeze blowing across the channel.

"That was a hell of a time to take a recreational dip," she snapped at him when she realized he had noticed her staring. She was aggravated by their close call and felt more worried than ever for their safety.

Alec narrowed his eyes at her but his voice was calm. "Sorry, love. I was just trying to clear my head. Well, now that you're packed up, how about that tea? Then we'll head out."

"Fine," Molly replied, "but why don't I cover the boys while you make the tea. I can watch from the galley steps."

Alec chuckled, then handed her the gun. She watched as he puttered around the kitchen, pulling out mugs and tea bags and sugar.

She watched as he competently put bottled water in the mugs and placed them in the microwave. While he worked, she eyed the walkway, then glanced at their two prisoners. She felt anxious, as if she had forgotten something important, but shook off the feeling.

The red timer readout was counting down, *four, three, two, one...* It went off at the same instant she cried out, "Alec, stop the microwave before it—"

The high-pitched wail of the timer cut off her words. In horror, she watched Alec grab his head and fall to his knees. His moan was more intense this time, as if the pain were greater.

Molly stood, her hand sweating around the gun as the two men stared at her, challenge in their eyes.

"Alec. Alec, are you all right?" she demanded. In response, he shuddered, then lay very, very still.

It was hard to swallow. Molly berated herself for not thinking faster. Alec was pale, and the prisoners' gazes grew more hostile by the second.

"Sit tight, boys," Molly heard herself say, then she took a step down into the galley, which was the last place on earth she wanted to be.

Chapter Eight

Alec bounced back from the inadvertent microwave attack after twenty minutes of unconsciousness. They were the longest twenty minutes Molly could ever remember spending. Not surprising, since she passed it holding a gun trained on two men who, if looks could kill, would have claimed her as their victim several times over.

With some gentle urging and that mug of tea, it took less than an hour after the incident for Alec to claim the helm of the *Geisha Empress* and steer her into the open waters of the Pacific. Molly was sorry they couldn't put her under sail power, but considering the fact she had to play guard, she settled for the smooth ride offered by the powerful inboard engine.

When they were four miles from the marina, Alec turned the boat toward the shore. A couple of hundred yards off land, near a deserted fishing dock, Alec dropped anchor. "We'll leave them here. The shore patrol will check them by tomorrow morning, if they haven't figured how to get themselves untied before then."

"I'm glad you're okay. Sorry about the ambush," Molly offered. "When I asked you to make the tea, I never thought about the timer."

"Hey, I understand. You weren't trying to cook my goose and repay me for that rough stuff last night, were you?"

He sounded his old cocky self. She realized it was Alec's nature to always put pressure on a sore spot. "Yeah. But you're too hard-boiled for that. Right, mate?"

They laughed, then hurried through the chores of securing the boat.

"I think it will be much safer leaving the *Geisha Empress* and traveling to Catalina by other means," Alec said, "considering your chat with the gal in the store. Why don't we drive their Mercedes to San Pedro, take the ferry over and rent a car to get out to the lodge? I don't think anyone will think to look for us there, once the *Empress* is recovered."

"It sounds fine to me," Molly offered, "except that whoever these guys are, they thought to look on Brooker's boat for us. Why not his lodge?"

Alec fell silent for a moment, then admitted, "Even though they aren't carrying ID, I think those guys are cops. Maybe the girl at the market called in a report."

"Can't have happened that way. They were out there waiting when I went into the store."

"Well, someone else could have seen us."

"Do you think we're that famous?" Molly asked, incredulous that anyone would recognize her in a moving car.

Alec nodded, then stopped winding up line and stood and faced her. "I was going to tell you as soon as you got back from shopping. I had the radio tuned in to a network news broadcast. They're describing us as fugitives."

"On the radio?" Molly shrieked. A local station she could understand, even a major Los Angeles station. But a national one? "Why?"

"Because someone tried to take Fred Brooker out in prison yesterday. Nearly did it, too. Electrocuted a guard instead, when the bloke pulled him away from a booby-trapped electrical line in the prison kitchen. This whole mess is shaping up very dramatically for those news barracudas. Nearly dead rich criminal, followed by dead bodies discovered this morning on the doorstep of a beautiful woman—a woman who happens to be a witness in the Brooker murder trial. I'm surprised we're not all over the media with that lead-in."

Molly slumped onto the deck and put her head onto her knees. Things were worse than she ever imagined they could be. "Are they saying we're involved?"

"One report made us out to be as bad as Bonnie and Clyde. Sorry, love, but it looks like your fifteen minutes of fame have arrived."

"Maybe we need to rethink this a bit, Alec. Even though we're innocent of everything else, we could go to jail for tying up two policemen." She gestured toward the cabin. "I think someone should contact Lieutenant Cortez and offer our explanation about the dead men they found at my home. Obviously Brooker's got people looking for you—for us now, I suppose. But even if they take you into custody, Dr. Chen could treat you."

Alec vehemently shook his head, then caught his forehead between his hands. The sudden motion seemed to have pained him. "No. Until I know who those gorillas were that met me at the airport, and who that punk was that was willing to kill us both at your house, I'm not going near the coppers. So let's just all drop that particular bag of bones.''

His handsome face hardened and the same, brook-no-argument expression she had seen last night during her abduction reappeared. Since she was in no position to force the point, Molly shut up.

But once they reached shore she was going to demand that Alec contact Alicia Chen again. He had to get medical treatment before he could shake some of the paranoia that she thought was making him even more jittery than their experiences warranted.

Molly shivered as she thought about what he had told her, that he had been ''programmed'' to kill someone. Was it safe to be alone with him? she wondered.

She stared at this man she'd known for such a short time under the strangest of circumstances. Though she felt no fear as she looked at him and had seldom been burned trusting her instincts, a flash of panic warmed her blood. They were together because of chance encounters and circumstance. Was her instinct that he was telling the truth about being tortured and brainwashed enough to make her stay with him?

The bandage on his neck reminded her of the proof she had seen of Alec's torture. She thought of his pain, his anger and also how he had saved her life this morning. If he'd been hired to kill her, why wouldn't he have done it last night or this morning? And anyway, why kill her at all? He was the eyewitness. None of it made sense.

Shaking off her doubts, Molly touched Alec's arm. ''How are you feeling, physically, I mean?'' she asked.

''Not quite kipper, but working on it.'' He flashed her a smile. ''How about yourself? You look damn normal despite no sleep and the mayhem you've witnessed." Though the words weren't effusive, his look was full of approval.

"Thanks, I think," she replied. "Can I help you with anything on the boat?"

"You ever sailed before, Molly?"

"No. Well, yes. I've been on a sailboat, but I didn't handle any of the ropes or anything."

"Lines."

"Lines, sorry. Now I need a sailing interpreter." Molly squinted up at the mast. "Okay, I've hung on to some lines once before. I did steer for a while, but the boat I was on didn't have a wheel, it had a tiller. All I remember about that was that the boat went in the opposite direction I steered."

"You don't have to worry about that with the *Empress*." He pointed toward the steering wheel. "Okay, love. Drive her just like a car while I set the lines. Then we'll be off. It's going to take us awhile to get to San Pedro from here."

Molly saluted and jumped up. "Aye-aye. Let's do it."

Alec reached out to brush her cheek. His hand trembled slightly, and his eyes were intense when he looked deep into hers. She felt as if she should say something but suddenly could think of nothing.

Alec, however, could think of everything that could have and should have been between them. He'd been attracted to Molly at their first meeting, not only for her looks, which were lovely and appealing and full of life, but for the air of openness and decency she wore.

It made him want to do daredevil stunts, to race under a summer sun at fourteen knots and hear her holler to stop, to take her back to Australia for a look-see at the dingos, sharks and sheer space he loved so.

But none of that was likely, he realized with a stab of realistic thinking. He'd entered her life again as a fugitive with a countdown to death ticking away. It was a bomb he couldn't control or defuse. The last thing he wanted, the last thing he'd be able to live with, was bringing this sunny, lovely young woman any more pain than she had already endured because of him over the past twenty-four hours. Turning his eyes away, Alec shut off the thoughts of what could be.

Alec moved away from Molly so quickly she wasn't sure if she had imagined his touch or not. Without another word, they worked to stabilize the boat, hauled their personal belongings up on deck, locked their prisoners in the galley and climbed down into the dinghy.

The tiny outboard engine started immediately, and they were back at the slip in a few minutes. Alec decided to deflate the dinghy and sink it with the engine, which they did unnoticed in the nearly deserted marina. They hauled their satchels out to the Mercedes. It was a rental, they discovered, and held nothing to help identify the men any further.

Alec started the engine. "It'll take a bit to get to San Pedro."

"We've got to get some hot food," Molly replied. So they headed first to a fast-food restaurant.

"Deep-fried tucker," Molly kidded.

"Pass the salt and ketchup," Alec kidded back.

Their meal was courtesy of the contents of one of the visitor's wallets, into which Alec had stuck a signed I.O.U.

Molly chanced a last furtive glance over her shoulder as they merged onto the freeway, but found no gunmen with cocked guns or swarming SWAT teams, or even an errant news helicopter circling above.

Delighted to have food in her stomach, she leaned back against the lovely leather seat and immediately fell asleep.

Alec drove on, unwilling to turn on the radio and wake his sleeping passenger, even though he knew he should be keeping track of the news reports.

"Rest a bit, love," he murmured softly, driving with a steadier hand than he had a right to have.

FREDERICK BROOKER WAS escorted by two uniformed guards into interview room number one. He had several inches of gauze taped to the right side of his face and both his hands were bandaged. He walked slowly to a chair and sat across from the woman already waiting at the table.

"Kind of you to come," he snapped, his greenish eyes like flint. "I want you to let Erik know I'm okay. You tell him I'm walking around on my own two feet, talking and thinking clearly. You tell him. I don't want him worrying."

"It would be a lie if I told him you were thinking clearly," the woman replied. "We both know that."

Brooker shook his bandaged right hand in her face. "Don't start with me. I'm doing what I've got to do, like always. You do what I tell you, and nothing will change." He leaned over close enough to smell her perfume. "But if you don't do what I tell you, everything will change. I promise you that."

"Have you ever known me to disobey?"

Brooker smiled, wincing as the raw flesh pulled away from the gauze. "No. But that doesn't stop me from wondering if you didn't have something to do with my little accident. I'm sure my dying behind bars would not cause you great sorrow, my love."

"Are you accusing me of attempted murder, Frederick? Shall I hire Mason Weil for myself?"

"No, of course not. Besides, I've already hired someone who can take care of what happened to me inside, as well as carry out my plans outside of these four walls. He's very expensive." Brooker reached across to stroke the woman's designer suit jacket. "But then, I've never regretted paying for quality. You know that."

"You heard that your boat burned yesterday?" the woman asked, hoping to see another trace of pain on Brooker's face.

"Yes. Regrettable. Erik was very fond of the *Geisha Empress*. But that had to be," Brooker whispered. "Seems someone tipped off the FBI about my plans for Mr. Steele. They came to put him in protective custody, but the fool tied them up." Brooker laughed, a high-pitched sound that did not match his voice at all.

The woman's left eyelid quivered, but she made no reply.

Brooker stopped laughing, then sighed. "Well, you can go now, dear heart. Take care of my boy. Tell him Daddy will be home very soon." His eyes traveled the length of the woman's neck. "I'm very, very anxious to sleep in my own bed again."

"I'll tell Erik," the woman said, standing abruptly. Without another word, she left.

"Back to your cell, Mr. Brooker," one of the two guards said.

Frederick Brooker stood and walked ahead of them, refusing to acknowledge their temporary existence in his life.

THE LIGHTS OF AVALON, Catalina Island's harbor town, snapped on and off like lightning bugs in the cool dusk as Alec and Molly sailed into the bay.

To their right, Catalina's landmark white marble ballroom dome sparkled, and off to the left, south of the half-mile-long development of the town proper, sat the Enchanted Cottage. A tiny white Victorian tucked into the rocky cliff, the cottage had been built by a captain for his fiancée as a wedding present. The woman had never seen it, however, breaking off the marriage plans when she decided the island was too desolate to live on.

The would-be groom died of a broken heart, according to local legend. Now, bright pots of orange flowers bloomed on the railing, so someone had eventually made it a home, Molly found herself thinking.

"There's always hope," Molly murmured.

"What?"

She looked at Alec, surprised that he'd heard her over the noise of the ferry and the waves. Quickly she told him the story of the cottage and the doomed lovers.

"I'd say he was better off dying. A love as strong as that, there's no getting over."

"Time heals all wounds, no?"

"Might scab them over a bit, but I doubt they truly heal. Man walks around more dead than alive the rest of his life. No good that, I'd say."

Unable to think of a reply to such a revealing remark and finding herself wondering if Alec had had such a love in his past, Molly changed the subject. She called his attention to the glass-bottom boats cruising the coast, then explained how she had visited as a child each summer.

"At that time the island was virtually uninhabited, bought outright by William Wrigley of chewing gum fame and then deeded as a wildlife preserve to the state of California. No more than two percent of the land can ever be developed."

"It reminds me of home," Alec replied. "A thousand times more space than men. Good proportion for thinking."

"Do you miss Australia?"

"Nah, not usually." He stood close to her and brushed a lock of hair away from her mouth. "Especially not today, at this moment. Although if we're trying to hide from someone, Alice Springs would have a lot more options than this place."

They both stared at the dock, which was looming closer. The trip to San Pedro, during which she was embarrassed to have fallen asleep, took two hours. The cruise took the same, though they had not been able to board until 2:30 p.m. It was still full daylight but clouding up over the Pacific.

"We'll pretty much have the town to ourselves by the time we get dinner tonight," Molly told Alec. "The day-trippers leave at 6:00 p.m. It might be safest to head to Brooker's lodge then."

"I think you're right," he replied. "I'll check into a motel somewhere, though, and we'll lie low until dark. Follow a bit behind me until I get a key. Our pictures are probably all over the news by now. It's very dangerous to be seen together."

Alec was wearing a cowboy hat, which covered his blond hair, and black sunglasses to hide his eyes. Molly had purchased a beige-and-green scarf to cover her mane and wore a bulky sweatshirt she'd stuffed into one of their bags. The bag also held the two guns, which she was petrified would set off some kind of alarm when they'd boarded the ferry, but no check of luggage had been made.

During the voyage, they sat apart, meeting up only now as the passengers were disembarking. Alec took her arm and guided her through the light crowd.

"I'm going to try to make a few calls tomorrow and find out what's going on," she whispered.

"To whom?"

"The phone companies have as much information on people as credit-reporting agencies, in some cases. I'm going to do a little research on Mr. Brooker. I've got a secretary who's as good as gold, Alec. I think she'll help us. Don't worry. I won't do anything to get us caught."

"I trust you, love. I told you that. Don't lose me." With a squeeze of her hand, Alec left her side and headed down the ferry plank to land.

Molly followed, not too closely, and made a mental note to try to get into the telephone company business office on Catalina and check out the records for Brooker's lodge. If memory served her, it was a three-person office, and if she went when they were busy, she'd probably get away with just flashing her ID, giving a phony name before they looked too closely at it and smiling a lot.

The actual plant facilities housing the network wiring and switching equipment were well guarded, but the business offices were notorious for having stringent rules about signing in and out that were seldom enforced.

Their records could possibly tell her about Brooker's other business holdings and real estate, two things that she felt she should look into. On the cruise over, Molly had devoured a stack of newspapers and a three-month-old *Newsweek* she had pinched from the cruise line's waiting area. The magazine contained a lengthy article on Frederick Brooker and Paul Buntz.

After reading it, she was convinced that Buntz must have been blackmailing Brooker over information about a string of robberies that had taken place at several of Brooker's clients' homes in the months before Buntz was killed.

It might even be that Buntz had fenced some of the stolen merchandise, as the *Newsweek* article had speculated, since he had once been arrested as a fence with organized-crime connections.

Molly was anxious to do a little sleuthing on her own in this matter, as well as to discuss what she had read with Alec.

One thing she found interesting was that Buntz and Brooker were both born in Kensington, Ohio. Buntz was the same age as Brooker, so there was a good possibility they had known each other growing up.

To Molly's way of thinking, it was a lead that might prove significant in tying Brooker more tightly to all that had happened so far. If someone could find the link between Paul Buntz and Frederick Brooker, maybe they could discover what the ex-sportscaster had been blackmailing Brooker over. The more Molly thought about it, the more she was convinced that the answer to that mystery would probably answer the question of whom Alec was programmed to kill.

Sleuthing single-handedly was a risky plan, but it was all Molly could think of at the moment. And a good Pacific Communications manager always worked with what she had, she told herself with a wry grin, which immediately turned to a grimace when she remembered Rafe Amundson.

Swallowing a new surge of emotion at the memory of this morning's tragedy, Molly managed to keep Alec in sight, though she had to wipe tears away several times.

Fifteen minutes after they walked off the ferry, Alec and Molly were locked into room 19 of the Devil Fish Motel. Alec used everything but fifty dollars of the money he had taken from the "visitors" to buy ferry tickets, lunch and rent for the night. The motel was the island's most secluded, and emptiest. Only two other guests were registered, Alec had heard from the manager. The motel was located high on a side street at the farthest settled point of the city of Avalon. Most visitors liked a more central location, the manager had explained.

Molly thought what he really meant was that they liked more civilized surroundings. After she had looked around, she wasn't too pleased with their accommodations. The room's good features were a double bed with an ominous, canyon-size cleft running down the middle, a television with three fuzzy channels and a bathroom whose grout had come over with the first settlers. The bad included a damp, cold draft under an ill-fitting door, no soap or tissues and two towels the size of sandwich Swiss—and nearly as holey.

"I'm sorry about the kip, Molly," Alec apologized as soon as she'd walked across the threshold. "We don't have enough cash for two rooms." He deposited what little money he had left on the small night table. "Your name is Margaret Day, by the way. I'm Robert."

"Where did you come up with those?"

"Bob Dylan's a favorite of mine. Peggy Day is one of his best." Alec shrugged, looked out the door in both directions, then shut and locked it.

Molly liked that song and found herself wondering if the lyrics she remembered from that folksy ballad, which revealed that Bob wanted to spend the night with Peggy Day, was pertinent.

Unwilling to ask Alec, Molly sat on the bed and nearly tilted over on the worn-out mattress. She kicked off her pink tennis shoes, which were smudged from the soot under the ferry seats, and pulled the scarf from her head. She shook her hair free and collapsed on the bed's lumpy surface.

"Money's a real problem, Alec. We've got to call Alicia, if you think we can still trust her and see if she can meet us somewhere soon."

"I know. But we can't call from the room. Your phone cards are surely being traced by now, and I don't have one."

"Wait a minute," Molly cried out. She rolled off the bed and grabbed one of the canvas satchels, emptying its contents onto the graying, threadbare carpet. Rafe's call-out book of emergency numbers was there. Bound in leather, its front flap held various items Rafe had never got around to putting anywhere else.

One of the items was his calling card. Another was a hundred-dollar bill. With a sigh, she tossed the two items onto the bed. "There's a little more money. And a way to try to reach Dr. Chen. That's Rafe's phone card from work. His PIN is 1551. That's the last four numbers of his Pacific Communications employee number. The crew always kidded him because everyone else's numbers ended in three thousand and something. He was there a long time."

It must have been something in her voice that made Alec kneel down beside her and take her in his arms.

"I'm so, so sorry, Molly. What happened wasn't your fault, though I know that doesn't help anything."

Molly fully lost her composure then. Her crying turned to sobbing, which turned into a hiccuping torrent and finally into exhaustion. Alec held her through the entire gamut, rubbing her back, smoothing her hair.

"It's so damned unfair," she finally said. "He never hurt anyone..."

"I know, Molly." Alec hugged her and stood, massaging the kinks out of his neck gently. "None of this is fair. Not the deaths of innocent people, not the hole this has made in your life, or mine."

She realized then that she knew almost nothing about him. "What do you do in Melbourne, Alec Steele?"

He grinned and sat down again, relaxing against the bed with his arms around her. "I own a charter boat, do day sailing, touring the coast a bit. I made a bit of money racing the past few years but gave it up after your Yankee, Dennis Connor, lost the America's Cup. Good bloke, that Connor. Never gives up." His voice grew huskier. "You can't give up, either, Molly girl. We'll get through this. Get some help. See some daylight. You can count on it."

At that second, she realized she would believe whatever he said to her. Her body was warm next to his and vulnerable in a thousand different ways. Without realizing what she was doing, Molly leaned into him.

Though she had begun the kiss, he immediately took control. His mouth was harder than she had imagined, and gentler. And hotter, as it moved against her lips, dueled with her tongue and devoured her conscious awareness. He squeezed her to him, and they tumbled onto the floor. His hands traveled the length of her, caressing her and hugging her to him. Now, for the first time, she understood the meaning of the word "bliss."

When he broke away from her, his breathing was ragged, his eyes bright and his voice silky and soft. "I've wanted to do that ever since I thought you were going to shoot me."

"When did you think I was going to shoot you? Last night, you mean?"

"No. Months ago, when I opened the door at Brooker's office and you were standing there, wild-eyed and grabbing for something in your purse as if it was the only protection between you and the hounds of hell."

Molly laughed low in her throat and shifted her hips closer to him. The movement put a much more serious look on Alec's face, and a much more reckless thought into hers. "I thought about you, too, that night. It was Valentine's Day. I was hoping I would see you again. And then—"

He raised two fingers to her lips and shushed her. "Don't, Molly girl. Don't go back. Stay here with me a bit more."

Alec kissed her again then, and she told him with her body that he could—*should*—make love to her, that she wanted him. He moved his hand under the sweatshirt, under her bra, stroking her breast, her stomach, coming back around to rub her nipples until she thought she would cry out.

But instead, he cried out. Forgetting his injury, Molly had dug her nails into his neck, accidentally touching his wound.

"Oh, no, I'm so sorry, Alec. Alec, are you okay?"

He waved her away and unsteadily moved up on his knees, grabbing his head with one hand and squeezing it. "It's okay, love. Really. Ah-g-g-gh."

She sat next to him now, rubbing his back, saying repeatedly she was sorry. Finally he grinned and patted her leg. "Hey, it's okay, honest. I think we pinched one of those bloody needles down, though. It hurts like hell. Can't you try to get it out now, love?"

She pulled back the adhesive tape and stared at the two tiny black needles. One spot seemed to be infected, which really scared her. What if she hit a nerve, or worse, and really incapacitated him?

"No, Alec, I can't. But let's try to reach your friend now. Really. Use Rafe's card to call Dr. Chen. That thing could be infected. Besides, she's bound to be worried about failing to connect with you earlier on the boat."

"I will, soon. Just let me sit here with you for a while. Tell me about what you were reading on the ferry over."

Molly related the facts about the Brooker case, as well as the information she'd gleaned about Paul Buntz growing up in Brooker's hometown, and of his connection to stolen goods.

"The magazine article noted that twenty-five of Brooker's company's clients in the Del Mar, Coronado area were robbed in one three-week period. It had to be an inside job according to the police, but they could never prove it by getting a lead from the burglars, so they concentrated on the items stolen, particularly the jewelry. Some of it was located in New York and traced back to Paul Buntz. Do you think that could be the thing he was blackmailing Brooker over?"

Alec's eyes seemed cloudy and he shook his head. "Could be, love. I didn't know Brooker long, but I'll tell you one thing. You wouldn't want to cross the man. Even before he shot that man in cold blood, I sensed he wouldn't let anyone get the best of him without paying the price."

"Did you cross him?"

"Not in business. But it's my word that could send him to death row. It's not likely that Brooker would take that lying down. Personalities like his never accept responsibility for their own fate."

"Well, that's enough of this for now," Molly said, noting that Alec's body language was becoming more and more distressed. "Please call Alicia now, before you fall asleep. Then we'll eat."

Reluctantly Alec agreed. She left him sitting on the bed, the phone cradled in his lap. Molly went into the bathroom and ran the water, not liking the way Alec's voice changed every time he said Alicia's name and not liking herself much at all for experiencing what felt a lot like jealousy. When Molly heard his voice rise and some teasing chatter begin, she slammed the door shut.

When she came out of the bathroom five minutes later, Alec was lying on his side in bed, sound asleep and snoring. She crept toward him and stared. He was gorgeous. There was no getting around that, she thought. His face, even gaunt with fatigue and bruised from the car accident last night, was smooth and full of character and masculine grace.

He was snoring as if he'd been sleeping for hours. She found a surprisingly new blanket on the narrow shelf in the closet and threw it over his long legs. She grabbed some money, flicked off the light and quashed a powerful urge to crawl in next to him as well as another no less powerful inclination to kiss him.

It was insane to have feelings for this man, this stranger, but she felt an irresistible tug of sensual attraction. Chemistry never makes sense, Molly told herself, then slipped soundlessly out the door.

Chapter Nine

The city of Avalon was, as is often the case of towns by the Pacific, settled by sailing men. Hundreds of tiny houses line streets too narrow for any traffic but foot or bicycle. Most buildings are over fifty years old and were constructed with pieces of debris from ships washed ashore or lumber bought and hauled by retired sailors who had once visited Catalina and vowed to return to live out their days there.

Zane Grey, the author famous for his classic Western tales of heroes and villains, had once owned a house on the island. Celebrities of all sorts landed at the tiny mountaintop airport. They walked or rode motor scooters and bought salt-water taffy and postcards of the lovely place memorialized as the island of romance, twenty-six miles across the sea from the mainland.

Molly stood on the pier and watched as night fell over the water and thought how much farther away than those twenty-six miles she felt. Her mind was awhirl with contradicting emotions, all centering on the events that had occurred since she first laid eyes on Alec Steele.

She had agreed to testify to do her civic duty, the same civic duty that had led her to place the call to the police the morning of February 15 after she'd heard the news report.

When she told the detectives that she witnessed Paul Buntz getting into the limo she had been told was Frederick Brooker's, she had caused quite a commotion. For a while, she felt as if her own rights were being infringed upon while they checked out her story, her job, her credit, everything.

The police finally told her she made a very credible witness and that the district attorney would be in touch. He had been, she had retold the story, and that was that. It never occurred to her to tell them she would refuse to testify as to what she'd seen, but now, twenty-six miles and seven months later, she wondered if she had been naive.

The police hadn't warned her she could be in danger. They had not revealed that they had an eyewitness.

They certainly hadn't told her that people close to her could be harmed! And for what?

After all, Molly realized for the first time, she had not actually seen Frederick Brooker the night of the murder. She couldn't really swear the man who got into the car was Paul Buntz, only that he was carrying a similar orange gym bag.

It had been enough, however, for the district attorney.

Molly wondered, as she blew on her hands and stared at the frenzy of whitecaps whipped up by the breeze, if it was also enough to make Brooker want to kill her.

When two young men jostled her and smiled, Molly pulled the terry-cloth hat she had bought to replace her forgotten scarf, down farther over her ears, wrapped her arms around her to keep warm and decided she would let Alec sleep while she found something to eat.

Molly walked toward the opposite end of the island from the motel and settled for a very busy, loud-music-playing fish house called Smokey's. She headed for the ladies' room and found an old-fashioned phone booth in the hallway outside. Seeing this chance to learn a few things, she used Rafe's card to make several calls. The first was to her own town house.

A male voice answered on the second ring. Molly hung up quickly and stared at the phone as if it were a snake. She glanced outside, as if expecting federal agents to be charging through the kitchen at Smokey's ready to arrest her.

At least the cops would lock up, she told herself, relieved that her belongings were safe despite her status as a fugitive.

The second call was to Sara Gillem's home phone. Her clerk picked up on the first ring.

"Hello?"

"Sara, it's me. I can't tell you where I am, but I'm going to be calling you back with some requests for microfiche records of long-distance calls."

Sara sucked in a mouthful of air. "Okay. When?"

"I don't know. Maybe Saturday. Can you get into the office on Saturday morning and wait for my call?"

"Yes. Although the you-know-who might be there, too."

Molly experienced a rush of guilt. "Sara, if you're the least bit worried that you might—"

"Stop right there, Boss. Call me Saturday. I'll say a prayer for you."

Molly had to wipe away a few tears over Sara's loyalty. Without dwelling on it, she made the third call to Information in Orange County and got three possible numbers for Sylvester Rojas, the assistant district attorney who had taken all her statements and run through her testimony for the trial.

The first two numbers elicited nonstop voice-mail transfers, but the third produced a real voice.

"Sylvester? I think I just saw him across the hall," a woman replied. "Can I tell him who is calling?"

Well, here goes nothing, Molly thought. In this era of automatic redial, caller ID, third-party calling, call waiting and speakerphones, she could be walking right into a trap. Taking a breath to steady her nerves, she answered, "Tell him it's Molly."

"Molly? Okay, hang on."

The woman had not sounded suspicious or alarmed. A few seconds later, Sylvester Rojas picked up the phone.

"Hello?" His voice sounded puzzled, as if her name had rung no bells.

"It's Molly Jakes, Sylvester. Can you talk to me for a minute?"

"Holy cow! Where are you? Are you okay?"

"Thanks for asking. Yes, I'm fine." In a torrent of words, Molly told him the bare bones of what had happened—that Alec had kidnapped her, that he'd been taken captive, tortured and brainwashed, that they had both nearly been killed, that they had left two men tied up on the *Geisha Empress*. Ninety seconds later she paused to catch her breath. "I can't tell you where I am, Sylvester. But please tell the district attorney that Alec Steele and I will be in touch. We still plan to testify. If Brooker doesn't get to us first."

"This is so incredible, Molly. But you know I must advise you to turn yourselves in. At least in protective custody, you'll be safe until—"

"I'm going now, Sylvester. Thank you. I'll call again when I can. Just tell the police the truth. It might help me stay alive."

Molly slammed down the phone. Her throat was raw, and her knees were shaking. She hurried out into the restaurant, hoping to disappear in a roomful of strange faces.

Grabbing a stool at the bar, she sat right in front of the television and ordered a meal, hoping someone would turn on the news. As if by telepathy, the bartender, a young, pony-tailed redhead with a gold earring in her nose, switched on headline news.

Molly watched the entire broadcast, ate but never tasted a huge plate of shrimp and French fries, and never heard the briefest mention of herself or Alec on the news.

Had he lied to her? she wondered. Or were double murder, kidnapping and all the other crimes such common things, that they were already old news? Suddenly the fatigue, anger and confusion over her physical attraction to the dangerous Mr. Alec Steele, swirled together in an overwhelming mass in her brain.

What was she doing, running off with him anyway? Granted, he'd saved her life at her town house, but how did she know he was right that *she was also in danger?*

Maybe she had only been in danger because of him!

"Now what?" she whispered, suddenly paranoid over the loud voices and the eyes of the men and women eating and drinking and enjoying themselves around her.

Molly stood, removed the twenty-dollar bill she'd folded into her sweatshirt pocket, paid for her meal and hurried out of the bar.

ALEC WOKE WITH A START, grabbing the mattress beneath him as if it were a lifeline which would keep him from falling from the cliff in his dreams. His heart was racing and his whole body ached, especially his neck.

Gingerly he looked around the motel room for Molly. In the dark he saw the bulky shape of a chair, the scuffed table with tape around one leg and the television. A clock, ticking loudly enough for him to hear, read 7:55.

For a moment more, Alec lay still, willing himself to relax, then he rolled off the bed. He went to the door, looked out in both directions and walked outside. A little girl with a pink sundress and bare feet was playing with a ball by the open door of a room four doors away.

Alec went back inside and showered. He was alarmed when he saw that Molly had taken the money, until he realized Rafe's hundred-dollar bill was still on the bed. Pocketing that, he donned the cowboy hat and one of the sweatshirts she'd packed for him and headed out to find her.

Alicia was due to fly in tomorrow. They were to call back tomorrow morning at nine to find out what time the plane she was going to charter would arrive. She was bringing money and some medication she hoped would prove helpful, though she had cautioned him that she had never heard of any therapy that utilized needles of the kind he had described as being imbedded in his skin.

Alec clenched his teeth and moved his head slowly. The pinch wasn't as bad as it had been. But it still hurt like a blackfly bite. At the corner of Main and Juanita, Alec stopped and looked down the street full of diners and bars.

Molly was nowhere to be seen. He ducked into a bar called The Red Tree and ordered a beer. The television was on, and as he took the mug the bartender handed him and walked around the pool table to grab a chair, the words Special Bulletin popped on the screen.

In what he hoped was a casual manner, he walked back to the bar and grabbed a handful of peanuts. A female broadcaster began to talk, too low for him to hear, but when the background picture changed to a shot of a classic Cheoy Lee yacht, bearing the name *Geisha Empress* that was burning, he barked, "Can you turn that up?" more loudly than he had intended.

The barkeep obliged and he listened, nearly choking when he tried to swallow the peanuts. They felt like marbles going down his tight throat. The broadcaster's words rang in his ears ". . . are speculating that the two federal agents, both shot execution-style, were murdered on the yacht and then the luxury vessel was set afire. No word yet on any witnesses, but authorities are questioning two fishermen who reportedly saw a couple in a dinghy at about the time police estimate the killings took place. Police and the FBI will not comment on the reports that this vessel is owned by Frederick Brooker, the multimillionaire businessman who is set to go on trial Tuesday. More news at eleven."

Alec finished the beer with one gulp, turned away from the bar and walked outside and into pouring rain. He felt light-headed and made of ice. A pulse point of pain beat in his neck, and he was convinced that he could feel the needles vibrating when a bolt of lightning struck nearby.

A single plan bounced around inside his skull like a ball in a Roadrunner cartoon. Find Molly and hide. Find Molly and hide.

Find Molly.

Hide.

Then a second thought hit, nearly paralyzing him. Did he want to find Molly and hide her? Or did he want to kill her and then hide? With a shudder, Alec took off at a dead run back to the motel.

He was back at the Devil Fish in less than ten minutes. As he hurried by the darkened office, he noticed the neon sign now glowed Evil Fish through the rain.

"I'm coming, Molly," he murmured under his breath. His heartbeat slowed a bit when he saw that a light was on inside the room. She was back, safe.

Alec stopped outside the door, poised to knock, when a movement to the left made him hesitate. He was hit from behind before he could turn to investigate and fell before he could call out her name.

Chapter Ten

Molly woke, uncomfortably tense and hot in the dark, still room. The light she had left on in the bathroom was out. Her eyes darted to the clock. When she realized it wasn't working, she relaxed a fraction, comforted that all the electricity was cut, surely by the storm. She glanced at her wristwatch, could not read the dial, but estimated it to be about ten-thirty.

Her body complained that she had not slept long enough.

When she'd arrived back at the motel and found that Alec wasn't in the room waiting for her, she had paced, but not panicked, reasoning that he had likely been hungry and gone out. When the storm kicked up, she told herself he probably stayed put, assuming she would do the same.

Now she didn't know what to think.

Listening intently, Molly heard the rain still falling. A second later, lightning flashed, illuminating the shabby room, which was as empty of Alec as before. Two seconds later, an enormous crack of thunder shook the motel room violently.

Rolling off the bed, Molly sighed and pulled off her heavy sweatshirt, then peeked out between the drapes.

Without Mother Nature's strikes of white heat, the sky was impenetrable. When another flash forewarned her, she tensed, but the thunder did not rumble until eight seconds later. "Eight miles away," she said, remembering her mother's words that each second counted meant the storm was a mile farther away.

The parking lot was empty except for a single car. The dark sedan was approximately twenty yards from the door. It looked to Molly like something—a bulky shape—was propped inside. Was someone sitting in the car? Molly wondered. Who sat in a car outside a motel room? she asked herself. The answer made her feel weak with fear.

Someone watching a room. Waiting. Waiting for her? Forcing herself to breathe evenly, Molly moved quickly to the door, turned the dead bolt and engaged the chain. She had foolishly left them off because she had assumed Alec would be back any second.

Maybe it was Alec in the car. The thought unnerved her further. Where would he get a car? Why would he be outside?

If it wasn't Alec, then where the devil was he?

Maybe Alicia Chen had wired him some money, she told herself, knowing she was losing control of her usual ability to reason. Her mind stayed on the same track. So if Alec had rented a car... Had he had another attack and passed out? There was no getting around it, Molly realized. She had to go outside if she was going to get a better look. With more bravado than she felt, she threw the sweatshirt around her shoulders, stuck the hat on her head and unlocked the door. Tentatively, she opened it a crack.

The rain fell steadily, a silver gray curtain of drops. She stepped outside and was immediately drenched.

Running quickly, she reached the end of the walkway before the next bolt of lightning flashed. Hiding behind a round concrete pillar, she tried to ascertain if there actually was someone in the car opposite the motel's small front office.

From this angle, she couldn't see as well as from her room, but it still looked like a person was in the front seat, slumped down as if asleep. Did she dare approach the car to see if it was Alec?

Thinking of every bad horror movie she'd ever seen, she realized the only sensible answer was no. It was too much to risk.

Exasperated, Molly decided to go back to the room and try the phone. She would call the office and ask the desk clerk to send someone out to check the car. But what if the motel called the police?

That thought made her heart pump faster. It was tough getting used to being a citizen who wanted to avoid the police, she realized. As a matter of fact, she cautioned herself, even though the motel seemed deserted except for her, she'd better watch her step—or someone else she hadn't seen would be calling the office about her.

With self-concealment foremost in her mind, Molly hugged the rear wall of the walkway, and slowly moved backward in the dark, letting her fingers feel for the open door. The rough, thick plaster of the outer wall met her blindly groping hand. She moved steadily, inch by inch, her gaze riveted on the sedan. Finally her fingers felt the smooth, painted wood door behind her, cracked open an inch.

With a brief, darting look around, she slipped into the room, locked the door and collapsed on the floor, only to be startled enough to cry out when the antique air-conditioning unit kicked in with a roar.

A half second later, a light, not in the bathroom, but on the table beside the bed, clicked on. The electricity was restored. Gratefully, Molly turned toward the light, and from the outermost edge of her consciousness, a warning bell sounded. The bed hadn't been slept in. The black leather jacket lying on the chair was not hers, or Alec's.

Nor was the small silver gun glowing on the floor, near an opened box of bullets.

She was in the wrong room! With her legs shaking and her vision blurring from the horror of her mistake, Molly scrambled to her knees and grabbed for the doorknob. Just then, a tiny click signaled that someone outside, an inch away from her, was about to enter.

ALEC HUNKERED DOWN in the rain beside the sedan, trying to see the man standing at the door of the room next to his and Molly's. He didn't have a clue whether it was one of his attackers or not. He hadn't got a look at them until he woke up, and then it was only at the backs of their heads.

They both had worn long trench coats and rain hats. One was a small guy, the second a burly six-footer. An older fellow, Alec had judged by catching the briefest of looks at his profile. They had knocked him out, dragged him to the car and left him tied up inside, where he watched his pair of attackers disappear on foot, headed toward the center of town.

For the past hour, he had struggled to free himself from the ropes around his wrists, managing it a few seconds ago, just in time to see this new stranger walk up to the room next to the one he hoped Molly was still locked inside.

During the physically taxing past hour, Alec wrestled with explanations as to why his abductors had tied him up and left him in the car. He thought they had given him some kind of drug, for he felt drowsy and nauseated, and he couldn't feel the pinch in his neck. But what it all meant he did not know.

All he knew was that when he woke up he was intent on finding Molly and getting the hell out of the motel and to Fred Brooker's secluded lodge, where they would have a better chance of planning their next move.

Alec wiped the rain out of his eyes with the back of a wet hand and watched as the stranger disappeared into the room. Running as quickly as he could, he crossed the lot and stopped in front of room 19. Raising his knuckles to rap against the door, he found to his surprise that it was unlocked and open.

Wide open.

Alec stepped inside. The bathroom light spilled over the vacant sleeping area. Molly was nowhere to be seen, but the satchel she had carried off with her while he slept was now on the floor beside the bed, and a small pile of money was on the table next to a bottle half-full of soda.

Which meant she had returned from dinner, but where the devil was she now?

The carpeting was soaked a foot inside the doorway. Alec pictured Molly opening the door and going out. But then what? he asked himself. The motel office was closed. With his pulse pounding in his ears, blocking out the sound of the storm, Alec braced himself against the open doorway. He scanned the parking lot and surrounding walkways for a sight of her. The only thing he saw was the car he had been locked inside, the front passenger door still open as he had inadvertently left it.

"Molly," he called hoarsely. The rain fell. Somewhere in the distance, he heard a foghorn, but no voice answered his call.

HUDDLED INSIDE THE CLOSET inside the stranger's room, Molly thought she heard Alec's voice. She held her breath, wondering what the man in the room would do if Alec pounded on the door and asked about her.

With every muscle in her body tensed in terror, she peeked through the crack at him. He was a slim, well-groomed young man. Short blond hair and a neatly trimmed mustache. His arms were sinewy and strong-looking. She couldn't get a clear look at his face, but she thought he looked very familiar.

As she watched, he bent down and loaded the gun. After closing the bullet box, he took from his back pocket what looked to Molly like a piece of panty hose and a pair of rubber gloves. He slipped something over his head and, with his back still to Molly, bent over and picked up the gun lying on the carpet.

Why hadn't she thought of that? Scolding herself silently, Molly watched nervously as the young man stood up and faced the door. He must have heard someone outside, she realized. Someone like Alec? she thought. "No," she whispered, covering her mouth in a panic that she had let a sound escape.

A moment later, Molly's worst fear was confirmed. There was a knock, then Alec's familiar voice called out, "Excuse me, sir. I need to ask you a question."

The man clicked off the light. Molly blinked her eyes, frantic to see, unable to make out anything but black and bulky shapes. She heard the metallic click of the chamber turning in the gun, and she realized the man was loading more bullets.

From somewhere deep within her, Molly found the strength to throw her safety lessons and procedures and cautious nature aside. She hurled herself out of the closet, shouting at the top of her lungs, "Watch out, Alec. There's a man in here with a gun!"

The next few seconds were madness. The man fired the gun at her. She felt the bullet buzz by her head at the same instant the shattering noise of the gun exploded through her senses.

Another crash in the darkness told her Alec had kicked open the door.

"Molly, where are you?" he yelled.

"Here," she screamed, just as a bony hand grabbed her in the dark.

"I'll kill you," the man shouted, his face now grotesque and unrecognizable, as he pushed her up against the wall. When her eyes adjusted to the half light, she realized the man had pulled a stocking mask over his face, which horribly disfigured his features.

He raised the gun in his left hand.

Before she could move, Alec rammed the stranger from behind. The gun flew out of the man's hand and discharged so close to Molly's face that she was deafened by the sound and burned by the acrid smoke of gunpowder.

The three of them fell to the ground as a bolt of lightning flashed through the door, followed in a millisecond by a shattering clap of thunder.

In a daze, Molly huddled against the wall and watched as the masked man kicked viciously at Alec. Alec managed to grab the man's leg and knock him down, but before he could grab him again, the smaller man broke free and ran out into the rain.

"Molly, Molly, you okay, love?" Alec quizzed, crawling back to where she had pressed against the cold plaster wall.

"I think so," she said uncertainly.

He grabbed her hand, which was impotently brushing at the dark powder speckling her face. He feared she was in shock but could not allow her time to compose herself. "Come on, get up. We've got to get our things and leave."

He pulled her to a standing position, but she sagged against him. "We have to go to the police, Alec. There are too many of them for us to run away. They're going to kill us!"

"We can't. We don't know who to trust, Molly." Though he knew it was a risk to tell her more bad news in her shaky condition, he recounted what he had seen on television. "That's four men dead, plus the guys on the freeway, Molly, and they're trying to hang it all on us. Every law enforcement officer in the state is ready to shoot first and ask about the details later. We've got to hide. Now."

Like a zombie, Molly let Alec pull her out of the stranger's room and into theirs. He put dry clothes on her, his hands gentle but impersonal. She watched without comment or complaint as he made a slit in the well-worn bedspread and tossed it over her head as a makeshift poncho.

Pulling her by the arm, Alec locked their room as well as the one next door, leaving the gun where it had landed but grabbing the stranger's leather jacket. The rain had stopped. They crept quickly out of the rear of the parking lot and along a short alley. Then they jumped a stone wall and hurried into the rolling, slick, muddy brushland, miles from anywhere.

FREDERICK BROOKER'S LODGE was not easy to find. Alec had had the foresight to pick up a map of Catalina Island when he'd checked into the Devil Fish, but as he stood reading it in the weak daylight at 6:00 a.m., he had to admit to Molly that he didn't know exactly where they were.

From the position of the mainland shoreline he could see that they had traveled approximately twelve miles. He looked over at Molly. She was literally asleep on her feet, legs slightly spread-eagled as she leaned against a tree, her eyes closed while she breathed the deep rhythm of exhausted sleep.

A stab of remorse reverberated through his aching body. Molly was lovely, even after a night of tromping through hell. She had said little as they walked, but he knew she was scared, confused and more than a little angry at finding herself a fugitive, falsely accused, chased by the law and an unknown group of assassins for God only knew what reason. It cheered neither of them that he felt the same way.

Alec removed the cowboy hat and shaded his eyes. The morning's sunrise was beyond describing as beautiful. It looked to him, with its opulent golds and pinks, as it must have the day the earth was created. The sky was now a restful shade of blue, and there were no clouds.

The rainstorm had left the air cooler and clearer than any he remembered breathing on land. The grandeur of the scenery made Alec feel all over again that, despite the mess, there was going to be a way to find the person responsible for all the misery of the past few days.

They would then be able to clear themselves of all the crimes they had been tied to.

With a last glance at the ocean, Alec made himself a promise that he would bring Molly back to Avalon when their problems were over, and show her the glorious natural view unhampered by the human dilemmas with which one evil person could poison the lives of others.

Shading his eyes against the glare off the ocean, Alec scanned the mountainside below him and located the narrow maintenance road he had seen on the map. It meandered downward, a few hundred feet from where he stood, until it disappeared from view. He could make out a work shed just beyond the bend in the road, beside which were parked two tan pickup trucks.

Striding to the tree where Molly slept, his boots squishing with water that had gotten in them when he stepped into a stream an hour ago, he took her in his arms and shifted her into a sitting position. She collapsed like a pup tent and briefly opened her eyes.

"Rest here," Alec told her, throwing the stranger's leather jacket across her arms, which she had folded over her chest. She blinked, nodded her head and fell asleep again in an instant.

Alec placed the satchels next to her to keep her from falling over sideways and headed down the incline to the road. Five minutes later, he cautiously approached the trucks. They both carried the emblem of the Catalina Island Conservancy on their doors. Both were locked up tight, as was the shed. Alec strained to see inside the dusty window of the aluminum-sided storage building. The best he could make out was a desk and a file cabinet and what looked like a small refrigerator with a hot plate on top.

Were the keys to the trucks inside? he wondered. Without a moment's hesitation, he picked up one of the hundreds of sea-smoothed rocks ringing the foundation of the building and hurled it through the bottom square of the six-paned window.

He was gratified when it went clear through, leaving a big enough hole for him to reach in, unlatch the window and crawl inside.

After a ten-minute search, he did not find any keys, but he did find a coffeepot and, wonder of wonders, a portable phone of some kind. It was in a black leather case the size of a lunch box in the bottom desk drawer. He fiddled with the buttons and dials but couldn't get a dial tone. Then he remembered Molly's field of expertise and grinned. If anyone could figure this contraption out, surely she could. Whistling with high spirits over this tiny piece of good fortune, Alec wrote out an I.O.U. for two hundred dollars. He left it unsigned, but promised to mail a check within the month to pay for the broken glass and missing items.

He then took the phone, a six-pack of bottled water he found in the refrigerator, a jar of powdered creamer and the blue-and-white-speckled enameled coffeepot.

First he would take a break and get something to eat and then come back and see about hot-wiring one of the trucks. He had never done such a thing before, but he had worked on more balky boat engines in his life than he cared to remember, and figured a car's ignition system couldn't be that different.

Heading back up the deserted hill to Molly, Alec found himself fighting to take each step. He felt hot. Sweaty and clammy. He wouldn't give in, though. To combat the light-headedness, he began whistling "Peggy Day." He couldn't fix *his* Peggy Day breakfast in bed, but he could at least make her some coffee and make some arrangements with Alicia Chen.

He glanced at his watch, which read 6:55. He hadn't slept, except for the two and a half hours yesterday in the motel. Despite the whistling, he had to admit that he might be getting sick. He would have to rest. As soon as they got to Brooker's.

The thought of lying down in a bed for ten or twelve hours—with Molly—brought a smile to his face and gave him the strength to make it back up the hill.

MOLLY WAS DREAMING of breakfast. Belgian waffles and strawberries, bacon and eggs and hash browns, bagels and cream cheese. And coffee, freshly ground, with real cream and a half spoonful of sugar. Served in a china cup with hand-painted red and yellow roses.

She opened her eyes and the dream disappeared, but thankfully, the smell of coffee did not. It wasn't freshly ground, and they had no fresh cream, but it was the best-tasting thing she had ever put in her mouth.

"I'm not even going to ask you where that came from," Molly said, nodding her head toward the tan pickup parked a few yards away from where she sat, "until you give me another cup of this coffee."

Alec poured another few ounces into the chipped mug he had taken from the Devil Fish Motel last night. He had left an I.O.U. for that, also. When this mess was over, he was going to have to book a lengthy charter just to cover his expenses of the past few days.

"How'd you sleep?"

"Like the dead," she replied, then drank another mouthful of coffee, scalding her throat but not caring.

Alec handed her a sandwich he had constructed out of some of the contents of the second satchel. Molly had filled it with some of the supplies she had purchased for the *Geisha Empress* trip. From the stores of the galley, she had added peanut butter, jelly, salt and pepper, a can opener, matches, a small pan, napkins and a pack of plastic utensils.

Molly devoured her food, despite the fact that Alec had been so generous with the peanut butter she could hardly move her mouth. As she swallowed the last bite, he handed her a peeled orange, which she also gulped down. With a sigh, she sat back and wiped her mouth with a napkin. "Okay. So where did you get the truck?"

"We're borrowing it from the rangers. I've located the lodge on the map. It's ten miles the other side of the airfield, which is about another five miles from where we're sitting. I thought we could drive to the airport and ditch the truck, wait for Alicia, then drive to the lodge with something she can rent for us."

Molly raised her eyebrows. "You need to call her at nine, right?" She glanced at her watch, which showed ten minutes to. "Did you steal a phone, too?"

"As a matter of fact," Alec said, standing and brushing the crumbs off his pants, "I did." He walked to the truck and retrieved the black case, presenting it to Molly with a flourish. "How's this for roughing it?"

She snapped open the lid of the leather case and stared at the contraption inside. It was unlike any telephone she had seen during her eleven years with Pacific Communications. "What is this thing?"

"You don't know?" Alec asked. "I thought it was a bloody telephone!"

"No, it's not any kind of phone I've ever seen." She cranked a small wheel with a handle, then frowned. "It might be some kind of field intercom." She flipped it over and found an empty compartment where some kind of battery pack might fit. "But it doesn't work now."

"Well, can't you make it work? It's got a dial, a handset and an antenna. Isn't that a pretty fair description of a telephone?"

Molly looked down, unable to keep a tiny smile from her face. "Well, yes, just like a pretty fair description of that truck would be a hunk of steel on wheels. But there are no wires to a central office to send or receive a dial tone, and no radio transmitter or cellular battery to transmit or receive frequencies." She opened her eyes wide and shook her head. "It's kind of like a truck with no engine."

Alec's face was turning a dark red. "Well, I'm sure no bloody telephone company expert! I sail boats for a living. And one thing about boats is if it looks like a boat and tastes like a boat, it is a boat!"

"Tastes like a boat?" she questioned with a grin.

"You know what I mean," Alec shouted. "All I'm saying is that I don't know how a damn telephone works! Is that a crime? Forgive me for stealing you the wrong thing!"

"You're forgiven," Molly whispered, unable to control the muscles in her face. She knew it was inappropriate, but she was beginning to feel giddy over Alec's totally misplaced anger. She also knew his behavior was stress- and fatigue-induced. If she started laughing, she was afraid she would get hysterical.

The whole thing was so utterly ridiculous. Here she was, on the lam from the law with a man she barely knew, who had kidnapped her at gunpoint thirty-six hours before, eating peanut butter sandwiches beside a stolen truck. Alec himself, accused of murder and mayhem, tortured and brainwashed and kidnapped, was choosing this moment to come unglued, not because of the cops, not because of Frederick Brooker, but because he had stolen a telephone that wouldn't work.

A giggle bubbled up her throat, and she covered her mouth and looked at Alec. He was glaring at her, long legs stiff, arms crossed defiantly over his big chest, leaning against the truck.

When he realized she was trying not to laugh at him, he stared at her as if she were losing her mind.

This sent Molly over the edge. She began to laugh so hard that she had to clutch her sides. Her laugh filled the morning air around them, bounced off the trees and rocks with its melody, and finally broke through Alec's frustration. He, too, gave in to the release only humor can sometimes provide in the midst of a very grim situation.

After several minutes of being helplessly overcome by emotions, they managed to compose themselves. Molly stood and walked over to Alec and gave him a quick hug. He held her close to him and kissed her softly on the top of her head, a last chuckle rumbling in his throat. "We'd best drive on over to the airport, then, love. We'll find a phone that works there. And brush our teeth."

"Let's do it," Molly agreed. "But first, tell me what happened to you last night. Why didn't you come back until so late?"

"This is getting to be a rather worn-out excuse, but I was abducted."

"By who? The guy with the gun?"

"Sorry to say, but I don't know. I was standing in front of our room. I never saw them, except when they were walking away. They left me tied up in a car in the motel parking lot.''

"So that *was* you! I went outside when I saw someone in the car."

''You shouldn't have done that,'' Alec chided.

''Yeah, and you shouldn't have been abducted again. But instead of arguing the point, tell me what they did.''

''Knocked me out. I don't know,'' he snapped, fighting a wave of weakness that nearly knocked him off his feet. ''It doesn't make any sense to me, either, Molly. But it seems we've got more than one group of people after us. Maybe more than two groups, come to think of it.''

Molly's eyes were huge. ''I don't understand any of this, Alec. But one thing I do know. We've got to prove our story somehow. And to do that, we need to get to a phone.''

''Come on, then, and let me show you how to hot-wire a car, Molly girl.'' Alec didn't add that he wanted to show her how to do it because he feared he might pass out.

''I'm game,'' she replied. ''I've broken all the other felony laws of the state of California this morning. Lead the way.''

They picked up the satchels with their meager supplies and, fortified in some measure for whatever was going to happen next, Molly followed Alec to the truck.

Chapter Eleven

The blond man with the mustache dropped a quarter into the phone and punched in a series of numbers. After a few moments, the mechanized voice requested, "Four-dol-lars-and-eight-y-cents-plea-ze."

Swearing in Gaelic, his native language, the man fed in nineteen quarters and then dropped the nickel on the pay phone's narrow shelf. It hit once, bouncing with a ping onto the floor.

"Son of a..." he said, reverting to English as he scrambled to retrieve his nickel before the connection was broken. He grabbed it and shoved it into the slot, and was rewarded by the sound of ringing.

"Maryland Relay. This is operator thirty-nine. What number may I dial for you?" asked a female voice.

"The number is 202-555-6825. This is Mr. Trent calling for Erik Brooker."

"One moment, Mr. Trent. I'll dial the number. This is a TTY telephone for hearing-impaired users. I'll be typing in your questions and reading them back to you. When I'm finished, I'll say go ahead. When you are finished, please say go ahead to me so I'll know you're through."

"I know the system, Operator. Please make the call."

"One moment."

Trent tapped his fingers on the shelf while the sounds of dialing echoed in his ear. "I have Erik Brooker on the line, Mr. Trent. He says, 'Hello, Mr. Trent. What is your message please?' Go ahead."

"My trip was not successful. I did not catch either fish or fowl, thanks to the work of a poacher. Am flying into San Diego within the hour. Go ahead, Operator."

The operator paused to read the response, then cleared her throat twice. "'I am very sorry your trip was not successful, Mr. Trent. Please wait while I verify if your travel arrangements are acceptable.'" The operator added, "Erik Brooker has put us on hold, Mr. Trent."

"Thank you," Trent said tersely. Several seconds passed. Trent looked toward the spot where he had gotten change for a five-dollar bill. This is taking too long, he thought. About to hang up to get more change, he heard the operator begin again. "'Mr. Trent. I have spoken to your employer. He advises you to stay where you are, please. He is very concerned about these new poachers. He was hoping the ones you eliminated at sea were the end of the problem. Leave your phone number so I may call you again in one hour.'" The operator stopped, then added, "Go ahead, please."

Trent read out the digits unhappily, then slammed down the phone before saying goodbye or go ahead. He was furious at being given that last instruction, furious at the entire series of missteps, including his own forgetfulness in leaving his favorite leather jacket in that seedy motel room. From the ambush on the freeway two days ago until now, everything about this contract had been disrupted by mistakes.

Trent stared at the departure board and saw he had just missed the 9:20 Los Angeles shuttle, where he could have caught the quickest flight to New York and from there to Dublin.

Well, he'd wait the damn hour then, he decided. He stalked over to the small snack counter and ordered breakfast. As he sipped tomato juice, Trent caught the waitress staring at the lump on his forehead he had received during his skirmish with the Aussie. He glared at her.

She scurried off to fix him three eggs up, runny, leaving him filled with a desire to track down and take care of Molly Jakes, contract or no.

MOLLY STRAINED TO SEE her reflection in the rearview mirror of the truck. She had hidden her tangled hair beneath the terry-cloth hat covered with pictures of dolphins, which she had purchased yesterday. But staring at her sallow skin and dark-ringed eyes, she realized she had no makeup with her at all. It had never occurred to her until this second that she didn't have so much as a powder puff to her name.

"I have to buy some makeup," she said to Alec, who was combing his hair with his fingers before smashing it down with the soft, slouchy cowboy hat.

"Nah, love, you look great. A bit light on kip, but a lovely lass, all the same."

She frowned and pulled up the collar of the warm-up jacket she had borrowed from the *Geisha Empress,* which she wore under their attacker's leather jacket. "Dressed by Murder, Inc.," she said with a sigh, eliciting a grin from Alec.

"Hopefully that little bastard from last night grabbed a charter boat off the island, or is holed up somewhere."

"Who do you think he's working for? Brooker or the bad cops?" Molly asked as scenes of that dreadful fight flashed through her mind.

"One and the same source, I'd bet," Alec replied.

"We're going to have to come up with more than opinion to prove that to the police, you know."

"I know. Got any ideas?"

"Yes. We need to get a base of operation so I can make some calls." Molly waved at the airline terminal. "Maybe we should fly back to Mission Verde and work from my house. With your theory, that might be the best place to look."

"No, we can't risk that, Molly. Besides—" he stopped himself before continuing "—there are all those horrible memories for you there." Even while he was speaking, he realized that she was going to have to face them sooner or later. "We'll be okay here. Sailors feel best on the water. But if they can't have that, then at least they need to smell it nearby. We'll get you what you need." Alec gave her an appraising look. "Like I said before, you look good to me."

Molly made a noise of dismissal in her throat, but became aware of a warm glow traveling through her. Suddenly, with an aching intensity, she remembered exactly how it felt to kiss Alec, to have him want her. Nervously she fussed with her hat and cast about for a change in subject.

"Well, at least I've got some clean socks and underwear in one of the satchels. I'll wash up in the rest room sink, slap on some makeup and feel better anyway. I need to get another pair of sunglasses, too. I lost the ones we got in San Pedro yesterday.''

"No problem," Alec said. He jumped out of the truck, which he had pulled into a space at the far side of the terminal designated Long Term/Overnight Parking and ran around to open her door.

He was worried that enough time had passed since the murder of Rafe Amundson for their pictures to be in the newspaper, but he didn't mention his concern to Molly before they walked into the tiny terminal. She seemed relaxed and at ease, and if he could give her a couple seconds more of that without fearing they were going to be thrown to the ground and arrested, then he would.

After he called Alicia, the first thing he planned to do while Molly hit the gift shop for makeup and sunglasses was to peruse all the news boxes lined up like prisoners outside the building. Like any living creature being stalked, he wanted to know where his enemy was so he could tell how far and how fast to run.

Alec held the door for Molly and looked over his shoulder. His jaw clenched and he hesitated. One of the fifteen or so cars parked in the front of the airport was a blue-and-white California Highway Patrol vehicle.

Molly didn't focus on the people. She was busy surveying the sunny little room. It smelled of coffee, syrup and burned hot dogs, but seemed clean enough. The airline reservation counter took up the back wall, and a small gift shop was tucked over to the left next to the public rest rooms, which had Telephone Inside signs mounted above the doors.

The entire right wall, windowed floor-to-ceiling, faced the airfield. A coffee shop and snack bar, which included six round tables, were the busiest part of the terminal. A dozen people sat singly or in twos, and four stools at the six-stool snack bar were taken.

"Strewth," Alec said in a low tone.

"What kind of word is that?" Molly asked. "An Australian curse?"

"Yeah. An all-purpose one."

The seriousness of his tone made Molly turn and look into Alec's eyes. She knew immediately that something was wrong. He was staring at one of the tables in the eating area. She followed his gaze and saw a burly, white-haired man in a police uniform, chatting with a young woman. He was sitting sideways to their position. The sunlight flashed off his sunglasses and the handle of his holstered gun.

"What should we do?" she whispered.

"Buy you some makeup," he replied, taking her by the arm and steering her into the gift shop.

There was one other customer inside, a young, pregnant woman who was chatting with the cashier about her baby's impending birth.

"Which bag are the guns in?" Alec asked.

Molly's eyes widened. He wasn't contemplating a shoot-out with the cops, was he? she asked herself. "Alec, you're not—"

"I need to know where they are," he interrupted, "in case we get stopped by that cop out there. Don't worry, I'm not going to hurt anyone I don't have to. Especially a cop."

"I'm not sure that's very reassuring," she whispered, glancing at the two women at the counter. So far, they had not noticed her anxious conversation with Alec. "They're in the blue bag," she answered.

Alec surprised her by giving her a sudden kiss on the mouth. In his normal voice he said, "All right, Peggy, you get what you need. I've got a call to make, then I'll buy you some lunch.''

He was attempting to speak without his Australian accent, and Molly frowned at him. Besides sounding like a drunk, it was only 10:00 a.m., hardly time for lunch! So much for Alec throwing people off their trail.

Without waiting for her response, Alec turned and walked casually out of the gift shop. Molly hurriedly picked out grooming essentials and a lipstick, a tube of tinted sunscreen and a bottle of shampoo. The display of sunglasses was at the counter. Trying to look normal, she strolled up to it just as a good-looking young man with a shaved head brought in two bundles of newspapers.

While Molly tried on several pairs of glasses, she positioned the mirror so she could watch the exit of the rest room. The mother-to-be said her goodbyes to the cashier, and Molly handed over her own purchases to be totaled up.

Alec had yet to reappear. It was after 10:00 a.m., however. He was probably having trouble getting through to Alicia Chen, since he had promised to call her at nine sharp.

Hoping Alec had the woman's work number, Molly reached into the side pocket of the leather jacket for her money. The pocket was empty except for a piece of paper. The phone number, 202-555-6825, was written on it.

Delighted at this clue left behind by the blond man, she hastily stuck it back in the jacket and found her money in the other pocket. As she was waiting for the woman to make change, she looked down at the stack of newspapers. Her mouth fell open and she gasped. The front page carried a picture of Alec Steele, alongside a three-by-five black-and-white photo of her. It was the one on her Pacific Communications security identification badge, taken three years ago.

"Miss, here's your change. You need some antacids, too?"

Molly jerked her head around to face the cashier. "What?"

The woman wiggled a roll of blue-and-white-wrapped tablets in her hand. "You like the last lady? God a bad stomach today?" she grinned and stared at Molly's midsection. "You going to be a mommy, too?"

"No, no, no, thank you," Molly rattled off. She turned and started walking toward the rest rooms. Her face was flushed and hot, and she damned the fact she had eaten those sandwiches. At that moment, they felt like ten pounds of rocks in her stomach.

"Miss, miss! Stop!" she heard the cashier yell behind her.

Molly stopped and turned, her eyes fearfully seeking out the police officer. He was facing in her direction, staring at her, as were most of the customers.

The cashier was running toward Molly, carrying a pastel-colored paper bag. "You forgot your things, miss."

With trembling hands, Molly reached out and took the package. "Thank you," she said, forcing herself to swallow the bile burning at the back of her throat.

The young woman walked back to her store as Molly slowly turned. Everyone began eating again. Without running, she covered the space between her and the ladies' room in record time.

"Oh, thank goodness," she said aloud when she found the outer waiting room vacant. But her relief was short-lived. With her picture on the front page of the

Los Angeles Times, she and Alec were running out of time. Hurrying through a rudimentary grooming, Molly was peeking out the door for Alec within five minutes of her arrival.

There was no sign of him. She shut the door and locked herself in one of the bathroom stalls. Sitting on the commode with the lid down, she tried to keep herself from hyperventilating. Her watch read 10:18. How long did it take to make arrangements? she wondered. They had to get out of here before someone looked up from their newly delivered newspaper and found themselves face-to-face with California's newest fugitives.

Molly looked at her watch again. It still read 10:18. With a sigh, she decided she would give Alec five more minutes to appear, then she was going to go in after him.

ALEC CHECKED HIS WATCH and stared down at his scuffed boots. He had left a message on Alicia's home answering machine twice and called her office. The receptionist had told him, "Dr. Chen is expected in at around ten, sir."

He'd replied, "It's five minutes after ten, miss. Do you have a more accurate estimate than that?" and been put on hold.

The young woman had returned curtly, "Please give me your name and number, and I'll have Dr. Chen ring you between sessions."

Alec had given her the number of the pay phone in the rest-room lounge. His message was "Sorry I wasn't available as arranged at nine. Please call." The receptionist had not wanted to let him hang up without leaving his name, so he did the honors for her.

Ten minutes later, he was still staring at the phone, willing it to ring. It wasn't safe for him and Molly to be mingling with strangers in a public facility, of that he was sure. But he had to get medical help. During the past few minutes, he had begun to ache badly. And to sweat.

If he wasn't mistaken, he had a fever along with his very stiff neck. He had risked a glance at the tape-covered alien on his neck and found it looked infected. As he paced a few steps back and forth, the minutes dripping by second by second, he began to worry he really might pass out.

It was Molly's worst fear coming true, he realized. The damn thing in his neck was stopping him in his tracks. When his pacing led him the three steps toward the bathroom door, he went on through, feeling more light-headed with each shallow breath. His chest hurt. His ears rang when he turned on the water, and the image he saw reflected in the mirror wasn't pretty. If he didn't know better, he would say the pupil in his left eye was dilated more than the one in his right eye.

He splashed cold water on his face and neck. When his hat fell into the sink, he took it out and shook it off, lost his balance and crashed to the floor. The room spun and his stomach clenched. Fighting to keep conscious, Alec was aware only of the bare bulb above him, the grimy white linoleum against his cheek and a pair of black leather boots on the floor in the stall three feet away.

"Mister," he rasped, trying to move up on his knees. "Please, I need help."

The door of the stall opened. The man spoke in a voice that floated above Alec like fog. "Well, then, I'm glad I'm here to help."

I must be hallucinating, Alec thought, for the man had a gun. With a last flush of lucidity, he realized it was the man from the Devil Fish Motel.

Mr. Evil himself, back to complete the job.

MOLLY CREPT OUT OF the ladies' room, slapped on her sunglasses, and, with a roll of her shoulders, pushed her way into the men's room. She had a story all ready for the first male occupant who raised a fuss, but she was greeted only by a small, empty waiting room.

With a phone. She stared at it and it rang, nearly making her shriek with nerves. Molly picked it up before the second ring ended. "Yes."

"Is this 708-555-1818?" a polished female voice asked.

Molly checked the plate on the phone. "Yes, it is."

"Is, ah, Mr. Steele available?"

"Alicia? I mean, Dr. Chen? Is that you?" Molly asked.

"Who is this speaking, please?"

"Peggy. Molly. I'm with Alec. His friend. I'm so glad you called, Dr. Chen. Alec told me you were coming to Catalina Island today. He really needs your help. *We* need your help." Molly bit her tongue and shook her head to slow herself down. "I'm sorry, Dr. Chen. Let me look in the other room and see if Alec's in there." She started to put the phone down, then quickly added, "You won't hang up, will you?"

"No, Molly, I'll wait for Alec."

"Good." She let the phone dangle on its silver cord and opened the door to the bathroom. No one stood by the urinals or the sinks. But she could see feet in the last stall. Molly moved a little closer. "Alec?" They looked like his boots.

"Alec? Is everything okay?"

At that moment, Molly felt a gun in the small of her back. Someone stepped up to her from behind the door and a bony hand covered her mouth. "Don't scream or I'll kill you right here," the male voice ordered.

Molly, as a senior manager of Pacific Communications, had been required to take several classes to benefit herself and her crew.

One of them was self-defense.

Molly's training ordered her left foot to stomp down on her attacker's ankle and then kick backward with all her weight into the man's shin. This same training led her to bite down on the hand over her mouth as if it were a beefsteak.

The man screamed in rage and surprise and pain. The gun flew when Molly lunged toward him, swinging the satchel full of guns and plates and peanut butter jars smack into the man's forehead. She was gratified to see the blond-haired man, who had nearly killed her last night, lying like a sack of old laundry on the floor.

Molly picked up the gun, the third in her rapidly growing collection, stuck it in the satchel and tried to think what to do next. If someone walked in, she would never be able to explain.

Hide the body, a voice inside her skull instructed. Without a moment's hesitation, she dragged the unconscious man into the stall next to Alec and left him in a sitting position against the wall. She locked the door from inside and crawled underneath to find Alec.

He was sprawled across the commode, his head resting against the paper dispenser. He looked dead. Molly did not allow herself to accept that as a possibility.

With both hands, she grabbed his shirt, immediately realizing how hot his skin was. "He's burning up," she said, the echo of her voice reverberating throughout the small space.

Alec's eyes fluttered and he made a movement as if he were going to fall. "Peggy," he mumbled. "It's okay."

"It will be, Alec. Hang on to me."

Somehow she got him on his feet and out of the stall. She half carried, half dragged him out of the bathroom into the lounge and propped him against the couch. Then she grabbed the phone. "Dr. Chen, are you still there?"

"Molly? What's going on? Where's Alec?"

"He's here but he's really, really sick. I need to get him somewhere quiet. Are you going to be able to come to the island?"

"Yes. Tonight. On a chartered helicopter out of Redondo Beach. It lands at 8:40." The doctor's voice dropped ominously. "Molly, things are very, very bad for you two. The police, the newspapers are both saying you are wanted for murder. I'm so worried."

"Don't worry, Alicia. Just come. I'll either be here or I'll call you at this same phone booth and tell you how to find us. You keep the number, okay? I've got to go, right now."

"All right, Molly. I'll see you one way or the other tonight. Godspeed."

Molly hung up the phone. Alec's eyes were open and he was staring at her as if he had never seen her before in his life. She somehow got him to his feet and out the door of the terminal without being stopped. The cop and his car were no longer to be seen.

"One tiny break," Molly whispered to Alec as they finally made it back to the stolen truck. "Now all I have to do is remember how to hot-wire this thing, find a lodge in the middle of nowhere and keep you alive. If I can do that, it will be a good day."

It was a big if, and she knew it. But she had no intention of letting anything stop her now.

AT 10:40, Trent picked up the pay phone and made a second call to the Maryland Relay number. This time he was patched through to a voice-mail system.

"Mr. Trent, please press one and the numbers of your prearranged security code to retrieve your messages."

With a bruised finger, Trent punched in the code and listened. A series of clicks told him he was being patched through a private network of circuits to the phone in interview room number one of the Summer Point Jail.

Frederick Brooker answered. "Mr. Trent, you are twenty-five minutes late."

Trent braced his hand against his forehead. It was the only thing that helped him control the pain enough to talk. "I'm sorry. What do you want me to do here?"

"You're sure about the poachers?"

"Yes. I saw two of them knock your pigeon out last night. I don't know what went on, but he's loose. He's with the girl. I think they just left on the shuttle to San Diego."

"You did nothing about this?"

"No," Trent replied, leaning against the booth to keep his weight off his sprained knee. For an instant, his mind wandered to Molly Jakes. He was going to kill her for his own personal satisfaction. Soon.

"Come back. I'm sending someone else to deal with this. My plan was for this to be taken care of before Tuesday, but..." Brooker let his voice trail off to humiliate the man on the other end of the line even more. The man's failure wasn't really important to the overall plan. His own preparations had seen to that. Brooker was a man who employed many people but depended on no one.

"I'll be in touch," Trent rasped.

Brooker stared at the receiver a second, then hung up. He looked across the table at his attorney. "Did you get that catalog I asked you to bring? The October issue? It has a most remarkable miniature radio-control device. Made completely of cellulose. I'm very anxious to see it and send it to my son. He's an expert on radio-control motors, you know. Only fourteen years old." Brooker thought briefly of his life at fourteen, then turned off his thoughts before any of the pain could return.

"You've told me about your son. You must be very proud." Mason Weil handed the catalog across the table so the guard could peruse it for drugs, weapons or explosives. The sergeant glanced at it, shook it, then handed it to Brooker and withdrew to the corner of the room.

"Thank you, Mason," Brooker replied. "When I'm out of here, I'm going to take Erik to Germany to visit the plant that manufactures these. Possibly a good investment for Erik, down the road."

Mason Weil nodded approvingly and decided Brooker was recovering rapidly from his near-fatal "accident" in the prison kitchen. "I may have a lead on Swenson, the man you thought might have been behind the kitchen thing."

Brooker smiled and glanced at the guard in the corner. "Don't waste any more time on that," he said. "It's forgotten. Taken care of," he added in a whisper.

"I see," the attorney replied carefully. He scribbled a note on the yellow pad and moved on to the next item on his list as Brooker continued to turn the pages of the catalog.

"We filed the motion I discussed. We should hear by 5:00 p.m."

"Good."

The attorney admired his client's faith that he would be set free but worried at the source of his optimism. The district attorney's office and police department had been joined by some suits from the FBI. Someone had tipped them off that Brooker had hired a known hit man, one Gerald Trent of Dublin, to kill Alec.

They were putting a lot of pressure on Mason's firm about Brooker's connection to the murders in Mission Verde and the disappearance of the two star witnesses in the trial.

Weil had told them, quite honestly, that he had absolutely no information about any of the happenings of the past few days. He had filed a motion on Thursday for a mistrial. That motion had been denied. He'd filed another one today, which probably would also be denied.

With any luck, the bodies of Alec Steele and/or Molly Jakes would turn up by Monday, thus saving him from having to file a third. After all, if the witnesses were "unavailable," as he had been quoted in today's edition of the *Times*, well, then, Mason would be done with Frederick Brooker for good. Except, of course, for cashing the checks.

That, after all, was what American justice was all about.

Weil straightened his tie and sniffed the air. Not that he ever actually went to the bank anymore. He had three administrative assistants and two law clerks who did that for him, and an accountant and bookkeeper.

Glancing at Brooker, who was completely absorbed in his catalog, the attorney picked up a yellow pad and wrote down a few errands for one of the law clerks to do. When he was finished, he said, "Well, Mr. Brooker, I think we're done for now."

Brooker waved him off with his gauze-wrapped hand and stood. "I'll see you tomorrow, Mason. Same time, same channel."

With a most uncharacteristic smile, Brooker left the room.

Chapter Twelve

Frederick Brooker's retreat was larger, more secluded and less appealing than Molly had imagined.

Fifteen miles from the city of Avalon, it was built on a low-lying piece of land that butted up against a scrub-covered hill. According to the historic landmark note on Alec's map, the area was famous for wild-boar hunting in the 1920s. Molly parked the truck and wondered if wild boar were still in residence, but glanced at Alec, asleep and ashen-faced inside the stolen vehicle, and figured a few wild pigs were the least of her worries.

The house, a rustic, rambling single-storied structure of weathered planks, faced with stone glittering with the mineral known as fool's gold, had the abandoned air of a place that no one had visited for years. Twenty yards behind the lodge and to the right was a two-storied wooden structure. Too small to be a barn, Molly thought, and judged it to be a garage of some kind, though the padlocked door at the front seemed a bit narrow for cars.

Molly hopped over a sagging log fence and crossed to the front door of the house, which was maybe fifteen hundred square feet in size. The brush had been cleared away from the yard, and a pile of firewood was stacked neatly against the side of the lodge, but the windows were covered with a thick layer of grime. For a moment she wondered about a caretaker, but dismissed that thought. If anything, Brooker probably had someone come by once or twice a year.

But what if this was one of those weekends? Shaking off her grim worries, Molly got down to the job at hand. She had expected the front door to have a strong lock and she wasn't wrong. Well, now that she and Alec had stolen food, a boat, a truck, guns and money, breaking a window shouldn't add much prison time, she thought sardonically. She went back to the truck, retrieved the ubiquitous satchels and returned to the house to set to work.

Within ten minutes, Molly had broken a window with one of the gun handles, entered and begun checking out the lodge. It was musty but serviceable, sparsely decorated with boring but sturdy furniture. The floors were wide-planked oak, dark with varnish and covered in several areas by hooked rugs. There was only one picture on the wall, a ten-by-twelve black-and-white photograph. It was of a toddler, a round-faced boy in jeans and a red shirt. He held a remote-control box, and a toy racing car lay at his feet.

Dark-eyed and Asian-looking, the child was beautiful, with an intelligent, watchful expression. Molly thought of the picture she had seen of Brooker and the teenager, and decided this must be a younger version of the child. This sign of parental affection and pride on the part of Frederick Brooker—a murderer, most likely the man behind the mayhem snapping at her and Alec's heels—did not comfort her.

Lee Harvey Oswald had kids, Molly thought. So did most of the tyrants in history. Loving children was no guarantee one wouldn't kill without batting an eye.

After rubbing her hands together to warm them, Molly stripped off the leather jacket. The first chore she tackled was building a fire in the potbellied stove. A cast-iron pail of kindling next to it, it sat in the large central room, which served as a living room and dining area. There was an electric match lying atop the stove. Magically, it worked. Once the fire was going, Molly began a search of the kitchen.

Surprisingly fresh water flowed from the pump into a stainless-steel sink. Tasting it a half teaspoon at a time, she judged it to be drinkable.

"It'll probably kill me before morning," she said aloud, feeling more and more nervous in the creaking, unfamiliar surroundings. Setting a teakettle to boil on top of the stove, Molly continued with a quick poke through the cabinets. There were dishes and pans, some paper goods, but no food save three cans of chili and one of mixed vegetables. There was a refrigerator, but it was empty and turned off.

The find of the day was in the last drawer she glanced into. A twelve-by-twelve-inch metal box, eight inches high, was wedged into the drawer. It had a red cross painted on the top and the words First Aid blazed in white letters.

Inside were bandages, alcohol wipes, gauze, a pair of tweezers and scissors, first-aid cream, an unopened bottle of aspirin and a small box of antihistamines. There was also a prescription bottle full of capsules. Molly held it up to the weak light filtering through the dirty windows.

The container was labeled for Erik Brooker. The instructions read: "Take one capsule three times a day with food." It was a bottle of Augmentin, a wide-spectrum antibiotic she had once taken for strep throat. The expiration date was three months ago.

Gripping it in her fist, she decided to risk it. It shouldn't make Alec any sicker, and it could give him a little jump on the infection before Alicia Chen arrived.

Cheered up a bit over her find, Molly continued her domestic chores and set about exploring the rest of the building. There were two bedrooms in the rear of the house, which shared an adjoining bath. Beyond the kitchen she found a smaller bedroom with bunk beds and a shower and sink. There was a narrow, locked room off that bedroom, not much wider than a closet.

There was no sign anywhere of a telephone or television, although there was an old-fashioned clock radio in the kitchen. When she had a moment, she would turn it on and find out how the search for her and the man outside was progressing.

Ignoring the wave of hunger that suddenly washed over her, Molly kept poking around. Inside the small bedroom she found sleeping bags and a cedar chest full of linens and blankets. The sheets smelled musty, but the blankets were zipped into plastic bags, and when she took them out, she found they were brand-new, pure wool and just what the doctor ordered for a house with a limited source of central heat.

Molly took two sleeping bags and three blankets and returned to the living room, opened one bag and draped it over the oversize corduroy sofa next to the stove. She tossed the other bag and the blankets onto the reclining chair next to the sofa and thought to herself that, even in the upright position, the recliner looked like a heavenly place to sleep for about thirty-six hours.

Suddenly worried that she had spent too much time away from Alec, Molly ran to the front and looked out. His blond head was still propped against the door. Hurrying across the yard, she opened the door of the truck. "Alec, Alec. Try to wake up."

His eyelids fluttered open and he looked at Molly. "What's happened?"

"We're at Brooker's lodge, Alec. I need you to help me as much as you can. I want to get you inside."

"The *Strewth* is sinking. The generator's shorted out," Alec announced. "We're not going to be able to get the pump to work."

"What?"

"Can you swim?"

"No," Molly replied. "But it's okay, Alec. We're going to be okay."

His eyes rolled back in his head and he slumped against her. Molly realized the fever was causing him to hallucinate. She felt his forehead. He seemed warmer than before. His skin was blotched-looking and very dry to the touch.

He was going to die, Molly thought, her panic sudden and overwhelming. She had met an improbable man during an impossible time, a man, she realized at that moment, who meant a great deal to her, and she was going to lose him. He was going to die before they had a chance to see what might develop between them. Alec was going to leave her all alone to face a million murder charges.

Fighting against the self-pity threatening to overtake her, Molly sucked in a huge lungful of air to calm herself and gently shook Alec's arm. "Alec, you've got to try to stand and walk. You outweigh me by a hundred pounds, mate. I can't do this alone.''

The stress and fatigue and despair in her voice seemed to cut through his fever. Alec opened his eyes and looked at Molly. "What's wrong? Where are we?"

"Come with me now, Alec. Trust me. I'm trying to help you."

"I'd trust you with my life, love."

And he had, Molly realized. Somehow he found the strength to move out of the truck, though he leaned heavily against her and had to fight to remain conscious. A noise in the distance caught Molly's attention and she looked around. Off to the east, over the ocean, a helicopter was on its approach to Catalina Island Airport.

The police had helicopters. The Coast Guard had helicopters. Hell, her mind chattered, even the forest rangers had helicopters. Molly's anxiety percolated up a degree. She had to get Alec inside the lodge and hide the truck. The barnlike building was the obvious choice, though she had no idea what was inside.

Even if she managed to fit the wide-beamed truck through the door, she realized, they would have to be very careful not to tip anyone flying over that they were in the house. Especially with smoke and lights. The lodge's electricity was off, but she had seen plenty of candles in the kitchen. She would have to be cautious with those since none of the windows had any kind of drapery. The one thing about hiding in the middle of nowhere was that you could be approached from all directions and never know it.

"Walk, Alec. Come on, it's not too far."

He looked at her and sighed. "I'm sick, Molly girl."

At least he recognized her, she thought. "I know you are, Alec, but you're going to get better if you can make it inside. I'll make some tea and some soup. Good tucker," she coaxed. "Then we can both rest. Dr. Chen is coming tonight. But you have to help me by walking. It's not much farther. Try to walk, Alec. Please try."

Somehow he managed to move the twenty yards necessary, but Molly couldn't keep him from collapsing like a felled tree once they crossed the entryway. With her heart pounding, she dragged him into the house by the cuffs of his jeans, went back out and closed the door.

She stopped at the sound of another aircraft in the area. A light plane was circling a few miles away. It seemed to have some type of seal on its side, and Molly panicked. She ran at top speed toward the wooden structure, looking up at the sky. She never saw the large boulder that caused her to stumble and fall. For a few seconds she lay there, wondering how it would be to give up. But Alec's warnings about cops with drawn guns, as well as her own feelings of rage, got her back on her feet.

Someone had gone to a lot of trouble to get the two of them together. Someone had gone to a lot of trouble to kill and maim many others. Before she left this life, Molly promised herself, she was damn sure going to try to return at least some of the pain she and Alec had received.

With a burst of energy, she soon found herself with the padlock pried off the shed door. Inside, it was dark and dank and empty save for two motorbikes and had a space large enough to park the truck in. An expert now at hot-wiring the truck's ignition, she backed it inside without so much as scraping the paint, then closed the door.

Feeling her energy faltering, Molly hurried back to the lodge and closed and locked the door from the safety of its sheltering walls.

She emptied the satchel with the foodstuffs on the kitchen table. With a minimum of fuss, she made herself a cup of tea and drank it down while fixing Alec a glass of beer.

Beer was a kind of food, she reasoned. Although everyone knew not to mix alcohol with drugs, Alec's condition warranted some action, and this was the best her sleep-deprived brain could manage. She pounded two of the capsules and three aspirins into powder and spooned three tablespoons of beer on top of it to make a frothy white mixture.

Returning to Alec, she turned him on his side enough to get some of the liquid into him. His eyes opened and he swallowed, coughed, then shook his head. She gave him a few ounces more of the beer, then picked up the smaller glass of medicine.

"This is going to taste like hell, mate, but it's good for what ails you."

He managed a weak smile and touched her face. "*You* are good for what ails me. Where are we?"

"Brooker's lodge," she told him once again. "Drink."

He drank it down, made a face and motioned for more beer. She gave him a bit, then let him relax. As soon as his head rested on the rug, he was out.

Molly knew she didn't have the strength to move him to the couch. She managed to throw two of the blankets over him and pull off his boots. Draping one of the sleeping bags around her shoulders, she fell into a heap beside him. With a final effort, she raised her hand and looked at her wristwatch. It was 11:55.

Without another thought, Molly dropped into sleep, her mind and body numb to all but Alec's warmth.

ALEC OPENED HIS EYES. In front of his face was a closed door. He could see a thin lip of light from outside and felt a chill draft on his face.

Why am I on the floor? he asked his sleep-fogged brain. Is this the rest room at the island airport? He supposed he couldn't be there still, but where he was, he hadn't a clue. Straining to push himself up, he suddenly became aware of a person next to him. It was Molly, warm and soft, snuggled into the small of his back. Her even breathing filled his mind, pushing the pain and worry away for a moment.

Somehow she had found Brooker's lodge, he realized. Although how she'd gotten him inside, he didn't have the vaguest memory. He brought his watch to within two inches of his face and forced himself to focus. It was 8:10. He assumed it was evening. His neck throbbed with pain, his bones ached and his mouth felt like an acid pit. Even more urgently, his bladder ordered him to get moving or else, but Alec willed himself to lie still and not wake Molly for a few seconds more.

He liked the feel of her next to him, more than he should, Alec found himself thinking. At least until this mess was over, he couldn't afford to lose control of himself as he had that night in the motel room. The thought of the blond man lying in wait for them in the next room sent a shudder of anger through him.

Molly stirred and slid her arm tenderly across his stomach. "Alec?" she whispered.

"Hey, Molly girl." Alec patted her hand. She moved enough for him to turn on his back and look up at her in the fast-darkening gloom. "Fred Brooker's place, I presume."

"Yes. Thanks to your map, I found it without too much trouble." She pushed herself upright and sat cross-legged, pulling her long hair with her fingers as if to straighten it.

"You look fine," he murmured.

"Yeah, right." She made a sound of disgust and bent closer to Alec's face. Quickly she felt his forehead. "How are you feeling?"

"Like I've been bitten off, chewed and spit out by a fiend who didn't like the taste of my Australian bones." He swallowed with difficulty. "I need to get up and get something to drink. And find a bathroom."

Molly grinned and stood, then stretched out her hand to assist. His skin was much cooler to her touch, but Alec was pale and, from the sight of his graceless stumbling as he walked with her toward the bathroom, very weak. She stopped at the doorway. "I'll leave you alone. There's no light. But there's fresh water in the kitchen if you want to wash up."

"I promise not to crawl out any windows," he replied.

Molly left him and crept back into the living room. The stove was full of hot ash and dying embers, but she quickly stoked it up again into a serviceable fire. The two burners on the top would do to heat dinner, she decided. She grabbed a blanket and headed into the kitchen.

Night was falling all around her. Outside she could see a last trace of sunlight reflected upward off the curve of horizon along the Pacific. Quickly she covered the wide windows over the sink with one of the blankets and lit a candle to work by.

Scrounging through the supply satchel, she pulled out the can opener from the *Geisha Empress,* as well as several packages of cheese and crackers. Her mouth began to water as the smells from the opened cans of chili reached her nose. Munching on a mouthful of crackers, she looked up to find Alec staring at her, huge and ghostly pale in the flickering light.

She pointed to the pump. "Water, soap and a roll of paper towels are there."

"Yes, Nurse Ratched," he retorted, but walked slowly to the sink. "Do we have any beer left?"

"Beer, chili casserole and bread sticks coming right up," she replied cheerfully. "Followed by medicine for you. How's the neck?"

Alec looked at her curiously, using his jeans instead of the paper towels to dry his hands. "I'm doing better, love. What kind of medicine are you talking about?"

His voice was edgy and suspicious and Molly realized he wasn't completely back to normal. Calmly she explained about the prescription and the aspirin.

"Well, that explains the way my mouth tastes," he replied, seeming to relax. "You don't happen to have a toothbrush in that magic bag of yours, do you?"

"As a matter of fact, I do. Look inside the paper bag with roses on it. I bought us each one at the airport."

At the reminder of the airport, Alec clutched at the table and let his body fall into the chair across from where Molly was working. "I remember arriving there. I remember the cop and the gift shop and that I couldn't reach Alicia on the phone. What the hell happened next?"

Quickly she explained as much as she knew. "So I went into the men's room and found you—"

"Cheeky American snips," Alec cut in.

"Don't interrupt," she returned with a smile. "Anyway, so I went in and found you, but I also got grabbed by our friend, the nut case in the nylon mask."

"Jeez," he exploded, "he didn't hurt you?"

Molly licked the warm chili from the spoon. "No, he didn't. Our satchel hurt him a bit, I'm glad to say." She summarized her run-in with the attacker and explained about answering the call from Dr. Chen. Peering at her wristwatch, she added breathlessly, "Alicia should be on the island soon. She's going to wait for me to come for her, or to call her in the ladies' room. I wrote down the number, so we could reach her with directions if it seemed too dangerous to go back to the airport." Molly pulled the scrap of paper on which she had scribbled the phone number out of her pants pocket, then stopped short. "Damn!"

"What?"

"I did write the number. But it's the men's-room number." Furious with herself, Molly slammed the mixing spoon down against the side of the pan. A huge dollop of chili flew off and smacked her in the cheek.

"Well, then we'll have to go to the airport."

"I don't think it's safe to take the truck," she protested as she wiped the chili from her face. "What if the island police are looking for it?"

"They probably aren't. It's Friday night."

"What about the pictures of us in the newspapers?" Quickly she told him what she had seen in the gift shop. "What if the cashier recognized us? It's probably staked out."

"She was pretty interested in that pregnant woman. I doubt anyone would recognize us."

"Right. You're six foot three and blond. You have cowboy boots, a cowboy hat and scratches on your face. I was wearing pink tennis shoes and a hat with dolphins. I'm sure we blended right into the scenery!"

"Calm down, Molly," Alec whispered, resting his elbows on the table so he could steady his head by leaning his chin on his hands. His voice was raspy and fading. "Don't give up now. That's what Brooker's planning on, don't you see? That we'll give up. If we can just hold out until Alicia gets here . . ."

"I never should have listened to you, Alec. I should have stayed in my apartment and called the police."

"You would have been killed."

"Well, then I should have gone to the police after we tied up those two men on the boat. Surrendered. I could have gotten a lawyer to bail me out."

"And Brooker would have sent someone like the creep last night to shut you up. Face it, Molly. We're targets. The only way to survive is to find out who was behind my abduction."

"That's not the only thing we need to do, Alec Steele. We need to prove why it happened, why you were tortured and me set up to be kidnapped. How in the world are we going to do that from here?"

"Together, we'll think of something, Molly. . . ." Alec's voice trailed off.

Molly realized how much of his stamina had been taxed just by walking through the house. He was going to drive back into Avalon on a dark and winding road to meet Dr. Chen? I don't think so, her brain taunted.

Suddenly it all seemed too impossible to contend with. Alec was too weak from being sick. There were too many people working for Brooker, too many cops looking for them, too many people to mistrust.

There was no phone to call Sylvester Rojas, or her assistant at work, so she couldn't even begin to do any sleuthing. And most of all, she, it seemed, did not have the kind of intelligence to outwit a gnat.

Slowly, Molly stirred the chili. Alec hadn't said a word for several seconds. When she looked up, she found him, head resting on arms crossed on the table-top, sound asleep. She crumbled a handful of cheese and crackers on top of the chili and walked out of the kitchen.

Placing the pan on the top of the stove, she stood in the dark and ate dry crackers so fast they scratched her throat.

An image of Rafe sprang into her mind. The first repair emergency they had worked together was a nightmare. An inept line assigner in the Mission Verde central office had given a new customer, a life insurance company, the same phone number already assigned to another customer, the area's biggest funeral home.

The owner of the insurance company called the repair line, screaming and complaining that his customers reporting claims were getting a recording about Perpetual Care Family Plots. The poorly trained frame repairman who got the complaint ticket couldn't figure out how to wire the lines to a live operator to intercept the calls and reroute them temporarily. So instead, he disconnected all the circuits, signed off the ticket as complete, and left the sixteen bereaved families who called over the next two hours to hear a recording which said, "The number you have called has been disconnected. There is no new number."

Molly's call from dispatch came at 6:00 a.m., reporting a man who complained that the funeral home had stolen his mother's body.

It had taken thirteen hours and two crews of installers to fix all the problems. When she'd arrived at the funeral home to try to explain things to the exasperated owner, Rafe had met her at the door.

"You must be the new boss lady," he had snarled. "All I can advise you to do is take one thing at a time, Miss Jakes. 'Cause if you don't, that man will make sure you end up a customer here, and it ain't gonna be of natural causes."

With those words of wisdom, Rafe had chuckled and left her to deal with the mess.

And she had, Molly remembered. By being patient, tactful and using her head, she had taken Rafe's advice and dealt with one issue at a time until both customers were, if not happy, at least satisfied.

As the spicy scent of chili filled the air, Molly felt herself regain some confidence. She could do this, she told herself. First she would eat and make Alec eat, then get him into bed.

Then she would go outside and hot-wire the truck one more time, drive over and get Dr. Chen from the airport and bring her back here.

Dr. Chen would help Alec.

She would find a way to get to a telephone and reach Sara Gillem at home and Sylvester Rojas at the office. They had both promised to help her.

She would have to trust them to do just that.

Molly was a manager—of people and of problems. She could do this. She could, she reassured herself.

"Thanks, Rafe," Molly whispered. With that, she used the arm of the stolen leather jacket as a pot holder, picked up the bubbly pan of chili and took it into the kitchen.

"Wake up, Alec Steele. Dinner's ready."

...

Chapter Thirteen

As the lights of Catalina's airport came into view, Molly realized she had no clue as to what Alicia Chen looked like. Well, to heck with her E.E.O. training, she thought, swinging the stolen truck into one of the darker parking spaces beside the terminal. She would do the obvious and assume Alicia Chen was Chinese and hope there wasn't more than one Asian waiting in the ladies' room by the telephone.

The terminal was as good as closed. The lights were out at the coffee shop and snack bar as well as the ticket counter. A wire-mesh door was pulled across the gift shop and secured with a huge padlock. Two men, one dressed like a pilot in a brown leather flight jacket and matching hat, sat smoking cigarettes at one of the round tables. Molly, pulling her dolphin cap lower over her forehead, made a beeline for the ladies' room.

Her heart rate increased when she glanced at the door leading to the men's room and remembered her encounter earlier that day. Where had the guy gone? she found herself wondering. Jeez, it was like walking through a snake farm, worrying whether that creep was going to slither across her path again.

Molly smiled as she thought of her counterattack on the thug. As she did, she suddenly realized why he'd looked familiar to her. He had been at the freeway crash. *He* was the man in the mechanic's uniform, who had been so helpful.

Molly shuddered. This business of trusting strangers was affecting her entire life. In his case, she had been wrong. In Alec's, right. At least, she hoped she was right. She thought of his kiss in the motel and wondered whether a man could hide a murderous heart behind a kiss that caused a woman to melt.

It happened all the time in the movies. Molly shook her head. She was no Sherlock Holmes, but Alec Steele wasn't a danger to her. She would bet her life on that opinion.

You already have, a voice inside her head observed.

Shrugging away her doubts, Molly thought of the blond man who had fired a gun at her even though she had never hurt him at all. It was becoming more and more obvious that she had been intentionally lured to the freeway to meet up with Alec. But why? And why had Alec been tortured and brainwashed? Why not just kill them both? Brooker would probably get off scot-free, unless there was someone else who could finger him.

Someone else. This hunch echoed inside her brain with the solid authority of truth. A truth Molly would have to pursue. Because if someone else knew what had happened that night, it must be someone Brooker couldn't get to.

Or wouldn't get to.

"Later, Miss Scarlett," Molly said with a sigh. "I'll think about that later." Though the hours of sleep she had managed to grab on the carpet next to Alec had restored some of her energy, she was exhausted. She was looking forward to getting Dr. Chen on the scene. Even if she couldn't help Alec psychologically, she would be another person to talk to about this mess.

Molly pushed against the ladies' room door, her step light and her spirits lifting. A woman dressed in a tailored red suit, a cashmere coat over her lap and a kid leather valise at her feet, was sitting on the sofa in the waiting area. She had a laptop computer open beside her and was speaking into a cellular phone.

Her dark eyes met Molly's and she held up a long-nailed finger in caution. "Yes, Operator, I'll wait. Thank you," the woman said.

She was stunning. Small-boned and willowy, Alicia Chen looked about thirty, although Molly immediately judged her poise to have ten or fifteen years more experience than that. Her eyes were small and gracefully set at a slant. Her hair, cut to chin length and parted on the side, was glossy blue-black in the fluorescent light.

Dr. Chen wore no makeup save for vivid red lipstick.

Molly licked her own chapped mouth and nodded. "Hello. How are you?" she whispered, then crossed to the rest-room area and checked to see that they were indeed completely alone. Satisfied no maniacs lurked inside, Molly took a seat across from Dr. Chen.

The woman's attention was drawn back to the voice in her ear. "Operator, you must have misdialed. The number is 202-555-6825. He has to be there! Please try again." Suddenly Dr. Chen held out her hand to Molly. "I'm sorry, dear. You must be Molly. I'll be right with you."

Molly shook her head that she understood, but she was distracted by the phone number. Since her business was phones, she heard and read and wrote down probably hundreds of phone numbers a year. But that one seemed very familiar. Letting her brain work at trying to remember, Molly tuned back into Dr. Chen's conversation.

"Yes, Operator?" Alicia Chen listened intently. "I see. No, I don't wish to leave a message on the recorder. Thank you." With an irritated flip of her wrist, the woman closed the phone, snapped down the laptop and slid both into her valise.

Alicia Chen stood and held her arms out to Molly. "Oh, Molly, I'm so relieved to find you safe. Where is Alec? Outside? Do you two have a car?" The doctor's fingers, surprisingly strong, dug into the flesh of Molly's arm. "How is Alec holding up?"

"He's running a fever, Dr. Chen. A pretty high one, by the way he was hallucinating earlier, but it's come down some now. I gave him two doses of antibiotic and aspirin, and got some food into him, and I think he's a little better. I didn't try to mess with the wound and the needles. But he needs your help. We both do."

"I'll do whatever I can, Molly," Dr. Chen replied. "We should go to him now, I think." She glanced at the thin gold watch that hung slackly on her slender wrist. "You're much later than I thought you would be. I nearly gave up."

"I'm sorry. It's been very difficult."

"Of course it has, dear," Dr. Chen replied. "Here, you take my valise. I've another bag under this sofa."

Molly took the expensive bag as Dr. Chen pulled out a beautiful overnighter from below. She certainly came prepared, Molly found herself thinking enviously. The identification tag on the bag read California Psychiatric Associates, 1810 Summer Point Towers. Alicia Chen, M.D., Psychiatry.

The address was the same as Frederick Brooker's building, Molly realized with a start. Wasn't it right next door to Brooker's office, as a matter of fact? Before she could think any more about this unsettling connection, Molly's attention was snagged by Alicia's move toward the door.

"Dr. Chen, I think it will be best if we go out separately. There's a beige pickup truck parked in the lot outside, with a conservancy seal on the door. I'll get it and meet you at the front. Then we'll go out to the lodge."

Alicia Chen blinked. "You're staying at a lodge?"

"I know this sounds crazy, but yes. It was Alec's idea that no one would look for us there since it's owned by Frederick Brooker. Alec was here one summer when he took Brooker's boat out for a test, I guess. But maybe you know all about that."

"No, I didn't know that. I mean, Alec told me he worked for Brooker when I saw him last winter, but Alec never mentioned visiting a lodge here. But his visit with me was very brief, as usual. The subject never came up."

For reasons unknown to Molly, Alicia Chen looked disturbed at the news about where they were headed. "It's very secluded, Doctor. And we've been careful not to draw any attention to ourselves."

"But is this safe? Doesn't Brooker have people who watch the property?"

"Not from the looks of it. But to tell you the truth, I'll be a lot more at ease if we leave now and talk on the way. Alec's out there alone."

"Certainly," Alicia replied. She made a shooing motion with her hands. "Go. I'll come out in a couple of minutes. I need to check in with my answering service, and I'll use this pay phone. Just be very, very careful, Molly. The police are looking everywhere for you and Alec."

"They don't really think we're killers, do they? I mean, surely they must see the connection between all that's happened and Frederick Brooker trying to weasel out of his trial."

"There is much speculation but little official comment in the press from the police or the FBI. I did hear a television report earlier tonight that Brooker's attorney has asked that all charges be dismissed because of major new evidence in the case."

Molly stood with her hand on the door. "Really? What kind of evidence?"

"It seems they've turned up information that Alec was once arrested for attempted murder. In Australia. Brooker's attorney hinted that Alec may have had a motive to kill Buntz himself and put the blame on Brooker."

"That's—that's ridiculous," Molly sputtered, forgetting for a few moments about rushing back to the lodge. "Alec's no killer. This is just another ploy on Brooker's part."

Alicia Chen arched her eyebrows at Molly. "How long have you known Alec Steele, Molly? I was under the impression when Alec called that you've just met."

"That's right." Molly bit her lip to keep from saying more. She had the uncomfortable feeling that Alicia Chen was sizing her up for some psychotherapy. "So what will the judge do? They won't just take some half-baked story as the truth, without any proof that Alec is connected, will they? If Brooker is released . . ."

"I don't know, Molly. All I can say is that it's a very bad time to be on the run. I'm hoping you'll help me convince Alec that he has to turn himself in, and you should, too. I don't know how long he, or you, can avoid arrest."

"But he can't do that until he gets himself unbrainwashed, or whatever you call it. I thought he explained all that to you."

"He did." Alicia's voice dropped down, as if she were talking to someone much younger—and much less capable—than herself. "But I could still treat him if he was in custody. Surely he must realize that. The more you two flee the police, the more it looks like you're guilty."

Molly felt her previous uplifted outlook wilt inside her. Of course Dr. Chen was right. What had they been thinking? Guilty people ran.

"You're probably right. Mr. Brooker's proving a rather formidable foe, even locked behind bars."

Alicia Chen nodded her head. "I believe Frederick Brooker will do whatever he needs to do to get out of jail, Molly. But please, I've held you up long enough. Go get the pickup. I'll see you in front."

Uncomfortable with the manner in which Dr. Chen seemed to be arrogantly taking charge of everything, Molly nonetheless did as she was told. She slipped out of the rest room and headed for the terminal's exit. Out of the corner of her eye, she saw that two other people had joined the pilot and his companion at their table. The four stopped talking when Molly entered the main room.

Her footsteps made the tiniest of sounds against the waxed linoleum, but Molly heard the echo and her body tensed. Had someone recognized her? Had the truck been reported missing? Were the police waiting outside?

"Miss," a male voice called out.

Molly stopped at the door, her sweating palms resting on the cool metal handle. Casually she turned.

"Yes?"

"We're getting ready to close up the building, hon. Did you see anyone else in the ladies'?"

The man in the pilot's cap was addressing her.

Molly swallowed. "Yes. There's one woman inside. I think she'll be right out, though."

"Okay, well, thank you. We're closing up early because the last shuttle from Redondo was canceled due to fog. Just wanted to be sure we weren't locking anyone inside."

"No, of course not," Molly replied, then hurried out into the cool night air. Her mind roamed over the hilly terrain to Alec, asleep in the lodge. She was glad he had told her about that bar fight in Australia. He was going to be shocked to find out that Brooker's people had found out about it.

Unfortunately, another shock was the last thing Alec Steele needed. But that couldn't be helped. If they were going to trust one another, they had to tell the truth.

Molly opened the truck's door and slid the valise onto the seat, elated at what she had seen Alicia tuck inside. A cellular and a laptop! She couldn't wait to borrow them. With those two little electronic toys, she could accomplish more in a few hours than she had in two days as far as finding information on Frederick Brooker was concerned.

Jumping up on the seat, Molly reached down and carefully unwrapped the electrical tape from the mass of wires hanging beneath the steering column and touched the correct two together. With a gratifying roar, the truck started. Molly rewrapped the tape and pulled out of her space. Off to the right she noticed a dark sedan parked with a single passenger inside.

Was it the same one she had seen last night? The same one Alec's attackers had locked him in for some reason? With her heart pounding, Molly debated what she should do. She rounded the side of the building and saw Alicia Chen walking toward the truck. Should I wave her off? Molly asked herself. If she drove away and the sedan followed her, she'd know it wasn't safe to go back to Alec. If they didn't follow, Alicia Chen might become the target.

Trusting her instincts, which told her it probably wasn't the same car, Molly slowed. Dr. Chen, with great agility, jumped up into the seat, overnighter and all, and slammed the door.

Molly sped off. Nervously she glanced into the rearview mirror, but no headlights lit up the glass.

"What's wrong?" Dr. Chen asked.

"Nothing." Molly turned and gave her a brief smile. "I just wanted to be sure we weren't followed. I saw Alec's and my pictures on the front page of the newspaper this morning, so I'm a little jittery about being recognized."

"The way you look now is not the way you looked in that picture," Alicia replied. "I wouldn't worry. Especially if Alec isn't with you. He's the more distinctive-looking of the two of you."

Feeling like the only girl without a date at the prom, Molly made a sound of agreement and watched the road ahead. There were few vehicles on this part of the island at night. The tour buses were tucked away in their garages and the maintenance workers, who were state employees, kept regular business hours.

"So, what do you think of Frederick Brooker, Dr. Chen? I never met him myself. What's he like?"

"Why would you think I know Brooker?" The doctor's voice was as cold as freezer burn.

"I just assumed. When I saw your ID tag on the valise, I realized I had seen your office the night I was at Summer Point Towers. Aren't you in the suite next to his?"

Was that where she remembered the number from, Molly's brain buzzed. Was it Brooker's?

Alicia Chen coughed. "You're very observant. Alec told me you work for the phone company. What do you do there?"

It was annoying not to be answered, even a little scary, but Molly kept her cool. "I'm a manager. I have a crew of eight installers." She pushed the accelerator pedal a little harder. "So, have you ever met Brooker?"

"I'll bet most of your crew are men. You have a very aggressive way of talking, as if you're used to dealing with men," Alicia replied. "Despite the American adage about catching more flies with honey, I find that they respond well to aggression. They respect it. Understand it. Sometimes compassion and implied directions are lost on their sex. Would you agree, Molly?"

"I'd agree that you're making me nervous," Molly found herself blurting out. "Why won't you answer my question about Brooker?"

"Because I'm not a good liar," the doctor replied.

Molly frowned, wondering what was wrong with Dr. Chen. Weren't shrinks supposed to be experts at communication? Maybe she would have more luck if she shifted to a less threatening topic. "How was your shuttle ride over? I've never ridden in a helicopter. I'm sure that was fun."

"It was loud. But one can see a great distance. It was very clear."

A memory scratched at her brain and Molly began to feel really uneasy. Maybe Alicia Chen was writing herself a few prescriptions. "Where did you fly out of?"

"Redondo Beach. I told you I was coming from there last night, remember?"

Molly did remember. Her hands gripped the steering wheel. She also remembered the pilot at the airport saying that the last shuttle from Redondo Beach had been canceled! "What time was the flight?"

"Your questions are exhausting, Molly."

"And so are your lack of answers, Dr. Chen," Molly barked, wishing Alec were on the seat beside her. In the dark she wasn't as confident about finding the road that led to Brooker's lodge. The fog off the ocean was creeping slowly over the island and she feared if they wasted any time at all, they would be stranded.

After several moments, Molly slowed to look for a landmark, luckily saw the clump of oaks with the small maintenance shed she was searching for, and turned left onto the road leading to Brooker's. "We'll be there in a few minutes. It's about three miles ahead."

Molly heard Alicia shift her slight weight on the crackling leather seat of the truck and fumble with the overnighter. Molly sighed. She would wait and try to talk to the doctor when Alec was around.

The truck hit a dip in the road and shuddered, and Molly caught a reflection in the rearview mirror. Twin headlights, as if dropped from the sky, lit up only fifty yards or so behind the truck.

"Damn. I think we're being followed," Molly warned.

"Stay calm, Molly," came the eerie reply.

"What? Jeez, Dr. Chen, there's someone following us! Don't tell me to be calm after what I've been through." Molly glanced over at the doctor and sucked in her breath.

Alicia Chen had turned toward her. She was staring at Molly with a blank look on her face. But it wasn't her look that made Molly nearly steer off the road.

It was the small, silver .22 pistol Alicia Chen was holding, pointed directly at her.

"I'm sorry, Molly," Alicia said. "But I'm going to have to ask you to pull over. Now."

"What is going on? My God, are you working with Brooker?"

"I don't have time to explain, Molly. Except to say no, no, no, I would rather die than do anything to help Frederick Brooker."

ALEC WAS READY TO TESTIFY.

"I saw the limo pull up in front of the dock where Frederick Brooker's yacht was moored. I was on board, checking out the sail cover that had just been delivered. I had taken a taxi over, thinking Mr. Brooker was waiting for me there, and not at his office. I saw Paul Buntz approach the car."

Alec suddenly couldn't speak.

"And then what happened?" a voice prompted.

"Buntz walked up to the car, someone inside spoke and Buntz reached for the door. I heard a shot, and Buntz fell to the ground. Frederick Brooker got out of the car and dragged Paul Buntz's body off the dock and dumped it in the river."

"Did you see Mr. Brooker with the gun?" the voice asked.

Alec turned to the right to face the judge. A person, wearing a black mask and black robes, sat silently. Alec looked out toward the courtroom. A woman was sit-

ting at a table. A lovely woman, with shining brown hair and brown eyes.

It was Molly.

"Do it, Alec. Get it over with," Molly said.

"No-o-o-o-o-o-o!" Alec screamed, as a buzzing, pounding pain seared through his body.

The masked judge pounded a huge gavel, once, twice, ten times. The rhythm of the gavel sounded like shots. Blood began to drip off the judge's bench, a river of blood that would drown them all . . .

ALEC SCREAMED and punched out at the air, managing to knock himself, entangled in the sleeping bag, off the side of the couch and onto the hard wooden floor with a crash.

For several seconds he lay there stunned, breathing hard. It was dark all around him, and cold. Orange-red embers burned in the belly of the stove a few feet from him, but he felt no warmth. Where was Molly?

"Molly," he called out, throwing the sleeping bag off so he could stand up. He walked toward the kitchen. "Molly? Are you here?"

A piece of paper, taped to the blue satchel, caught his attention. Bracing his woozy body with his arms, Alec fumbled with the box of matches on the table and lit the small candle Molly had stuck in a water glass. The wick caught and flamed. He moved the paper closer.

It's 9:30 p.m. I've gone to get Dr. Chen at the air-port. Take more aspirin and two of the capsules in the bottle if you wake up before I get back.

    Take care

                                  M

Alec reached for the bottle, dumped four capsules

into his hand, grabbed the last can of beer and popped the pills into his mouth. He flexed his shoulders and tentatively rolled his head from side to side. His neck still throbbed, but more as if he had a bee sting than a knife sticking in it. Molly had nursed him through, he realized. Holding the bottle up to toast her in absentia, he drank it down.

After he made a trip to the head to wash up as best he could without shaving, Alec rummaged around in the satchel and found cookies and a can of tuna. He opened the tuna as he ate a dozen of the vanilla snaps, then ate the tuna from the can. He followed that meal with one of the remaining oranges, which he peeled and ate in the dark, then returned to find his boots.

His watch read 10:55. He was angry that Molly had gone for Alicia without him, and fear burned in his chest that she had been apprehended by the cops—or worse, by that punk with the mustache—at the airport.

It was just like the headstrong chit, he thought, anger and admiration running a tag relay through his veins. Molly Jakes was a hell of a spunky woman. One in a million. Which was only one of the reasons he wasn't going to let anything else happen to her.

Alec walked to the front windows of the lodge and peered toward the road, hoping to see the truck headlights approaching. But the fog had rolled in. Pearl gray and slate gray and gray gray wisps of heavy, wet air the consistency of cotton candy blocked the view all around.

"Well, how the hell are you going to find the road, Molly girl?" he asked aloud. It was going to be touch and go for her just to stay out of a ditch, much less find the lodge, Alec realized. He would have to get her some light.

Hurrying into the kitchen, he grabbed the two boxes of eight-inch candles he had seen on the table, as well as a box of matches. He might burn down the island, but if he stuck enough of them along the road, maybe Molly would have a better chance of finding her way.

Without bothering to grab a sweatshirt, Alec raced out into the soupy air.

Chapter Fourteen

Molly's reaction to having about the twenty-fifth gun pointed at her in as many hours was to go off the deep end.

"Yeah, right," she screamed at Alicia, then turned the truck sharply to the left while flooring the accelerator. The truck careered wildly, bucking over gopher holes and boulders, jostling the gun out of Alicia Chen's hand and Alicia Chen's head against the dashboard of the truck.

Molly considered slowing enough to try to retrieve the gun, but the guy in the sedan behind her was nearly in the flatbed, so she ignored the urge and prayed Alicia would stay in the unconscious heap on the floor.

Speeding toward a copse of trees that leapt out of the fog, Molly frantically turned to the right to avoid them. The tires squealed and the truck shuddered but missed smashing into them. Molly accelerated again, feeling as though the lodge had to be behind her now. She turned again and nearly smashed into the sedan, which materialized out of the mist and swerved madly to avoid a head-on collision.

Gunning the engine, Molly looked back. At that moment, the crack of a shotgun rang out and the windshield shattered.

Hunching over the steering wheel, Molly kept her foot firmly on the pedal. Two more shots were fired, accompanied by the sounds of ripping metal.

Whoever it was was determined to stop the truck, no matter who he killed, Molly knew. She had to get to Alec, wherever the hell that was. As she zigged and zagged over the terrain, Molly realized that she was no longer sure in what direction she was headed, or in what direction the lodge was. The fog swirled around her, blocking all vision, then disappeared in a misty cloud to reveal ten yards of black night.

Risking a glance in the rearview mirror, Molly saw she had gained a few yards on the sedan, which was tilting wildly to one side. Figuring he must have blown a tire, she pushed the accelerator to the floor again. The truck jumped forward into a clearing where the fog thinned out. Ahead and to her right, at a distance her brain estimated was a quarter mile, a strange row of lights was flickering along the ground.

Flares—it was the police!

Molly's heart leapt against her chest and her mouth went dry. The police must have Alec, she thought, shivering at the memory of what he had said. "They'll fire first and get the details later...."

"Don't hurt him, please. Please," Molly prayed, a part of her, however, a bit relieved that the police could at least end the immediate threat of pistol-packing Alicia Chen and her sidekick in the psycho sedan behind her. Flicking a last look in the mirror, Molly was stunned to see no trace of the sedan. She slowed and turned her head to look. The car was nowhere in sight.

"I'll send AAA," Molly muttered, then drove in the direction of the flares, more than ready to surrender.

But there were no police cars, no news vans. No vehicles at all. A few hundred feet from the lodge, she found only Alec, waving both arms at her, surrounded by candles.

Skidding in the loose gravel, Molly stopped the truck and jumped out. "Alec, what's happened?"

"Molly! Thank God you found your way back. I thought I heard shots—"

She pointed to the shattered glass, which remained, remarkably, in one piece. "You did. Look."

"I knew it! You should never have gone alone." He wrapped his arms around her and hugged her so tightly she could hardly breathe, then he released her and looked at the truck. "But where's Alicia? Didn't her shuttle make it over?"

"No, it didn't," Molly replied. She suddenly felt out of breath. "I mean, she's here, but I don't think she just arrived on the shuttle. Alec, she pulled a gun on me. She's crazy!"

"What are you talking about, love?" Alec held her at arm's length. "Alicia pulled a gun on you? Where is she?"

"She's in the truck, Alec. Be careful," she shouted to his broad shoulders as he hurried away. "She had a gun, Alec."

Alec pulled open the truck door and lifted the unconscious Alicia Chen into his arms. "Open the door, Molly," he yelled.

Molly ran ahead and opened the lodge door, holding it against the wind, which was rising from the east, and watched. "Did you see the gun?"

"It's on the floor. Come inside with me, though. I'll put the truck away. The fog's lifting and I thought I saw some headlights down the road a mile or so."

"I'll get the truck. You take care of Alicia," Molly countered. Then she thought of the candles. Running down the road as fast as she could, Molly was gratified to see most were dark because of the breeze.

She kicked sand on those that were still flickering and jumped into the truck. The noise of some kind of engine carried over the rolling terrain and made her fumble as she tried to start the pickup. Was the sedan, with Dr. Chen's probable accomplice, back again?

Grabbing Alicia's gun, Molly stuck it in her pocket and ducked lower in the seat. Panting as if she had run five miles, she tried the ignition wires. Finally the switch kicked in and she raced the truck around and jammed it into the shed but not before ripping a huge dent in the left side panel.

Add one more felony to the list, thought Molly with a sigh, glaring at the broken windshield. Ducking low and running in a zigzag pattern, she hurried into the lodge. Only when she was back inside, with the door locked, did she allow herself a sigh of relief. But her calmness did not last long.

Alec was sitting and staring at Alicia Chen.

The doctor was lying on her back, one arm dangling lifelessly off the side of the couch. She was covered with a blanket, but Molly knew as soon as she saw the anguished pain grooved into Alec's face that Dr. Chen was dead.

Molly walked up behind Alec, hearing a roaring noise in her ears as she placed a hand on Alec's shoulder. He covered it with his hand, and squeezed, but his fingers were as cold as stream rock in winter.

"Oh, no, Alec. She hit her head. I didn't think it was serious. My God . . ."

Alec flipped the edge of the blanket. "It wasn't your fault, Molly. She's been shot." A huge stain blackened the red suit coat.

"The guy in the sedan. He killed her."

Alec rested his head in his hands and she saw tears glimmering on his face. "I did it, Molly. I'm the one who asked her to come. To risk trouble with the police, trouble like this." He shook his hand at her dead body, his voice rising.

"Stop it, Alec." Molly spoke in a firm, quiet tone. "Alicia Chen lied about the time she came over, and she pulled a gun on me. I think she was working with a man driving the sedan. The same man who knocked you out last night and left you in the parking lot, if I'm not mistaken." She knelt beside him and made him look at her. "It's not your fault, Alec. She was involved, somehow, with Brooker." He was staring at her as if she were speaking a language he didn't understand. "I'm sorry. I know you cared about her, Alec. But we've got to get out of here now. It's not safe for us to stay, but we'll have to go on foot. I need your help, Alec."

With a deep sigh, Alec put both arms around Molly and hugged her to him. For a long moment they said nothing. Then he kissed her hair, her cheek, her mouth, as if he wished he could kiss her forever, and pulled her to her feet. "Let's hit the road, then. It's the midnight hour. Our usual time to be tromping through the underbrush."

"We'll be in great shape by the time this is all over," Molly replied.

If we live through it, she thought. While Alec added a sweatshirt to his outfit and grabbed his hat, Molly layered another pair of borrowed pants over the ones she was wearing and shrugged into the leather jacket. She grabbed Alicia's valise with the laptop and phone, stuck the gun inside and followed Alec out of the door.

The first thing tomorrow, when they were safely hidden somewhere, she would call and alert the authorities that they could find Alicia's body at Frederick Brooker's lodge. "We'd better find a way to get off the island," she cautioned Alec as they cut across the back of the property and headed down toward Avalon Bay.

"My thoughts exactly, love. I think maybe it's time to pinch another boat."

Molly sighed in resignation. "I knew the punishment for rustling cattle in the States was hanging. What is it for stealing boats?"

"Don't ask, love." Alec's Australian baritone drifted on the thinning midnight air.

SYLVESTER ROJAS LOOKED UP from his cluttered desk in exasperation. "What do you mean, you think they're on Catalina Island? If you think that's where they are, why don't you go back there and get them?"

Trent took a drag on his cigarette and leaned back into the thick bed pillows of the San Diego Excelsior Hotel, where he had just checked in. "Because Brooker ordered me to come back. He said he would take care of them. That he had someone else working on things."

"Someone else other than us?" Rojas gasped. "That sounds like trouble, Trent."

"Look, rookie, this is your first hire-out. Don't worry about it. Brooker thinks he's going to skate on this rap. Me, I think he's doing big time, but my opinion don't count, since I'm not on the jury. Though from what I just heard on the news, the trial isn't even going to happen."

"That's not true," Rojas hissed. "I just got word from my boss that the judge ruled against Mason Weil's request for a mistrial. The cops are crawling on all fours, trying to dig up Alec Steele and Molly Jakes. The trial's going ahead on Tuesday. And someone here thinks both will be available to testify."

"Huh? Well, that don't concern me, Sylvester. All that I care about now is that you get me what's owed me." Trent paused while he took another hit off his cigarette, thinking about Molly Jakes. He should have stayed around to even the score. "Besides, don't play dumb with me. It was getting too hot on that little island. I saw one of the police shrinks along with the lieutenant Brooker says he turned come into town. Didn't he tell you about that?"

"No. What shrink?"

"That Oriental gal. You know, that works in the office next to Brooker's. Isn't she a cop?"

Rojas felt sick. He had accepted money, more than he would make in twenty years, to feed this lowlife on the other end of the phone information from the D.A. about Alec Steele. If he had it all to do over right now, he would never have accepted the bribe. Rojas darted his gaze around the nearly empty office. "Look, I don't know what you're talking about. I just got directions to pull out all the stops to eliminate those two. I assumed you were going to do it."

"Well, boyo, you assumed wrong." Trent hung up and sucked on the cigarette. A knock at the door signaled that room service had arrived. Trent got up and eyeballed the peephole. A man in a white coat, with a wheeled cart full of covered dishes, stood outside.

Trent opened the door and waved the man in. Before he could reach his gun, two men jumped out of the door of the room next to his while the man in the white jacket put a very impressive semiautomatic right up against his left nostril.

"FBI, Trent. Hit the floor."

"Can I see some ID?" he asked, his arms held high. Two men in suits knocked him to the floor on his face and cuffed him.

Chapter Fifteen

It took them only three hours to walk to Avalon Harbor, in most part because of Alec's sense of direction and revived condition.

Within twenty minutes, he had slipped aboard a Cal 28 sailboat the owners had obviously stored for the season. With the stealth of U.S. Navy Seals, Alec and Molly guided the *Pie-Rat* out of Avalon Harbor and into the dark, fog-shrouded Pacific.

Ten minutes out, Alec accepted a cup of steaming tea Molly offered him with a grateful smile. "We'll stay under power for a couple of hours. By dawn we can put up the sails. We can be in Marina del Rey by nine."

Marina del Rey was the destination they settled on at Molly's suggestion. Her assistant, Sara Gillem, lived there, and Molly felt sure the woman would offer them some shelter while they regrouped and decided what to do.

While Alec hadn't admitted it in so many words, Molly believed he was ready to surrender. Their main concern was that they avoid surrendering to a cop who might be under the guidance of Lieutenant Cortez, who they decided had to be the key hit man hired by Brooker.

"You're the one who should get some sleep, Alec. What with the fever and everything." She handed him two more antibiotic capsules she had brought up from the galley with her. "How are you doing now anyway?"

Alec threw the pills into his mouth and gulped his tea. "Peachy."

"I know you're hurting about Alicia. I'm going to use her phone to call the police before we dock in Marina del Rey. They'll go pick her up."

He nodded but said nothing, just frowned into the wall of fog surrounding them.

"Do you feel up to answering a couple of questions for me, Alec?"

"Sure. Shoot."

Molly licked the salt spray from her lips and took a step away from him. It seemed heartless to be asking him while he was suffering, but she knew they were running out of time. If they were taken into custody, they would have no further chance to talk, that much she knew for sure.

"Did you know Alicia knew Brooker?"

"No, I didn't. Although it makes sense now. Brooker contacted me a couple of years ago, said he heard of me because of my experience with the America's Cup races. But I knew they were in the same office building. I should have realized Alicia probably put a bug in his ear about me." Alec shrugged and threw the last dregs of tea overboard. "I still can't believe he got to her, though."

"What do you mean?"

"It's pretty obvious she was working for him, don't you think?"

"No. I didn't come to that conclusion at all. That's the major thing I can't figure out about all of this. Brooker wanted us found and/or dead. Alicia wanted . . . I don't know."

"She pulled a gun on you, Molly. She must have been in Brooker's pocket. I just can't imagine how someone that classy let him get to her."

"Alicia seemed very confident and strong willed," Molly offered. "Could it have been money?"

Alec scowled and squeezed the stainless-steel wheel until his knuckles were white. "I guess it can always be money or love behind a crime. Isn't that what they say? But I don't know. Alicia was loaded. Had enough money to support her mom, even. Set her up in a condominium back East, in Maryland, from what I heard." Alec shook his head. "But what can she have been doing?"

Molly hated herself for saying it, but she had to ask Alec the question that had been gnawing at her for hours. "Do you think she was the masked person who was brainwashing you, Alec?"

Alec stared upward for a moment. His face was a study in dueling emotions of fury and betrayal. "Maybe. I thought of that. I can't be sure, thanks to the drugs, that it was a woman under the mask. I do think Alicia may have been with the man who knocked me out and stuck me in the car at the Devil Fish."

"What did they do to you? Can you remember at all?"

He sighed and rubbed his forehead. "No. Maybe checked out the thing on my neck. I don't know."

Molly settled into the cushion-covered seat beside Alec and pulled a blanket around her. Along with the boat, her mind was racing through the waves of mysterious and impenetrable motives of people she barely knew. One thing was certain in her mind.

Alicia Chen wasn't working with Frederick Brooker, but against him.

"What does it mean, Alec?"

"What does what mean?"

"The brainwashing. That has to be the key to this. Why such an elaborate plan?"

"You said Brooker's attorney is trying to build a case that I'm a murderous type. Isn't that a good enough reason? The way I see it, I was going to kill you that night on the freeway and remember nothing. That way, they'd hit the district attorney's only two witnesses with one stone and raise the possibility I was lying all along."

Molly's blood ran cold listening to Alec's words. She met his eyes, which were navy blue and frigid like the midnight sea. "And your memory about having to kill someone?"

"Might be bogus...I don't know. I guess we'll never know, unless I do freak out..."

The wind swallowed his words. Molly grabbed the railing behind her and stared at the profile of the man she had spent so much time with, yet still knew only by instinct. "You're no killer, Alec Steele."

He left the wheel of the boat and pulled Molly into his arms, crushing her against him. Then he kissed her, a kiss of thanks and of wanting. A wave splashed over the side and Molly shrieked from the cold, making Alec laugh, the first sound of happiness he'd felt like making for days.

"Here, love, sit leeward. You'll do better." Gently he wrapped her in the blanket.

Molly settled herself next to him. "You know, Alec, we may be missing the biggest clue here. I think what we're not looking at is motive. The why of this mess. Isn't that always the key thing cops look for?''

"I think the district attorney is sticking with the line that Paul Buntz was fencing goods stolen during robberies of Brooker's clients. Which means they think Brooker set up his own clients. Motive enough, no?''

"Because Buntz was blackmailing him?''

"That would be my guess. And Brooker got tired of paying him off. So he got rid of him.''

"On the spur of the moment like that? It just doesn't fit with what we know about Brooker. Besides, I saw Paul Buntz that night. He had an orange bag with computer disks in it that I think belonged to Inscrutable Security. He was looking for Brooker and was very nervous. But he didn't seem frightened. After all, he went very willingly with him in the car. I don't think Buntz was blackmailing him. I think it was just a business-as-usual night, but something went wrong.''

"Yeah. Something called a gun.''

"Several other people saw Brooker pull into the office complex around the time I did. So why would he, without trying to hide it, pick up Buntz, drive him to the marina and kill him near his own yacht?''

"It was a crime of passion, Molly. Even the rich and famous fall victim to that. The cops found the murder weapon in the Dumpster a block from his estate.'' Alec shook his head again. "At least he wiped his prints off.''

"But don't you see, Alec? That series of events is poorly planned. Actually, it cries out amateur. Whereas all of this drama with us—impersonating cops, kidnapping you, calling me out on a phony complaint, planning for us to meet on the freeway, brainwashing—all of that is very sophisticated and complicated. Did the same mind plan both?''

"So what's the point, Molly?"

"I think the killing of Paul Buntz was an accident."

Alec made a noise of disbelief. "Yeah, he accidentally shot Buntz twice in the head and then accidentally dragged his body across ten yards of concrete and accidentally dumped him into the ocean in front of me."

"Yes. I think that's pretty much what happened," Molly replied. "I just can't understand *why* he resorted to a cover-up. With all his money, he knew he could hire the best and beat any kind of case about premeditated murder. Why not say, hey, I had a gun for protection, it went off when I dropped it? Why make up that whole story about never meeting Buntz before and Buntz trying to rob him and all?"

"Strewth, woman! Because he's a psychopath with no conscience, that's why," Alec barked. The boat was set on autosteer, but Alec kept his hands on the wheel, wanting to be ready to correct their course if he heard any foghorns or spotted any running lights. "After all, his own damn kid was in the car with him when it happened. Anyone who would set an example like that for a thirteen-year-old kid isn't real big on morals, if you ask me."

"His son was in the car?" Molly repeated. She had forgotten that fact, or had never known it. "Did he confirm his dad's story?"

"To the letter, no pun intended. The kid is deaf and doesn't speak, but he wrote out a statement that the cops told me matched his dad's deposition perfectly. Well coached, I think they called it. Protecting the old man's butt, like any kid would."

Molly began to shiver and realized that the fog and mist from the ocean had succeeded in drenching her. "I'm going to go below and change and get a little rest,

Alec.'' Standing next to him, she had the urge to hug him, but his stance implied he was back to not wanting anyone to touch him.

She knew about that kind of pain. It's what she felt when her father had died last year—without warning—and also how she felt after she had watched Rafe being gunned down.

Knowing Alec needed to withdraw to deal privately with his sorrow, Molly left it at that and hurried down the narrow stairs.

The boat they had commandeered was luxurious and well stocked. She shook out a packet of soup into a cup, added water from the bottled stock on board and put it in the microwave. Throwing a glance above, she retrieved the steaming cup before the timer beeped. She changed out of her wet clothes and curled up on the bed in the vee-berth tucked into the boat's bow.

As she sipped her soup, she emptied Alicia Chen's valise. The laptop was fully operational and loaded with software that allowed for faxing and calling up a variety of functions. Molly set it aside and flipped open the cellular phone. There was no number strip inside.

Suddenly she thought of the blond man, his bony hand, the vacant, disengaged look in his eye that told her he could kill her and feel nothing.

Molly went cold and nearly choked on a mouthful of soup. At that moment she remembered watching Alicia Chen making her call to the phone number—202-555-6825—Molly knew she had heard before. Or rather, had *read* before. On the slip of paper inside the blond attacker's black leather jacket.

Molly scrambled into the galley, grabbed the jacket and searched the pockets. The slip of paper was creased and a bit damp. But still legible was the number 202-555-6825.

She was right! Hurrying back to the cellular phone, she picked it up and dialed. On the fourth ring, a female voice answered. "Maryland Relay. What number may I dial for you, please?"

"Maryland Relay?" Molly echoed. What was Maryland Relay? "I'm sorry, Operator. This is Ms. Jakes with Pacific Communications Repair. We've got some AT&T long-line trunks crossed in the San Diego area and we're getting your numbers on our RMATS feeds as fiber optic feed. Can you tell me what kind of circuit I've called into?"

"What's your ID number, please?"

So much for intimidating the operator with repair-speak. Quickly Molly rattled off Rafe's ID and waited. Finally the voice spoke.

"We're TTY intercept, Ms. Jakes. Our clients are hearing impaired and we type in messages, then verbally pass on the typed responses from our clients. How can I assist you?"

"Oh, you already have, Operator. Thank you." Molly flipped the phone closed, her heart racing, her stomach a cramped ball.

TTY intercept. For the deaf. My God, was Frederick Brooker a monster so corrupt he would have his own child not only lie for him but pass messages on to a hired assassin?

But, more importantly, what reason would Alicia Chen have for calling that boy?

Molly put the phone down slowly and took everything else out of the valise. There was a burgundy Gucci notebook, a newspaper folded inside. A leather case with a gold zipper, four keys on a ring inside. A small package of tissues. A gold tube of red, red lipstick. A thin wallet with the initials AAC emblazoned in gold.

Molly opened it, knowing a woman's wallet usually offered a very intimate peek into her life. The clues were varied. Six hundred-dollar bills and four twenties, all crisp and new. An ATM receipt from Alicia's bank. Two quarters. A California driver's license, a gold credit card, a hospital ID for Summer Point General and a temporary visitor's pass for the city jail stamped "3 Day" were, one to a slot, lined up like trophies on a shelf.

Exasperated, Molly stuffed the items inside. When she tried to close the wallet, she realized she hadn't shoved the money in neatly enough, so she took it out and tried again. Then she noticed the secret compartment. Tucked under the lining of the currency fold was a flap, which flipped up.

Behind the flap was a picture, a small black-and-white photograph. It was of a handsome young man, intently operating a remote-control box while a toy car sat waiting at his feet. In the background, smiling down at him, stood Alicia Chen. With a shaking hand, Molly turned it over. Written in a smooth, lovely stroke were the words "Erik Chen Brooker—my *son*—age 8, Summer Vacation, Catalina Island."

"Alec!" Molly called out, too stunned to move.

ALEC WAS AS FLABBERGASTED as Molly at the revelation that Alicia Chen was the mother of Frederick Brooker's son.

"When my dad and her mom were married, I remember him telling me she and Alicia didn't speak for two years. Her mom would never tell my old man what the beef was. But it must have been over the marriage."

"Didn't you say Alicia's mother lived in the East?" Molly asked. "I think Erik Brooker goes to school there. Maybe she cares for him." She stared at the youngster's picture. "Such a handsome child. If Alicia knew what Brooker had done—getting Erik to lie for him—that might have been enough to make her want to do away with him. Maybe she was going to try to get you to do that for her."

For a moment, Alec and Molly stared at one another. "You mean you think Alicia was trying to brainwash me to kill Brooker before the trial?"

Molly's face mirrored her confusion. "I don't know, Alec. I know she hated the man. What doesn't make sense is how she could have expected you to pull that off. Brooker's in jail. And in the courtroom, he's going to have ten armed guards within striking distance at all times!"

"Someone did try to kill him in jail already," Alec replied. "Maybe Alicia hired someone to do that deed. But nothing we've found out about her tonight can convince me she wanted me to kill someone, or that she would have gone along with Brooker's plan to screw around with my head."

"There has to be some connection, though," Molly argued. "But I think you're right. Brooker wants you to take someone else out, so he has you brainwashed. I just don't know who." As soon as she said the words, goose bumps skittered down her arms.

She met Alec's eyes. They were bloodshot and bright. The dark circles under them looked as if they were drawn on with markers, they were so vivid.

Unable to keep from touching him, Molly reached out a hand to his face. He was cool, his beard stubbly. Alec turned his mouth to her fingers and kissed her. A moment later they were deep in an embrace as passionate as it was unexpected.

Breaking away gently from her mouth, he looked into her eyes. "You're a brave girl, Molly Jakes. You got me back on my feet without a peep. I feel like an albatross around your neck."

"Please don't say that, Alec. We're in this mess together, or haven't you noticed?"

"I've noticed." Alec allowed himself to drink in Molly's warmth and softness for a minute more, before forcing himself to set her free from his embrace. "I best be getting up on deck. I don't want to be surprised by a bump in the night out on this much ocean." He nodded at the clock on the wall beside Molly. "It'll be dawn soon enough. Why don't you get some sleep? We're going to be out in the open when we leave the boat and try to get to your friend's place. You're going to have to be quick on your feet."

Molly smiled. "I found some black hair dye down below. I was thinking it was time to do something about disguising your down-under thatch of hair."

"Whoa now, gal." Alec held his hands palm down. "That's what my hat is for. No one will recognize me."

Molly handed Alec the folded copy of the newspaper she had found stuck in Alicia's valise. "Yeah? Take a look."

Alec stared at it for a long minute, then threw it down in disgust. "I see what you mean." Suddenly all the strength seemed to leave his body and he sagged to the mattress beside her. "You know, love, it may be time to give this up. If we go to the coppers, tell the whole story, they'll have to believe us. This is too damn weird for anyone to have made up.''

Molly's pulse was pounding in her ears. While she had plans to do some sleuthing once they got to Sara's, what Alec said made more sense. They just had to be sure they stayed out of the grip of one cop in particular—Lieutenant Cortez.

Molly felt certain that he was responsible for Alicia Chen's death last night. His career was over, meaning he had nothing to lose. ''I can call Sylvester Rojas from Sara's in the morning. And an attorney. We're going to need one.'' She stopped and put her hand on his shoulder. ''Are you sure, Alec?''

''I think I am, Molly girl.'' He slapped his hands on his thighs and stood. ''Look, you nap for a bit. I'll get us closer to the harbor, then let you steer her in while I put that—'' he stopped and gripped ''—that junk on my hair. Think you can take her in by yourself? We'll dock her at one of the temporary tie-ups near the Excelsior Hotel and get to your mate's house somehow.''

''Turns the same way as a car, right?''

''Right.'' He pushed her gently and watched as she fell onto the mattress. ''Now sleep,'' he ordered, his voice gruff with a sudden aching to lie down beside her.

Molly watched Alec walk away. She wanted more than anything she could think of for Alec Steele to lie down beside her and hold her. But she knew they had no time for that, or for anything else but surviving.

Glancing up at the light, Molly thought about turning it off, but before her fatigued brain could give her hand the message, she was fast asleep.

FREDERICK BROOKER WAS quite alarmed to be summoned to interview room number one at 9:30 a.m. It was Sunday, and the interview rooms were generally closed to inmates on Sundays. The only thing that could warrant such a summons was an emergency.

The guard removed Brooker's handcuffs, careful not to knock the gauze bandages off, and opened the door.

"What's wrong, Mason? Is it Erik?" Brooker demanded.

Mason Weil raised his hand as if to calm Brooker, then dropped it to his side. "Your son is fine, Mr. Brooker. He arrived on the flight from Baltimore last night. He and his grandmother are at the Excelsior." Mason put a piece of paper on the table for the guard's inspection.

The burly redhead looked it over, then nodded for Brooker to pick it up. "Dear Father," the note began in the perfect typing of Erik's laptop printer.

I am looking forward very much to seeing you. I will be with Oona in the courthouse on Tuesday. I would like to come to visit you, but Mr. Weil said I should not do that. I received my new radio-controlled plane yesterday from Munich. Can we try it out at the Rose Bowl, like you promised, before we leave?

Love,
Your son, Erik

Brooker blinked several times in rapid succession and averted his eyes from Mason. Once he regained his composure, he folded the letter and handed it back to the attorney. "Keep that with the others, please."

"Of course, Mr. Brooker. Now, for the reason I'm here today." Weil leaned closer and folded his aristocratic hands on the table. "I'm afraid I have some very shocking news, Mr. Brooker. Your ex-wife, Alicia Chen, was reportedly found dead this morning at the lodge you own on Catalina Island."

"Alicia? Dead?" Brooker took an uncharacteristically ragged breath. "How?"

"Officially, I have no information. Unofficially, she was shot." Weil pulled on his tie delicately. "Please let me extend my deepest condol—"

"How does this affect the trial?" Brooker interrupted.

Weil was shocked at Brooker's complete lack of grief, but recovered quickly. "I—I don't know. But since the judge denied our request for a mistrial yesterday, I think this may buy a couple more postponements, which, as you know, I've been pushing for—"

"I don't want any postponements," Brooker yelled, slamming his thick-fingered fist onto the wooden surface, forgetting about the blistered flesh. He made no sign admitting pain.

Behind him, the guard crossed his arms over his chest but made no move toward Brooker.

Weil flexed his chin. "Well, you may have to accept one. I've other news for you, as well. The FBI picked up a man named Gerald Trent yesterday, in Marina del Rey. An Irish national they're claiming is a hired hit man. They've arrested him for the murder of the two FBI agents found on board the *Geisha Empress*. Word is they're playing hardball with him to make him talk or face the death penalty."

"Talk?" Brooker echoed quietly. "About what?"

"About who paid him to come to town to kidnap and/or kill Alec Steele, to begin with." Weil leaned farther forward. "I can tell you one thing for sure, Mr.

Brooker. The best, the very best deal this guy can hope to cut is to do life in prison with no chance of parole."

"So why did the FBI call you, Mason? Do they want you to take on Mr. Trent's case, *pro bono?*"

"They called me as a courtesy, Mr. Brooker. They're coming to question you soon, and they wanted me to be available when they show up."

"I have nothing to say to those men," Brooker replied. He glanced over at the huge, gunmetal gray clock hanging on the wall.

"I need to try to call my son before noon, Mason. So I'd better get in line now. We prisoners make a lot of calls on Sunday, you know." Brooker pushed his chair back, scraping the legs against the pitted linoleum floor. "I'll see you in court Tuesday, then. And if I were you, I wouldn't wear that tie. It makes you look effeminate."

The guard pulled open the door, and Brooker walked out, leaving Mason Weil ashen-faced, gripping the letter from Erik.

Chapter Sixteen

Lt. Henry Cortez had nineteen years' service on the police force, three commendations from three different mayors, and no chance of retiring with a twenty-year pension. A fact he could blame on his affair with Alicia Chen, the beautiful, manipulative psychiatrist who, because he thought it would win her love, he had agreed to help.

When Alicia, three weeks before, had told him of the preposterous plan she had learned her ex-husband was about to carry out and asked for his help, he should have gone to the captain.

But when she'd told him this, Alicia was lying in his arms, naked. Henry Cortez had never been happier—or more scared. Not of helping her "interfere" with Brooker's plan, but of losing her if he didn't.

So Cortez hadn't gone to his captain. And he had watched helplessly as Alicia, riding beside him in the front seat of his van, had fired a gun into a Bronco and killed the man driving. He couldn't have stopped her, he told himself many times.

But he could have refused to assault Alec Steele with a blackjack when he stood in front of room 19 at the Devil Fish Motel. And he could have refused to carry Steele to the rented sedan—technically, felonious kidnapping, just as he could have refused to let Alicia then inject Steele with some drug and mess with what looked like a vampire's bite on his neck.

But he had not refused, because he loved Alicia, and he had not refused her request that he follow her when she drove off last night with Molly Jakes.

Cortez knew Alicia had a gun with her. What he didn't know and couldn't have known and didn't want to face now as he stood outside Sara Gillem's condominium and waited for Molly Jakes and Alec Steele to show, was that he was going to lose Alicia last night.

That in the mud and the fog and the black, starless night, he was going to lose everything.

He had finally found Brooker's lodge at 3:00 a.m. Inside at 3:05, he saw Alicia lying on the couch, her pale skin glowing like an angel in stone. And just as cold.

Alicia was dead.

Molly Jakes and Alec Steele must have found out what she had done and killed her, then fled Catalina Island, Cortez told himself.

Probably by stealing another boat.

By flashing his badge, he had roused a helicopter pilot. By flashing his .38, he had convinced the guy that "police business" was important enough for him to fly in zero visibility and land on guts.

Operating on nineteen years of experience, deliberately deadening his heart to the unbearable pain inside, Cortez followed his hunch and now found himself in the shadows in front of Sara Gillem's place. She was Molly Jakes's most loyal supporter at her office. If the woman and Alec Steele were going to try to come ashore, this would be the place.

The Gillem woman had come down and bought five papers at 7:00 a.m. Cortez glanced at his watch. It was now 8:10. He would give them another hour to show, then he would visit Miss Gillem himself and wait upstairs.

As Cortez settled into the shadows of the parking garage, the sound of footsteps—rubber soles running on concrete—tipped him that someone was approaching. He took another step back and pulled out his gun but left the safety on. No use blowing away a jogger, though it wouldn't alter his future much now.

A few seconds later, two people hurried past, ten feet from his hiding place, and raced up the stairs toward the third floor. Sara Gillem's apartment was on the third floor, facing the ocean.

Cortez moved his head. A husky man, six foot plus with long, inky black hair, stood beside a woman, five foot six, buried under three layers of clothes, her hair shoved under a hat. They were in front of Gillem's door.

The cop flipped off the gun's safety and measured the shot. Too far away to be sure, and he couldn't get them both. Cortez holstered his gun and watched as the couple slipped inside. He could bust them all now as fugitives.

He could kill them all now and claim self-defense.

Trying not to think of Alicia, Cortez blinked the tears away and shuddered, thinking how little any of it mattered.

SARA GILLEM OPENED her door as far as the security chain would allow and peeked through the crack.

"Molly," she whispered, "is it really you?" The woman's gaze darted back and forth nervously between Molly, her dolphin-covered terry-cloth hat pulled low over her face, and the tall, dark-haired man standing next to her.

"It is, Sara," Molly answered. "And this is Alec. Please, let us in."

Quickly Sara disengaged the lock and opened the door. She hugged Molly, shook hands formally with Alec, then relocked the door, the dead bolt and the chain and led the exhausted pair into her kitchen.

"Why don't I fix breakfast while you two rest and tell me the real scoop on what's been going on."

Alec settled uneasily into one of Sara's cane-backed chairs, shooting Molly a look that told her he was questioning Sara's trustworthiness.

"I'd trust her with my life, mate," Molly offered with a wink, then leaned against the counter next to Sara, who was beating eggs. "I'll tell you the whole thing, but first tell me how things are at work."

Sara shook her head slowly. "Bad. Real bad. I saw a lot of men cry I didn't think knew the meaning of the word when we all heard about Rafe Thursday afternoon." Sara was forty-four and looked fifteen years younger. She was slim and had a no-nonsense, no-frills air of confidence about her which had served her well the past twenty years she had spent running the administrative side of an installation office. It was populated almost entirely by men, and if they worked there longer than ten minutes, they learned not to mess with Sara Gillem.

Sara met Molly's eyes, cutting directly to what she knew lay at the heart of her boss's question. "Everyone—to a person—is very worried about you, too. Real worried whether you are going to be okay. And furious that the police, especially that Cortez fellow, and the newspapers or anyone would say you had anything to do with Rafe getting killed."

Sara flashed her gaze at Alec, as if to warn him that if the same couldn't be said of him, he'd better leave now.

"It was terrible, Sara. Neither Alec nor I had any chance to warn him. And to have to leave him like we did..." Molly wiped away a tear and cleared her throat. She gave Sara a concise summary of the events leading up to Rafe's murder, then a thumbnail sketch of the Catalina Island odyssey she and Alec had endured the past three days.

The only details she left out were Alec's brainwashing and the parentage of Erik Brooker. Molly felt those were dangerously unresolved issues that might be too hot for anyone to handle, especially someone not involved.

Ten minutes later, grabbing a plate of buttered toast, Molly followed Sara over to the table, where her hostess was dishing Alec a helping of scrambled eggs the size of a dinner plate.

"So what are you two going to do now?" Sara asked, sitting beside Molly and pointing to the fork so her boss would eat.

"Well, I called Sylvester Rojas right after I called you this morning. I told him we'd be back in touch, but that I thought we were ready to surrender. But we need a lawyer first and some reassurances from the authorities that the dirty cop we're sure is out there has been apprehended."

"Does that guy Rojas have enough clout to guarantee that?" Sara asked.

Molly and Alec exchanged glances. After working for the telephone company, Sara was an expert on authority. She knew firsthand that promises came cheap but that action happened only when the person doing the promising had the power to get the job done. "He said he couldn't promise anything."

"Well then, wait until he gets to someone who can." Sara smiled for the first time since their arrival. "You two can wait here until then. And when it's all over with, we'll all go on "Hard Copy" or "Geraldo" and tell this whole story."

"For a good price, eh, love?" Alec added with a wink.

"You got that straight, honey," Sara said. "Now you two eat. Then you read the morning papers. I ran down at seven and bought one of each kind from the boxes outside. They're in the living room waiting for you. There's even an open letter in the *News* from the FBI to you, Molly."

"Quite the celebrities, are we?"

"Yep. Everyone's talking about you. One report said you had been arrested in San Francisco Friday night and were being held in secret. It was wrong, I guess."

"Can't trust those tabloids," Molly reminded her grimly. "Well, I told Rojas I'd call him back at twelve noon. Until then, I'm going to make a couple of calls and try to find a lawyer on Sunday."

"If you call Rojas from here, won't they just trace the call?" Alec asked. He was pacing the floor of Sara's living room, his face a mask of white against his unnaturally dark hair. He peeked through the drapes drawn across the sliding glass door leading out to Sara's deck. Stairs led down from the deck to the sand, giving Alec a new worry about their vulnerability to being ambushed.

"Not if I use Alicia's cellular. They are nearly impossible to pull out of the air and ID, although the FBI can do it. Don't worry," she said to the two of them. "I'll be careful."

Alec looked unconvinced. "Maybe we should go back to the boat, Molly. Keep your friend here out of it."

"I'm not worried about being in trouble," Sara said cheerfully. "When all the truth comes out, I'll be fine. And so will you two, you'll see."

Molly and Alec exchanged a grim glance, not at all as optimistic as Sara. But they sat together on the sofa, however, and ran through the newspapers Sara had thoughtfully obtained. Molly read aloud the statement from the FBI, urging her to turn herself in or, if she was being held captive by Alec Steele, to remain calm.

"I didn't realize that they thought I was holding you against your will," Alec replied when she finished.

"Well, who would imagine I'd go with a lug like you willingly?" she replied. She smiled to soften the words, but Alec seemed to be settling into a funk.

While Sara bustled around in the kitchen and brought them fresh coffee and sweet rolls, Molly and Alec continued perusing the newspapers. Both were amazed by the amount of ink that the story, and their lives, had received.

"My God, here's an interview with my father," Alec announced in a shocked voice. He ran through it quickly. "Yeah, that's my father, all right. Basically told the reporter to sod off and leave him alone. Said, 'I didn't raise that boy to run from nothing.' Now there's a character reference if I ever heard one."

For the first time, Molly stopped and realized how worried her own family must be about her safety. Her mom and only sibling, her older sister, Jeannie, both lived in Sacramento.

Molly threw a glance at the cellular phone but decided that was a call that would have to wait. If anyone's lines were tapped, it would be her mother's. Molly looked at the clock again. It was only 9:35. "Hang on till noon, everyone. Then we'll know where we stand."

She continued to read, fascinated by a biographical story about Frederick Brooker. It mentioned that he had been raised by a father who had died when he was sixteen, and that his mother had abandoned the family when he was born.

"There's no mention of Brooker's ex-wife by name," Molly said softly to Alec, who looked up from his reading, "but this says they were divorced after the birth of Brooker's only child. It also says Erik's been flown in for the trial but that his attorney does not want him to take the stand."

"Bloody bastard, Fred Brooker is," Alec snapped. "Maybe they won't call Erik as a witness once they find out about his mother. That poor little bloke is going to have to face more pain than he should have to in his life."

Molly touched Alec's leg gently. "I know. But at least he'll have his grandmother to help get him through this."

Alec nodded, but looked grimmer than ever. Molly had dyed his eyebrows to match his hair but had not attempted the eyelashes. With the black hair, he had a ghostly, gaunt look about him, like an Australian version of a vampire. Shaking off this silly image, Molly stiffened at the approaching sound of a Coast Guard helicopter.

Sara ran into the room and looked up tensely, and Alec jumped off the couch and ran to the drapes. Risking a peek outside, he saw the chopper continue down the coastline.

"Shore patrol," Sara announced. "We're all too jumpy." She looked at Molly. "How about if I loan you something to wear and let you take a shower? You got some time to kill, and if you don't mind me saying, your grooming is not quite up to Pacific Communications management standards.''

Molly laughed at Sara's words and saw that Alec, too, relaxed.

''I'd offer you something, too, honey, but my son's clothes are too short and too small for you. But you're welcome to a shower.''

''Thanks,'' Alec replied. He took the newspapers out of Molly's hands. ''But why don't you go ahead? If Sara doesn't mind, I'm going to take off my boots and rest here for a few minutes. If we're going to have company later, I could use a little sleep.''

Molly allowed Sara to hustle her off but not before she threw Alec a kiss, which he rewarded by smiling at her before he leaned back and closed his eyes.

''SO WHAT'S THE SCOOP, Miss Molly? Is this guy for real?''

Molly was sitting, wrapped in Sara's thick terry-cloth robe, staring into her friend's dressing-table mirror while Sara combed out Molly's hair.

''He's for real, all right.''

Sara gave an appreciative whistle. ''He's a hunk, which I knew from his pictures, but he's also got a lot of sex appeal with a capital *S!*'' Sara wagged her head back and forth. ''You sure you can trust him? A man like that is used to getting his way with women, you know. No chance he did kill that man Buntz, is there? One of the callers on the radio show said he thought that was what happened.''

''There was a show on us?'' Molly asked in horror. ''When?''

"Friday night, I think it was. Had on that lawyer of Frederick Brooker's, Mason Weil. What a creep he is," Sara offered.

"I can't believe I'm in the middle of this—this circus," Molly said.

"You are. Wait until the trial. Things are only going to get worse, I'd say."

"If they ever have the trial," Molly answered. "With all that's happened—"

"That judge said last night they're going on with it. We'll see what he says tomorrow, once you and Alec Steele turn yourselves in. Think that will change his mind? He looks like the stubborn type, you ask me."

"I agree," Molly answered. "I don't know what he'll say about things when Alec and I get a chance to explain what's happened to us. I would think a lot more charges could be filed against Brooker. Of course, how we're going to prove anything is another matter."

"That's the truth right there, Molly. We've seen enough guilty-as-sin murderers walking around free lately. California's wild with them. I'm just glad we've got a death penalty."

Too weary to even begin arguing about her friend's views on that topic, Molly sat mute while Sara dried her hair and fussed with it.

"Now you can look halfway decent for those surrender pictures," Sara kidded when she was finally done. "You stay in there and rest awhile," she added, as Molly went into Sara's tidy, sun-filled room to dress. "I'm going to clean up the kitchen, then do some paperwork at my desk. I'll let you know when it's twelve o'clock."

Thanking Sara profusely, Molly shut herself into Sara's bedroom. Resisting the urge to dive into bed, she tossed off the robe and stretched. She was beyond tired, Molly realized. Exhausted in mind and body, she felt numb, as if feelings of hunger or fright or passion or pain would never again touch her.

Her mind flew to the other room, to Alec, who had lost as much as she these past few days. Privacy, dear friends, reputation. None of it was fair, but it was all reality.

And, as the down-to-earth Sara had just reminded her, it wasn't over yet.

With a sigh, Molly pulled on the pink silk blouse Sara had set out for her and buttoned it up. She had never seen Sara wear this before and felt her eyes sting with gratitude that her friend was loaning her something brand-new.

Shaking out the freshly ironed khaki slacks, Molly sat on the bed and tugged them on. They were a bit snug around the hips but felt heavenly soft and clean. As she zipped them up, the sheer bedroom curtain fluttered inward toward Molly. The sounds of seabirds and waves reached her ears and an ocean breeze, fresh and cool, filled the room.

Molly walked toward the deck, pleased that Sara had left the door cracked open. The sunlight would feel delicious on her face, Molly realized. Maybe she could sit outside for just a few moments. Like Alicia Chen had commented, she wasn't the distinctive-looking fugitive of the two. With a sad smile, Molly lifted her hand to push aside the drapery and step out.

At that second, a man burst through the door and grabbed her. He held one hand around her throat. The other hand held his gun, which he pressed against Molly's right ear.

Lieutenant Cortez looked like hell, she found herself thinking. His gray hair had a slick yellow sheen to it, and his lined face was blotched and stubbly.

"Not a peep, Miss Jakes. Not a peep."

Fighting to swallow, Molly nodded slightly and let the obviously deranged cop push her slowly backward into Sara's bedroom.

SYLVESTER ROJAS was sweating. He looked around the table in the district attorney's conference room, searching for a sign that anyone believed his story. Four FBI agents, two Orange County cops and his boss, Lynn Nicholson, all stared back.

"I didn't know Trent was going to kill anyone. The plan was to kidnap Steele, but not to kill him. Just to talk some sense into him. Bribe him, even," Rojas said brightly, hoping that a lesser felony admission would help his credibility.

"We want to know where Molly Jakes and Alec Steele are," the FBI agent in charge, Jeffrey Yamamoto, demanded. "We know you talked with her this morning. Where was she?"

"I have no idea. She said she was going to call back at twelve. Honestly, I don't know where she is. Trent might know. After all, he saw them on Catalina Island. Where is he?"

"That's none of your concern, Mr. Rojas," the agent snapped. "Now let's get on with how you were contacted about setting up this bribe. Did Frederick Brooker call you directly?"

Rojas sat back defiantly in his chair and crossed his arms. "I want my attorney. I called him an hour ago. I am not going to answer any more questions until he gets here."

Yamamoto nodded to another agent and then to the Mission Verde District Attorney.

"Your request for Mr. Mason Weil was denied by Mr. Weil's office. A public defender has been called. Unless you know of another private attorney who might consider taking your case.''

''Weil won't come?'' Rojas uncrossed his arms. So it was going to be like that, he realized. Trent's going to make a deal, even though he brainwashed Steele and killed those agents. Brooker's going to make a deal, even though he planned and paid for the whole thing.

And he'd be left holding the bag. He'd grown up in the middle-class section of San Diego, been the first in his family to graduate from college. His parents, first-generation Americans, were proud of their son, the lawyer. Not for long. Not once the press had him for lunch, Sylvester admitted to himself.

''I'll make a statement,'' he said. ''Where do you want me to begin?''

A shared sigh of relief traveled the room.

''Tell us what you know about the murders on the *Geisha Empress*,'' Yamamoto demanded. ''Were Alec Steele and Molly Jakes involved?''

''No,'' Rojas answered.

''Who decided to kill them?''

''Trent. He thought it would make you all look harder for Jakes and Steele, and make his job easier.''

''And who hired Trent?'' Yamamoto pressed. ''Frederick Brooker?''

Four years of experience in the prosecutor's office told Sylvester Rojas he should keep his mouth shut. He had information to bargain with. Information that could reduce his prison time substantially. But at that moment he didn't care.

''Yes,'' he said, letting go of his guilt. ''Frederick Brooker bought and paid for us both.''

Chapter Seventeen

Alec woke with a start, his eyes flying open to find disquieting sunlight instead of the gray and chilling fog of his dreams. With a quick movement, he looked around the room. Sara Gillem sat in the corner, stereo headphones over her ears, doing paperwork at her desk.

Molly was nowhere in sight.

But, unlike the past days of fear and hiding, Alec didn't panic when the lovely lady he felt so much for was not within reach. Though that's where he hoped to keep her, he realized as he stretched his arms and sat up, as soon as they got out of this mess. With deliberate care, Alec moved his neck gingerly from side to side.

The medication Molly had been pumping into him had done the trick. Whatever infection had troubled him, he seemed to have shaken off. Now, if he could just get the damn needles taken out.

Alec realized that need could wait because he had a more urgent one to find the john. Maybe give himself a quick shave. He looked across at Sara just as she glanced over.

"Hey, there," she called out, lifting one of the headphones off her ear. "Why don't you wash up while Molly's napping? Bathroom's the first door on your left. Extra shaving gear under the sink, if you want to help yourself.''

"Thanks, Sara,'' Alec replied with a smile. Molly's friend went back to her music and her bookkeeping, and Alec padded down the hallway in his socks. It felt great to be out of those boots, he thought, pausing in front of the bathroom and staring at the closed door behind which, he assumed, Molly was sleeping.

Walking as quietly as he could, he put his ear against the door and listened. He didn't hear anything. Gently he put his hand on the doorknob and slowly it turned. The last thing he wanted to do was wake the poor girl, but he would feel better if he could just make sure she was okay.

Although there was no way she wasn't going to be okay, tucked into a cozy bed in the sunny apartment of her dear friend.

Alec cracked open the door and looked in.

Molly was not on the bed.

A bell of fear, like a fire alarm, went off in his head and he ran into the room. "Molly!" Alec yelled, crossing to the open glass door.

Before he could step outside, his attention was diverted to the mirror. In it he saw a reflection that stopped him dead in his tracks.

Behind him was the cop, Cortez, holding on to a bound and gagged Molly Jakes. Cortez was pointing a gun at him. "Hold it right there, cowboy.''

"Let her go, Cortez.''

"Yeah, sure thing, cowboy,'' the cop replied, pressing his free hand down against Molly's shoulder so she would fall to her knees. "Where's the other broad? The helpful Miss Gillem?''

Alec met Molly's terror-filled eyes. She seemed to be begging him to do something, anything, to keep another friend of hers from being hurt. "She's in the other room, with headphones on, working at her desk. I don't think she'll be a problem anytime soon." Alec nodded at the open door. "So why don't you head out the way you came in, Cortez. Give yourself a running start to make it to Mexico before your mates come after you for murder."

"I didn't murder anyone," Cortez said, his voice a growl of pain. He brought the pistol up even with Alec's eyes. "But you did. Both of you did. You killed Alicia. And for that, I'm not waiting around for courthouse justice. I'm going to deal it out right here, right now."

"Had a thing with Alicia, did you? Is that how you got her to work with you for that slime, Brooker? He bribed you and you pressured her?"

Cortez squinted his black eyes at Alec. "You've got that all wrong, Steele. Alicia hated Brooker. She's the one who got me involved in all this! She found out Brooker was going to shanghai you with a couple of ex-cops turned bad. Don't ask me why she cared what happened to you, but she did. She told me you'd been given a posthypnotic suggestion you were going to be powerless to overcome. I think she undid it the night she fooled with your bandages at the motel, but she wasn't sure. That's why she came to see you the other night, to check. She was terrified Brooker was going to get away with murder."

"Yeah? Then why did she pull the gun on Molly? Why not tell us the whole story herself?"

"Because she was hiding something else that even I don't understand," Cortez said in a flat voice. "Something about Paul Buntz's murder. Something she was afraid you knew but didn't even realize was the way she put it."

The cop's finger tightened on the gun's trigger. "You didn't need to kill her, Steele. I saw what you two did to her. Shot her like a dog, then left her all alone."

"I didn't kill Alicia, you moron. You killed her yourself, when you fired at Molly and the truck last night!"

Alec's words hit Cortez like a fist. For a moment, he relaxed his grip on Molly, which was the chance she was waiting for. Throwing herself sideways, she knocked Cortez off balance. The gun went flying and landed on Sara's bed.

With the yell of a banshee, Alec leapt across the room on top of Cortez. He caught the cop in the chest and smashed him against the wall. For a few furious seconds, he pummeled him senselessly, halting only when he realized Molly was kicking at his leg in an effort to make him stop.

Alec let Cortez, battered and bloody, fall into a heap. He picked Molly up from the floor and placed her gently on the bed. After sticking the cop's gun in his belt, he removed her gag and began to untie her.

"Are you nuts?" Molly rewarded him by screaming. "You almost killed him. Jeez, Alec, don't give them a legitimate charge to pile on all the ones they've made up."

Alec cupped Molly's tear-strained face in his hands and kissed her, then folded her into his arms. "It's okay, love. We're both safe now. Don't cry." When she finally gave in to his embrace, he pulled her against him and kissed the top of her head. "It's okay, Molly. It's nearly over."

At that second, he heard the metallic click of a gun and spun Molly away in time to stare at Cortez. The cop had drawn a second, smaller gun from a holster at his ankle. Before Alec could do a single thing to stop him, the cop fired.

Molly screamed, a sound that reached through the headphones and sent Sara Gillem running to her neighbor's to call for the cops, the army, anyone who would help.

MOLLY SAT RIGIDLY, dressed all in black, in the third row of the courtroom. She waited, like the other hundred people packed tightly into the chamber, for the bailiff to bring in the next witness.

Frederick Brooker and his attorney were directly in front of her. Brooker sat sideways, often looking at his son, Erik, who sat with his grandmother in the front row.

Lynn Nicholson, the red-haired district attorney, seated at a table to the right of Brooker, was holding a whispered conversation with one of her young associates.

FBI agent Yamamoto, Molly was surprised to see, was also in court. She had developed a rapport with the agent in the three weeks since she had surrendered herself to his protective custody in the living room of Sara Gillem's condominium. She found him kind and intelligent and nonreactionary, allowing each piece of her story to be recorded and verified before interrupting her with any questions.

Molly found that a great relief, since the details of the days between Thursday at 3:00 a.m. when she was stopped by a freeway wreck and abducted at gunpoint, and 11:00 a.m. on Sunday when Henry Cortez shot himself, seemed surrealistic and difficult to comprehend, to say the least. She smiled and mouthed hello when Agent Yamamoto looked her way. He nodded.

"Please approach the bench and be sworn in, Mr. Steele," Molly heard the judge direct. She turned and met Alec's eyes. They were boring into her, blue and full of enough emotion to make her smile amid this grim proceeding.

They had not been alone together for three weeks. Both had been in protective custody and sequestered, the judge giving in to a delay in the trial due to the hoopla of their capture.

One call had been allowed, but Molly learned nothing but the fact that Alec had had the dye taken out of his hair and had the needles in his neck removed, except for a tiny piece that had separated from the shaft.

"Looks like a tick head, the doctor said. Nothing to worry about. I'm good as new."

"I can't wait to see for myself," Molly had told him.

Alec did look good as new, even better, she thought to herself. Handsome in a navy jacket and gray slacks, white shirt and red paisley tie and—a sexy touch of pure Alec—his ever-present cowboy boots.

They would be together tonight, she realized. Once his testimony was over, the trial was history. Lynn Nicholson had promised that.

For the past week, Molly had testified and listened to the other evidence.

The ballistics tie-in to the gun.

The gun store's records indicating the gun belonged to Brooker.

The powder burns on the front, driver's side of the limo.

The coroner's grisly details of death.

Now she could listen to Alec Steele. His voice was firm and full of energy, the lilt and music of Australia charming everyone within hearing distance.

Mason Weil was cross-examining him. "So, your testimony is that you had boarded Mr. Brooker's yacht illegally, were rummaging around and then heard a car engine from twenty feet away."

"No," Alec replied cheerfully. "My testimony is that I boarded Mr. Brooker's boat to wait for him, concerned we may have gotten our appointment mixed up. I heard a car, so I went to the fence to see if it was Mr. Brooker."

They went back and forth, over the same material three more times. Lynn Nicholson objected that Weil was being argumentative.

Her objection was sustained.

"Please move on, Mr. Weil," the judge ordered.

"Tell the court again, please, what you saw when Mr. Buntz leaned into the car window."

"As I said before, Mr. Buntz leaned into the car and I heard the sound of a gun going off. Mr. Buntz fell to the ground, and Mr. Brooker got out of the car and dragged the body to the dock and rolled it into the water."

Molly cringed at the graphic depiction and glanced at young Erik Brooker. As she did, she caught Brooker signing to the boy. His motions were subtle and quick.

Index finger to thumb, palm up. Do it, she remembered from her sign language course. Then Brooker made the sign for what Molly remembered was *Y,* a stiff pinky and thumb, three fingers bent, closed onto the palm, palm side toward the reader.

She tried to remember what *Y* also meant. Was it "now"? Had Brooker just told Erik to "do it now"?

Molly stared at the boy, who nodded and reached his left hand to his right wrist. On it was a tiny device resembling a calculator. Erik pressed a button.

And Alec screamed.

Molly jumped from her seat and stared at Alec, who was holding his hands to the sides of his head in anguish. "Alec!" she cried out.

"Sit down, Mr. Steele!" the judge ordered.

"Order. We'll have order!" the court clerk bellowed.

Two armed courtroom guards approached the front of the bench, their hands on their holsters.

Slowly Alec lowered his hands and stared at Brooker.

"Mr. Steele?" the judge said. "What is it, Mr. Steele? Are you ill?"

Molly glanced at the jury. The gazes of the twelve men and women were riveted to Alec, as were all those of the spectators. Except one. Frederick Brooker turned and signed, "Do it now," once more to his son.

Before Molly could cry out, Erik pressed the button again and Alec howled in pain, then leapt off the witness stand and made a beeline for Brooker. Guards scurried, people screamed, and the district attorney stood in shocked disbelief as everyone ran for cover.

"Alec!" Molly yelled helplessly as one of the guards tackled Alec from behind. They fell to the floor, but not before Alec grabbed Brooker by the pant leg and pulled him out of his chair with a crash.

The second guard joined in the fray, and Alec grabbed his gun, held his arm stiffly and tried to aim at Brooker, who was crawling toward the jury.

Agent Yamamoto leapt onto the prosecutor's table, gripping what looked like a small shotgun in his hands. "Put it down, Mr. Steele," he ordered.

"He's got a gun!" Mason Weil screamed, scurrying behind Lynn Nicholson. "Shoot Steele, for God's sake. He'll murder us all."

Suddenly the last piece of the puzzle fell into place in Molly's brain. Alec had been brainwashed to kill someone, and that someone was himself.

Frederick Brooker's plan was to brainwash the man and trigger, via a remote control in the hand of his son, a command to make Alec act in a way that was sure to cause Alec's own death.

Molly reeled with the truth of her judgment, then understood the last mystery. The reason Alicia Chen had tried to have Brooker killed in prison, but might also have let Alec die.

It was to protect her son.

Alec testified just now that Brooker got out of the car from the side that faced him. But he had earlier said that the car was heading away from him, meaning Brooker had to exit on the passenger's side! Everyone else had testified that the shots had been fired from the driver's side.

Which meant someone else was driving. And someone else had fired the gun, probably in error. Brooker's son, Erik, was getting a driving lesson from his old man. A lesson that had turned into a nightmare, caused by an accident that Brooker thought he could cover up with murder.

Leaping over people screaming and pushing and trying to get to safety, Molly grabbed Erik Brooker by the arm and yanked the radio-control device off his arm. She had no idea how to counteract the command that must have triggered Alec's behavior, but at least she could keep him from pressing it again.

She jumped over the low barrier partitioning the spectators from the front of the courtroom and put her hand over the end of the gun Alec held pointed at Brooker's head. "Don't do it, Alec. You're no murderer."

"Drop the gun, Mr. Steele. Now!" the guard yelled.

"Step away, Miss Jakes," Yamamoto ordered.

Molly stood her ground, the gun an inch from her heart. With her free hand, she dangled the radio-control wristband in front of Alec's raging eyes. "It's a trick, Alec. But it's over. You've got to trust me, mate. Don't you remember? You said you would trust me."

While one hundred and twenty-five people held their breaths, Alec Steele blinked. His eyes rolled back into his head. Molly grabbed the gun but could not grab Alec before he fell with a groan onto the cold marble floor.

Epilogue

February 14
The following year

Alec steadied Molly as she walked beside him down the ferry's gangplank. Around her she heard the whispers and giggles of strangers, but she endured this scene good-naturedly. She would react like those strangers if she saw a handsome hunk leading a woman wearing a blindfold and a red chiffon cocktail dress onto Catalina Island for a romantic dinner on Valentine's Day. Molly hugged Alec's arm. "You should have warned me about the blindfold, mate. I'd have worn my new pink tennis shoes for the occasion."

"You've got to be kidding. And risk the chance to see those legs in red satin dancing shoes, love? You can call me lots of things, but don't call me crazy."

Molly wrinkled her nose as the smell of horse, followed by the sound of hooves, pricked her senses. After much clattering, Alec ordered her to step up.

She did, into a carriage of some kind. In an instant, Alec was snuggled beside her. Scattered applause and "Great idea, buddy!" drifted up from the crowd around her. Call him anything, Molly thought to herself. As long as it's romantic.

In the five months since the trial, they had tried to settle into a life together. Alec had rented an apartment, at which she'd slept many nights while she looked for a new house. As much as she loved her town house, after Rafe's death, Molly knew it would never feel like home.

But she'd held off buying anything new, just as Alec had put off returning to his business in Australia. She had promised to go with him at Easter time and wondered if this night was a prelude to something connected to that.

Did he want her to move there with him? Molly wondered.

Alec rested his finger against Molly's brow. "I can hear you thinking in there, love. This is a night to relax and enjoy, remember? I promised you we'd come back to Catalina Island someday and have a happier time than last."

"It's already happier, Alec. Brooker's in jail. I'm back at work." Her voice wavered. "I have you in my life. Just don't tell me you've booked us a room at the Devil Fish Motel."

Alec laughed, a hearty, infectious laugh, joined by Molly and the voice of an unseen male she assumed was the carriage driver. The breeze in her hair, the smell of the Pacific and Alec by her side were potent inducements to relax. Still, she worried. Could she leave America? Would she be happy leaving her job? Alec had told her that women had a much harder time with careers in Australia.

"Are there really a lot of flies?" Molly asked.

"What?" Alec asked. "Did you get bitten?"

"No, silly, I mean in Australia. You're always complaining about flies and sharks and heat. Is it really as bad as all that?"

"No, it's quite wonderful, in its way. Wide open. Room to roam, find yourself. And you'll find nowhere with nicer people, I think. But what brought that on? Worried about our trip? My dad's really looking forward to our visit."

"He is?" Molly asked in surprise. "And why is that? Wants to meet your partner in crime?"

The carriage halted and Alec moved closer to Molly to reach for the door. "No, what he said was 'I'm looking forward to seeing with my own eyes the chit that you can't live without marrying.'"

Molly gasped at his unexpected words. He loosened the blindfold and met her eyes. She saw a touch of fear on his handsome face, though of the emotion-tugging, vulnerable variety.

"Well, as proposals go, I guess that was a clunker." Alec grinned. "Which is why I brought you here to spend some time convincing you to say yes."

Through glowing eyes, Molly looked past Alec. They were at the foot of the stairs leading up to the Enchanted Cottage. The Victorian beauty's white clapboards shone in the dusky light.

"You rented the cottage? How on earth...?"

"Hey, Molly girl. This here's the U.S. of A. Money talks. People listen."

"This is the most special Valentine's Day gift a woman ever had, Alec Steele. Thank you." She leaned across to kiss him, then let him help her down. The carriage driver waved and drove away, and Alec led her up the steps.

"Yeah, well, a man should take a woman to a special place when he's going to ask her to be his wife."

It was the most gloriously sentimental event she had ever experienced. A Valentine's Day proposal. How corny. How sweet. How perfect.

They stood on the porch, embracing, watching the boats of Avalon bob in the breeze . . . twenty-six miles away from all the troubles of the world. Molly turned Alec's face to hers and kissed him again, then whispered into his ear just what special thing she had planned for him tonight.

He grinned wolfishly. "Can't I have it now?"

"Out here? I don't think so. But it'll keep, mate. I promise."

"Well then," Alec said, "I'll get my gift giving out of the way. Miss Jakes," he said, pulling a small blue box out of the jacket of his tuxedo with a flourish, "I believe this has your name on it."

Trembling, Molly accepted the gift. With a flick of her finger, she opened the box and gasped.

Alec was romantic and corny as hell, but he also had fabulous taste. Nested in white velvet was an exquisite sapphire, the color of a summer sea and the exact shade of Alec Steele's eyes.

The ring, encircled with tiny, winking diamonds, sparkled like stars. "Oh, Alec!" she cried. "It's beautiful. Put it on me, please."

"Well, I'll take that as a yes, then?"

"Yes. Take it most definitely as a yes, Alec. As long as you promise you will always trust me," she countered, tears streaming down her face.

"With my life, love. With my life."

HARLEQUIN®

I N T R I G U E ®

WHO IS THIS

They say what makes a woman alluring is her air of mystery. Next month, Harlequin Intrigue brings you another *very* mysterious woman of mystery—Laura Parker. We're proud to introduce another writer to Harlequin Intrigue, as the Woman of Mystery program continues.

And not only is the author a "Woman of Mystery"— the heroine is, too!

Andrea Uchello thinks she has outrun her jaded past—until she runs smack into treasury agent Victor Mondragon. He knows he shouldn't trust her, and she's afraid he'll find out why. But from the very start, Andy and Victor have two things in common: they've both been had by a very clever thief, and they share an attraction that is immediate, explosive and probably a crime!

Don't miss
#327 INDISCREET
by Laura Parker
June 1995

Be on the lookout for more "Woman of Mystery" books in the months ahead, as we search out the best new writers, just for you—only from Harlequin Intrigue!

WOMEN9

HARLEQUIN®

I N T R I G U E ®

Into a world where danger lurks around
every corner, and there's a fine line between trust
and betrayal, comes a tall, dark and handsome man.

Intuition draws you to him...but instinct keeps you
away. Is he really one of those...

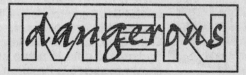

Don't miss even one of the twelve sexy but secretive
men, coming to you one per month in 1995.

In June, look for:
#325 TALL, DARK AND DEADLY
by Madeline Harper

Take a walk on the wild side...with our
"DANGEROUS MEN"!

DM-5

ANNOUNCING THE

FLYAWAY VACATION SWEEPSTAKES!

This month's destination:

Beautiful SAN FRANCISCO!

This month, as a special surprise, we're offering an exciting FREE VACATION!

Think how much fun it would be to visit San Francisco "on us"! You could ride cable cars, visit Chinatown, see the Golden Gate Bridge and dine in some of the finest restaurants in America!

The facing page contains two Entry Coupons (as does every book you received this shipment). Complete and return *all* the entry coupons; **the more times you enter, the better your chances of winning!**

Then keep your fingers crossed, because you'll find out by June 15, 1995 if you're the winner! If you are, here's what you'll get:

- Round-trip airfare for two to beautiful San Francisco!
- 4 days/3 nights at a first-class hotel!
- $500.00 pocket money for meals and sightseeing!

Remember: The more times you enter, the better your chances of winning!*

*NO PURCHASE OR OBLIGATION TO CONTINUE BEING A SUBSCRIBER NECESSARY TO ENTER. SEE REVERSE SIDE OR ANY ENTRY COUPON FOR ALTERNATIVE MEANS OF ENTRY.

VSF KAL

FLYAWAY VACATION
SWEEPSTAKES
OFFICIAL ENTRY COUPON

This entry must be received by: MAY 30, 1995
This month's winner will be notified by: JUNE 15, 1995
Trip must be taken between: JULY 30, 1995-JULY 30, 1996

YES, I want to win the San Francisco vacation for two. I understand the prize includes round-trip airfare, first-class hotel and $500.00 spending money. Please let me know if I'm the winner!

Name_____

Address _____ Apt. _____

City   State/Prov.   Zip/Postal Code

Account #_____

Return entry with invoice in reply envelope.

© 1995 HARLEQUIN ENTERPRISES LTD.   CSF KAL

FLYAWAY VACATION
SWEEPSTAKES
OFFICIAL ENTRY COUPON

This entry must be received by: MAY 30, 1995
This month's winner will be notified by: JUNE 15, 1995
Trip must be taken between: JULY 30, 1995-JULY 30, 1996

YES, I want to win the San Francisco vacation for two. I understand the prize includes round-trip airfare, first-class hotel and $500.00 spending money. Please let me know if I'm the winner!

Name_____

Address _____ Apt. _____

City   State/Prov.   Zip/Postal Code

Account #_____

Return entry with invoice in reply envelope.

© 1995 HARLEQUIN ENTERPRISES LTD.   CSF KAL

OFFICIAL RULES
FLYAWAY VACATION SWEEPSTAKES 3449
NO PURCHASE OR OBLIGATION NECESSARY

Three Harlequin Reader Service 1995 shipments will contain respectively, coupons for entry into three different prize drawings, one for a trip for two to San Francisco, another for a trip for two to Las Vegas and the third for a trip for two to Orlando, Florida. To enter any drawing using an Entry Coupon, simply complete and mail according to directions.

There is no obligation to continue using the Reader Service to enter and be eligible for any prize drawing. You may also enter any drawing by hand printing the words "Flyaway Vacation," your name and address on a 3"x5" card and the destination of the prize you wish that entry to be considered for (i.e., San Francisco trip, Las Vegas trip or Orlando trip). Send your 3"x5" entries via first-class mail (limit: one entry per envelope) to: Flyaway Vacation Sweepstakes 3449, c/o Prize Destination you wish that entry to be considered for, P.O. Box 1315, Buffalo, NY 14269-1315, USA or P.O. Box 610, Fort Erie, Ontario L2A 5X3, Canada.

To be eligible for the San Francisco trip, entries must be received by 5/30/95; for the Las Vegas trip, 7/30/95; and for the Orlando trip, 9/30/95.

Winners will be determined in random drawings conducted under the supervision of D.L. Blair, Inc., an independent judging organization whose decisions are final, from among all eligible entries received for that drawing. San Francisco trip prize includes round-trip airfare for two, 4-day/3-night weekend accommodations at a first-class hotel, and $500 in cash (trip must be taken between 7/30/95—7/30/96, approximate prize value—$3,500); Las Vegas trip includes round-trip airfare for two, 4-day/3-night weekend accommodations at a first-class hotel, and $500 in cash (trip must be taken between 9/30/95—9/30/96, approximate prize value—$3,500); Orlando trip includes round-trip airfare for two, 4-day/3-night weekend accommodations at a first-class hotel, and $500 in cash (trip must be taken between 11/30/95—11/30/96, approximate prize value—$3,500). All travelers must sign and return a Release of Liability prior to travel. Hotel accommodations and flights are subject to accommodation and schedule availability. Sweepstakes open to residents of the U.S. (except Puerto Rico) and Canada, 18 years of age or older. Employees and immediate family members of Harlequin Enterprises, Ltd., D.L. Blair, Inc., their affiliates, subsidiaries and all other agencies, entities and persons connected with the use, marketing or conduct of this sweepstakes are not eligible. Odds of winning a prize are dependent upon the number of eligible entries received for that drawing. Prize drawing and winner notification for each drawing will occur no later than 15 days after deadline for entry eligibility for that drawing. Limit: one prize to an individual, family or organization. All applicable laws and regulations apply. Sweepstakes offer void wherever prohibited by law. Any litigation within the province of Quebec respecting the conduct and awarding of the prizes in this sweepstakes must be submitted to the Regies des loteries et Courses du Quebec. In order to win a prize, residents of Canada will be required to correctly answer a time-limited arithmetical skill-testing question. Value of prizes are in U.S. currency.

Winners will be obligated to sign and return an Affidavit of Eligibility within 30 days of notification. In the event of noncompliance within this time period, prize may not be awarded. If any prize or prize notification is returned as undeliverable, that prize will not be awarded. By acceptance of a prize, winner consents to use of his/her name, photograph or other likeness for purposes of advertising, trade and promotion on behalf of Harlequin Enterprises, Ltd., without further compensation, unless prohibited by law.

For the names of prizewinners (available after 12/31/95), send a self-addressed, stamped envelope to: Flyaway Vacation Sweepstakes 3449 Winners, P.O. Box 4200, Blair, NE 68009.

RVC KAL